TO THE END OF THE WAR

TO THE END OF THE WAR

UNPUBLISHED STORIES BY JAMES JONES

Edited and with Introductions
by George Hendrick

INTEGRATED MEDIA

NEW YORK

To My Father

Nothing in his life
Became him like the leaving it; he died
As one that had been studied in his death
To throw away the dearest thing he owed.
As 't were a careless trifle.—Macbeth

CONTENTS

INTRODUCTION

FROM *THEY SHALL INHERIT THE LAUGHTER* TO *TO THE END OF THE WAR*

JAMES JONES WROTE TO HIS editor, Maxwell Perkins, about his first, unpublished novel, *They Shall Inherit the Laughter*: "*Laughter* was largely autobiographical and I had a readymade plot and characters who followed it; all that I had to do was heighten it and use my imagination." He wrote the truth; he used his own life in a story set during a dramatic period when World War II still raged and he went over the hill, returning to his hometown, Robinson, Illinois. Almost every character in the novel was based on someone he knew, or knew about, in East-Central Illinois.

A soldier named James Jones went AWOL, probably November 1, 1943, and went back to Robinson, where he had been born in 1921. His grandfather George Jones had once lived on a nearby farm but became prosperous after oil was discovered on his property. He moved into Robinson, studied law, established a practice, and became sheriff of the county for four years. He was a leading citizen and moved his family into a three-story Southern-style mansion.

George Jones was a religious man, a Methodist, a teetotaler, domineering. He demanded that his four sons become professionals: two doctors and two lawyers. He sent his sons to Northwestern University, where one son took his own life. Ramon Jones, father of James Jones, was destined for medicine, but he convinced his father to allow him to go into dentistry, which demanded fewer years of study, in order to marry more quickly. He married Ada Blessing in 1908, and soon established his practice in Robinson. Dr. Jones was a handsome, outgoing man, but he began to drink heavily. Ada Jones was a vain, beautiful woman, obsessed with social status. Eventually she became religious and turned to Christian Science. James Jones, deeply attached to his father, came to despise his mother, who often quarreled with her husband.

George Jones died in 1929, and the family at first was partially immune from the economic depression, which began that year, for he left a significant estate. In 1932, with the collapse of the Samuel Insull public utilities empire, where George Jones had heavily invested, the largest part of the family fortune disappeared. Dr. Jones lost his inheritance and was losing his patients since they could no longer afford dental care.

After Dr. Jones was forced to give up his house, he moved his family into rented quarters. His wife was acutely unhappy about her decline in social standing, and Dr. Jones withdrew more and more into alcoholism. In this bitterly divided family, struggling through the long depression, Jones had an unhappy, rebellious adolescence. As soon as he completed high school and turned eighteen, in 1939, he joined the Army Air Corps but eventually transferred to the Infantry and was stationed in Hawaii. His service in the peacetime army, concluding with the attack on Pearl Harbor on December 7, 1941, became the subject matter of his second novel, *From Here to Eternity.*

Jones's personal world was shaken while he was in Hawaii; his mother died and his father committed suicide. The most positive thing that happened in this period of his life was his discovery of the novels of Thomas Wolfe, who wrote about a family much like his own. From reading Wolfe, Jones wrote, he realized that "I had been a writer all my life without knowing it or having written." He began to write poetry and prose sketches.

Jones had been assigned to Company F, Second Battalion, Twenty-Seventh Infantry Regiment, which was ordered to go to Guadalcanal.

The troopship he was on arrived December 30, 1942. The battles on that island were fierce, and the troops suffered from dengue fever, malaria, and other tropical diseases, and continual fear.

In an undated manuscript, he wrote, "I might be dead in a month, which would mean that I would never learn to say and never get said those things which proved I had once existed somewhere." Every soldier "accepted," Jones wrote in *WWII*, "that his name is already written down in the rolls of the already dead."

Jones often told the story of a day on Guadalcanal when he killed a Japanese soldier and found in the man's billfold a picture of his wife and child. Jones then viewed war in a different way, recognizing he had obliterated a so-called enemy who was a fellow human being. He wanted to be finished with killing. Jones's most dramatic retelling of the incident is in his novel *The Thin Red Line*.

Jones was saved from taking another man's life. On January 12, 1943, he was hit in the head by a fragment from a mortar shell. There was blood everywhere, and his glasses were shattered. Had he not been in a shallow foxhole, he would have soon been in a deeper grave.

Jones was taken to a field hospital where he stayed a week before rejoining his company. The battle for Guadalcanal was basically over then; the Japanese troops were being evacuated. The U.S. troops there expected to be sent to New Georgia in the Solomon Islands for more combat. Jones felt his luck had run out. He wrote his brother that until a soldier was hit, he was confident it would happen to other guys but not to him. Once hit, he wrote, "You lose that confidence."

He was spared a landing and battles on New Georgia by another piece of luck. He was having trouble with his ankle, which he had injured playing football at Schofield Barracks. After it became increasingly difficult for him to walk, he was sent home by hospital ship, first to New Zealand for a short time and then on to San Francisco. He was then transferred to Kennedy General Hospital near Memphis, Tennessee.

At Kennedy General Hospital, he received a course of therapy and then was sent to a convalescent barracks for a month, but the treatments had to be extended and went on month after month. In the months he was hospitalized, he came into contact with large numbers of men from two battle zones: Attu and Guadalcanal.

Attu is in the fog-shrouded Aleutians off the coast of Alaska. In an attempt to retake the island from the Japanese, American troops landed on May 11, 1943. From the first, the battle for Attu was a fiasco. The practice landings for the officers and men took place on warm California beaches, giving them no worthwhile knowledge about what they would face in the fog and on the tundra of Attu. In addition, through faulty intelligence, the army believed that 500 Japanese were stationed on the island. In fact, there were 2,300.

To make matters even worse, the map available to those planning and supervising the operation showed the topography only up to a thousand yards from the shoreline. In the uncharted interior of Attu, companies were lost and wandered for days in the eternal fog.

The absolute disaster came early. The troops landed wearing ordinary winter uniforms, not suitable for the fierce winds and rain of the island. They wore leather boots, which were not waterproofed. Men had cold, wet feet, rubbed raw. Gangrene followed. Whole wards were soon filled with Attu survivors who had lost their feet. The Japanese commander decided to stage a banzai attack, said to be the first of the war, on American forces, May 29, 1943. His men had suffered large-scale casualties in the past eighteen days. He had only a thousand men who could bear arms. His men who were ill or who could not walk were ordered to kill themselves. At three a.m., the Japanese began a silent attack, bayoneting U.S. troops in their sleeping bags. Then shooting began and grenades were exploded. According to one account, once the silence was broken the Japanese were screaming, "Japanese drink blood like wine."

After the Japanese slaughtered the first American troops they came upon, they moved on and finally met resistance. The Japanese then began killing themselves, mostly by holding grenades to their bodies. Of 2,300 Japanese men on Attu, 29 were prisoners. The rest were dead. The U.S. troops also suffered heavy losses: 549 were killed, 1,148 wounded, 2,100 with gangrene, exposure, and shock. The Attu survivors in the hospital had many stories to tell Jones.

The survivors of the Guadalcanal battles had their tales, and Jones had his. His dreams were crowded with scenes he could not forget, scenes largely connected with ridges named the Galloping Horse. General Collins on January 8, 1943, gave the order to take those mountain ridges. Later, in *The Thin Red Line*, Jones wrote an unforgettable account of that battle. He also wrote a long poem called "The Hill They Call the Horse" sometime after that battle. Sleepless in a hospital—New Zealand? San Francisco? a hospital ship? the hospital near Memphis? We do not know—he relived scenes in the concluding section of the long poem:

> And my fear crawls up and chokes me.
> This is why I came:
> This is the force of madness that took me by the hand
> And would not let me cringe! Why me! Why me!
> Dumbly with cloven tongue I stand in the bloody dawn
> Atop, the Horse.
>   I would run: my legs laugh in my face.
> For across the crest they come
> In solitary line
> As I last saw them:
>   Dried mud ground into their green fatigues, gritty to the touch;
> Helmets, those who have them, rusty, caked with mud;
> Sweat streaming down, faces twisted with the agony of fear
>   and tension.
> They pass by me with stumbling tread,
> And each looks at me reproachfully and sadly:
> They died: I lived. They resent my luck.
> They cannot see that I am not the lucky one.
> As they pass, I see them as I saw them last:
> George Creel—
> A little string of brains hanging down between his eyes;
> Joe Dommicci—
> His eyes big between his glasses and a gaping hole where once
>   had been his ear; . . .

Hannon—
Stumbling along, face gone below the eyes;
Big Kraus—
No marks, no blood, just dead with hard-set lips and
    unbelieving eyes; . . .
    The line goes on—for there are many.
Red Johansson—
    Both legs gone and spouting fountains while he drags
        himself across the ground.
The line goes on—for there are many more.
There is the boy (I never knew his name)
Who was lying wounded on a litter,
Glad he had been wounded,
And believing he was safe at last
When a sniper blew his brains out
And filled the litter with a pool of blood.
The line goes on—
    I see it in the distance, climbing,
Groping blindly up that hill,
The hill they call The Horse.
And my unseen chains release me,
    And I am away—through swirling wisps of madness and
        of pain.
I am back inside my body with its straining antenna of fear.
I am safe—at least for now,
But I cannot relax:
I know I must go back some day—provided that I live.
I must see this place in stillness—when the jungle has reclaimed it.
Or I shall never rest.
I cannot sleep tonight. . . . Perhaps a pill.

Once his ankle began to improve, Jones was given passes to go into Memphis, where he rented a suite in the Peabody Hotel for six weeks. It was a wild, drunken time for him, with local women ready to go to bed with him. For a time, he wrote that he didn't get pleasure from laying a woman unless he was drunk.

Jones's psychological state worsened, and he began to pick fights in bars. Not only was he haunted by the memories of death and destruction on Guadalcanal, but also he faced being sent to England preparing for the coming invasion of the Continent. Hospital personnel seem not to have recognized his psychological state at this time. He did get some relief from the horrors when he was engrossed in writing sketches of his wartime experiences and those told him by the men in the Memphis hospital. At this point, his fiction had not been shaped or put into any discernible order.

This is the backstory for the novel he was beginning, a work eventually called *They Shall Inherit the Laughter.*

Callous doctors certified this man Jones, with a weak ankle and with severe psychological problems, to be fit for duty. Disgusted, he went over the hill, heading for Robinson, probably on November 1, 1943. He stayed with his uncle Charles Jones and wife, Sadie, who now lived in the mansion once owned by George Jones. Jones and other members of his family believed that Uncle Charlie had managed to possess more of George Jones's estate than was legal or ethical.

Uncle Charlie was a staid attorney offended by his nephew's drunkenness and public scenes. The uncle was more interested in protecting the family name than helping his troubled nephew. He even let the drunken Jones spend the night in jail to teach him a lesson. Jones wanted to become a writer, but Uncle Charlie could not understand that. His advice: Jones should get a job once he was discharged from the army and do his writing in his spare time.

After a few days in Robinson, with all the memories of the past and the problems of the present, Jones was intoxicated most of the time, out of control, headed for a scene with his uncle or with leaders of the community whom he considered hypocrites. Aunt Sadie was more sympathetic to Jones than her husband was, and she decided to ask Lowney Handy to help Jones.

Lowney was an unconventional woman married to the superintendent of the Ohio Oil Refinery there in Robinson. She was about forty, childless, something of an unofficial social worker, early on helping the down-and-out, and during the war, servicemen. Kentucky-born, she was a brilliant conversationalist. She had read widely but unsystematically. She attempted to write fiction but was not successful, for she lacked control over her material. Her husband, Harry, was one of the most important men in Robinson. Once she played a role in social events, but she retreated from such activities. She was at times eccentric and often quixotic. She was an early New Ager, interested in Madame Blavatsky and Theosophy, Hindu religious texts, and other Eastern religions. She was a good listener and would give full attention to the stories of the troubled people who sought her out. She was, in this early period when she knew Jones, an admirable person. Jones did not do her justice in *They Shall Inherit the Laughter*, in *Some Came Running*, and in *Go to the Widow-Maker*, where she was caricatured. Later, she became autocratic, possessive, and destructive.

Aunt Sadie brought Jones to see Lowney early in November, 1943. A.B.C. Whipple in "James Jones and His Angel," *Life*, May 7, 1951, gave Lowney's account of the meeting: "He swaggered; he wore dark glasses; he even asked me to read his poetry aloud. He had obviously come over for a free drink. Then he saw my books. . . . He flipped through them and plopped them back as if he were gulping down what they had in them." Jones's account of this meeting is in "Johnny Meets Sandy."

Jones returned to the Handy home the next day, and he and Lowney spent the rest of the day in bed. Because she liked his writing and believed in his future as a writer, Jones wrote that "she subjected herself to me and made herself my disciple in everything from writing to love." Lowney certainly did not believe what she told this young man she had just met. She made quick decisions; after seeing a part of what he had written, she set out to help him be a published writer. In order to do that she began to control his antisocial activities, and she became his warden, his keeper. She certainly did not become his subject. She was not an experienced teacher, but she decided to help him learn to write.

As part of Lowney's control over Jones, she met his sexual needs. She had little interest in sex. Her husband had passed on gonorrhea to her, and as part of the treatment, she had a hysterectomy. In their fashion, Harry and Lowney loved each other; he supported her expensive book-buying and did not ask her to return to the social life in Robinson she now scorned. She stayed with him through his alcoholism and his own affairs.

Before Jones returned to army duty in Camp Campbell in Kentucky, he wrote the Handys that he wanted to live with them, and Lowney and Harry decided to take Jones into their home. In reality, Lowney decided and Harry offered no opposition. Once Jones was back on duty, Lowney began to maneuver to get him released from the army. Jones continued to go AWOL to work on his novel, which had been nebulous until after he met Lowney.

At Camp Campbell, he became company clerk but was disgusted when the army mistreated a Jewish officer whom Jones admired. Again, he went AWOL; when he returned, he was placed in the stockade and then transferred to a prison ward in the hospital. He saw a psychiatrist, and Jones wrote his older brother, Jeff, a summary: He told the doctor "that I am genius (altho they probably won't believe that); that if they attempt to send me overseas again, I'll commit suicide; that if I don't get out of the army I'll either go mad or turn into a criminal—which is just next door to a writer anyway. . . ." All he wanted to do was write. Jones obviously had all these feelings, but Lowney probably helped him shape them into a narrative for the psychiatrist. Lowney was persistent: Jones the genius needed to get out of the army and fulfill his destiny. Jones was also persevering. He had done his part in the war. He had no luck left. He wanted out.

Jones received an honorable discharge on July 6, 1944. Before he returned to Robinson, he traveled to Asheville, North Carolina, where Thomas Wolfe was born and lived with his dysfunctional family until he went away to college. Then Jones went to live with Lowney and Harry, with Harry providing money for him until *From Here to Eternity* was completed in 1950. Harry had a room built for Jones at the back of the family home and later bought Jones a Jeep and a trailer, which allowed him to get away from Robinson for short periods of time. Harry seems to have been completely aware of the sexual relationship of his wife and her young writer and raised no objections. In many ways, Harry was the unsung hero in this story. He gave Jones a home and an allowance, providing the time for the young veteran to learn to write.

Jones began to shape his novel, and Lowney must have played a major part in crafting an outline and in providing special details about Robinsonians. By the time he left the army in 1944, he probably had written some battle scenes and accounts of his first going AWOL and the drunken episode on the night train. He had undoubtedly written some account of his hell-raising in Robinson and about his quarrel with Uncle Charlie (named Erskine Carter in the novel). When he came to writing about Lowney, he omitted their love affair and did little with her interest in teaching him to write.

For many years, Jones was besotted with Lowney, but even early in their relationships he subconsciously seemed to have misgivings about her. In *They Shall Inherit the Laughter*, Lowney is given the name Cornelia but is always called by her nickname, Corny. In many sections of the novel, she fits the classic definitions of that word: trite, banal.

One of Jones's successes in his first novel was his dialogue, especially among servicemen. All the resentments come pouring out, overbearing, pompous, insolent officers; doctors who were indifferent to suffering and were little better than butchers; self-righteous chief clerks; the politics in the army; anti-Semitism and discrimination against people of color; the hypocrisy of mindless religious support of war by ministers and civilians alike; the civilian and military misunderstanding of the walking wounded. Few wanted to listen to the army groundlings who came from poor families and who had little education. Veterans of Korea, Vietnam, Iraq, Afghanistan, and assorted mini-wars would understand the dissatisfactions of Jones's combat soldiers in World War II.

Jones in *They Shall Inherit the Laughter* dared to discuss taboo subjects. He defended a musician friend who was alleged to be gay; he wrote sensitively about the musician's friend who was an African-American; and he opposed anti-Semitism in the army.

What kind of framework would allow Jones to put the parts together? Undoubtedly with the help of Lowney, the decision was made to have two central characters—Johnny Carter (based on Jones) and Corny Marion (based on Lowney). Physically or psychologically wounded men would meet at the home of Corny and Eddie Marion. These men who were not getting the help they needed from military personnel or the understanding they needed from family on the home front had turned to mindless carousing, fueled by alcohol. Corny and her husband provided them with a refuge to talk to other servicemen who understood what they had gone through. Corny, in the latter part of the novel, becomes the men's therapist, trying to help them solve their intractable problems. Jones the student/lover of Lowney, appears to be a true believer in Corny's solutions, but Perkins and other editors at Scribner's understood the novel was flawed. Unfortunately, Perkins did not work with Jones to tear the novel apart and remove much of the material based on Lowney. Perkins helped Wolfe revise and reduce the size of the immense manuscript *Look Homeward, Angel*, but Perkins was in ill health when he began reading *They Shall Inherit the Laughter* and unable to do for Jones what he did for Wolfe.

It is likely that Lowney suggested the title for this first novel, using words from beatitudes from Jesus' Sermon on the Mount:

"Blessed are the meek, for they shall inherit the earth." (Matthew 5:5)

"Blessed are ye that weep now, for ye shall laugh." (Luke 6:21)

In addition to references to Theosophy and to Hindu texts, Lowney often used biblical quotations. She interested Jones in religious views drawn from many sources, including the Bible, but in *They Shall Inherit the Laughter*, Jones had not internalized these ideas and they seem awkwardly attached to quite unaccepting materials. In the war stories and the talk of enlisted men, Jones had a tragic view of life. Emersonian Transcendentalism, Theosophy, and Eastern texts, interesting and useful as they are, did not mesh with his core beliefs.

Jones worked on the novel from the time he left the army in July 1944 until January 1945, when he had a finished manuscript. He then decided to enroll for the spring semester at New York University, where Wolfe had once taught. He wanted to submit the novel to the fabled editor Maxwell Perkins, who had worked with Wolfe, Hemingway, and Fitzgerald. He arrived at Perkins's office without an appointment, carrying with him his manuscript. The receptionist told Jones that Perkins was out of the office, but that if he would leave his manuscript it would be read. Jones was not willing to do that. The receptionist disappeared, then returned to say that Perkins had returned by way of a back entrance and would see him. The story was fictional: There was no back entrance.

The two men began an intense discussion of the war, ignoring the novel itself. Finally, late in the afternoon, Perkins suggested the two adjourn to the Ritz Bar for "tea." Jones impressed Perkins, who clearly wanted to find a new World War II writer for the Scribner's list. He passed the manuscript on to other editors, who read it but sensibly recommended against publication. The poet John Hall Wheelock, an editor at Scribner's, wrote Maxwell Aley, Jones's agent, that the novel was "a serious attempt to do a big piece of work." Perkins wrote Aley that *Laughter* lacked "the technique" to make it publishable. Left open was the resubmission of a revised manuscript. Unfortunately, Jones was not given the specifics he needed to make successful changes.

Maxwell Aley did give the manuscript a thorough reading. He wrote Jones on March 25, 1945: "The problem of the book remains Corny." He was frank: "She sounds like a high school girl not a mature woman. . . . your reader would laugh because Corny is grandiose. She speaks like a second-rate editorial in a Southern newspaper." Still, Aley did not recommend that Corny's role in the novel be severely diminished; instead, he gave general advice: "Make it human. Break it up. You're writing a novel not a tract, and when you are writing about Johnny you are usually adult and often first-rate by any standards." Aley was correct about the Johnny sections, but many of the Corny sections needed to be abandoned.

It is safe to speculate that Lowney did not see her fictional portrait as Aley did. Jones, no doubt with Lowney's strong support, dropped Aley as his agent. Without the editorial help he needed, Jones started to work with his revisions. He wrote Perkins on November 20, 1945, that he would be ready to resubmit the manuscript in four or five weeks. In that letter, he noted that Perkins had told him that the novel had "lacked resolution," and that he had corrected that problem. He did submit the manuscript on January 17, 1946.

One of the readers for Perkins was Burroughs Mitchell, to be Jones's editor after Perkins's death. Mitchell thought the novel was "a clumsy, ill-proportioned book." He believed the faults were too large to make another revision promising.

One of the faults of the novel, which made it clumsy, was the spewing out of gossip in the exposés of wealthy or prominent citizens of Robinson. A close friend of Lowney and Jones wrote on December 9, 2010: "It was Lowney's experiences as part of Robinson bridge playing and golfing partners at the country club that supplied Jim with material for *Laughter.* He had been too young to know his characters. And I now realize that it was more gossip than true portrayals." Jones did know his fellow soldiers.

Writing to Perkins on February 10, 1946, to ask about Scribner's decision concerning publishing *They Shall Inherit the Laughter*, Jones mentioned that he wanted to do a novel about his friend Stewart and the peacetime army.

Perkins telegraphed Jones on February 16, 1946: WOULD YOU CONSIDER PAYMENT FIVE HUNDRED NOW FOR OPTION ON STEWART NOVEL [FROM HERE TO ETERNITY] AND SETTING ASIDE INHERIT LAUGHTER FOR REASON ILL WRITE SOME FURTHER PAYMENT TO BE MADE AFTER WE APPROVE SOME FIFTY THOUSAND WORDS. WISH TO COOPERATE BUT HAVE MORE FAITH IN SECOND NOVEL, AND HAVE FURTHER REVISIONS TO PROPOSED [SIC] FOR LAUGHTER.

Jones wired Perkins on February 17: PROPOSITION ACCEPTED PLACING MYSELF IN YOUR HANDS AND AWAITING LETTER HERE. . . . In Maxwell Perkins, Jones had found another person who believed in his promise as a writer.

Perkins sent Jones an encouraging letter and explained his reasons for not accepting *They Shall Inherit the Laughter.* He felt the public was not interested in the subject at that time and that the novel would seem insulting by military people and by civilians. It might be more acceptable at a later time, Perkins believed. Jones never revised the novel, but *Some Came Running* and *Whistle* were indebted to it.

The editors at Scribner's were correct; *They Shall Inherit the Laughter* should not be published, but there are chapters and parts of chapters that deserve to appear as stories.

I have rescued the best parts of the manuscript, but this publication is not *They Shall Inherit the Laughter.* It is a collection of interrelated stories now titled *To the End of the War*, a toast given by servicemen suffering from remembrances of death and destruction and fear, always fear, and at present they were possessed by anger, confusion, and guilt. They drank to stilled guns and to peace.

The best stories are about the autobiographic hero, Johnny Carter, and his friends. Corny has not disappeared, but her role is diminished, and she has been renamed. Jones turned a chapter about his friend George in the novel into the short story "Two Legs for the Two of Us" (which was eventually published elsewhere). He changed Corny's name to Sandy to distance that story from Corny. I have followed Jones's lead and used the name *Sandy* throughout. All other names remain the same.

Chapters based on gossip about prominent Robinsonians have been omitted.

Sections of the novel that read like book reports on Eugene Debs, Prince Kropotkin, Thorstein Veblen, and other radicals have been omitted. Reading in Lowney's library, Jones caught the excitement of college students taking the course "Great Ideas of the World" and wanted to let the whole world know about his intellectual discoveries. Again, he had not internalized these ideas. That material is omitted.

Lessons on Emersonian Transcendentalism have been omitted, as has a lecture on the yin-yang symbol. Lowney's comments on art and politics are not included.

Johnny's rage remains, the causes near the surface and deep, deep.

One man whom Johnny once liked now gleefully wants to drop bombs. He remains in all his sinfulness.

Hypocrisy on the home front remains, as do war-mongering ministers, businessmen, and citizens.

Johnny and friends remain, frozen in time, as are their anger, frustration, pain, and humanity.

A toast: "To the end of the war."

From his first writings about army life, James Jones had a gift for dialogue. In this story, probably written in 1944, he explores the mistreatment and resentments of enlisted men. Wounded and with physical or psychological impairments, they were now declared fit for additional combat service. Desertion was an option.

Little has changed since 1944: the Walter Reed Medical Center scandal, the repeated deployments, the refusal to give benefits to some wounded men and women, and the need for wartime cannon fodder, even if the soldier is not physically fit.

*The widow of a fifty-year-old reservist in one of our current wars "said her husband suffered from a bad knee, a bum shoulder, and high blood pressure—and never should never have been sent to Iraq in the first place, given his physical ailments" (*Newsweek*, February 14, 2011, p. 34).*

OVER THE HILL

ON THE ROAD, AUTUMN 1943

THE HOSPITAL RECEIVING OFFICE WAS a small wooden building set in the large quadrangle of brick buildings that held the wards and the various branches of Surgery and Therapy and Pharmacy. Through an opening in this brick bulwark the trucks brought the newly arrived patients from the hospital trains, and long lines of the walking sick and wounded twined in and out around the inner sanctum and passed through the Receiving Office to be assigned and checked and looked over. The hospital, originally built to handle three thousand patients, was already becoming overcrowded and plans were being figured as to how to handle the influx that swept in like waves from the hospital trains that pulled into the hospital siding downtown in Memphis every few days.

This day, however, was not one of those in which a wild scramble was enacted to get the patients settled before dark. There was no influx of patients in the quadrangle, and its largeness looked deserted and lonely except for the occasional uniformed figures going back and forth on some kind of duty.

Corporal Johnny Carter, formerly of Endymion, Indiana, carrying the black gladstone which held all his earthly possessions, limped indifferently across the expanse of dusty sparsely grassed red earth from the

Convalescent Barracks to the Receiving Office. He was on his way out, back to duty.

He left his bag on the porch of the white wooden building and went inside to pick up his records and travel orders. He didn't know yet where he was going, and he didn't care much since one place would be about the same as another: The best he could hope for would be a camp near or in a large town. He was not happy at the prospect of going back to duty.

The chief clerk, who handed him the orders and the large brown envelope of records, was a tall slim arrogantly intelligent young man, after the usual pattern of army clerks. He was a technical sergeant and his black wavy hair was worn long in defiance of tradition, showing proudly that he did not spend time in the field as do the less intelligent common ruck of soldiery.

"Corporal," he said. "You will have a two-man detail to report in with you. Here are the train tickets. That two-and-a-half-ton job out in front is the truck to take you to the station. Your detail hasn't shown up yet. When they do, have them load their equipment in the back and get in. All three Service Records are in that envelope. Be very careful of them. In the army, a man's Service Record is more important than anything else. Including the man."

Johnny did not like the chief clerk's long hair or his arrogant intelligence that he wore like chevrons. He grunted an "Okay," and turned to the door. In his four and a half years in the army, he had done some clerical work himself and had come in contact with a great many clerks.

The chief clerk leaned his elbows on the counter behind which he stood and elaborately lighted a cigaret with a silver Dunhill lighter which he took from his pocket.

"Is that that Camp Campbell detail?" A first lieutenant sat behind the counter, his feet—encased in the prescribed leggings—cocked up on a typing table, a pencil behind his ear, reading a newspaper. "Yessir," said the chief clerk. "I want to talk to him," said the lieutenant, "Corporal," said the chief clerk. "The lieutenant wants to speak to you."

Johnny came back and stood at a weary attention before the lieutenant. The lieutenant put down his newspaper irritably, took down his feet, stood up, took the pencil from behind his ear and turned it over and over in his bands. He neglected to give Johnny "at ease," and Johnny continued to stand at attention. The chief clerk stood respectfully near, a little behind the lieutenant. "These two men you're in charge of are bad ones," the lieutenant said. "One of them, Wilkinsson, has been over the hill four times since he came here. The other one—what's his name?" he turned to the chief clerk who handed him a copy of the Special Orders and murmured a respectful "Gettinger."

The lieutenant took the paper and ran his pencil down the page line by line as a pointer. "Gettinger," he said finally. "The other one, Gettinger, has been over twice. You may have trouble with them. If they try to get away from you, put the hammer on 'em." The lieutenant gave Johnny a sharp glance to impress his order. Johnny was not an MP and did not carry sidearms. He had a wild vision of himself throwing rocks at two retreating figures. But being more or less experienced in the army, he refrained from asking for clarification as to with what he would put the hammer on 'em.

"If they get away from you," the lieutenant said, "report them to the nearest Provost Marshall." Outside of downtown Memphis, Johnny had no idea of the whereabouts of any Provost Marshall in the country. However, he did not interrupt the lieutenant to ask. Johnny, who was still standing at attention, snapped out a belligerent salute, said "Yessir," and walked outside. The lieutenant returned the salute with a casual gesture and, his duty attended to, sat back down, replaced the pencil behind his ear, recocked his feet, and took up his interrupted newspaper. He began to speak authoritatively about the Russians to the chief clerk, who successfully accomplished the feat of listening respectfully and comradely at the same time.

Outside Johnny tossed his bag into the back and then sat down on the running board of the empty truck to wait, feeling vaguely resentful and irritated. In 1945 the fall was a long one, and in November the weather was still hot out in the sun. Johnny scraped little crosses in the dust with the toe of his shoe and felt the sweat begin to trickle down his spine and drip from his armpits. His vague irritation rose and became specific: He was wearing one of his good uniforms. He possessed four; two of them had been issued by the hospital, the other two he had bought downtown in Memphis. The issue uniforms were khaki chenille summer uniforms; they fitted him like bags, and there are no post tailors or regimental tailors here as there had been at Schofield Barracks in Hawaii to put them down. He wore them as little as possible. The other two uniforms were officer uniforms with shoulder straps and were of tropical worsted wool. He had been ordered by several MPs to remove the shoulder straps, but up to now he had been able to wriggle out of doing so, although he never considered why it was so necessary to him to keep the unauthorized officer shoulder straps. He got up from the running board and moved out of the sun to sit on the edge of the little porch of the Receiving Office.

Presently, he saw the other two men coming. They struggled down the dusty road, each carrying his two blue barracks bags, heavily stuffed and awkward. Johnny watched them sympathetically. He was glad he had lost all his gear; when he came back to the States he wore hospital pajamas and had nothing left of four years' accumulation of property except a toothbrush, razor, a minute can of Dr Lyon's toothpowder, and a GI shaving brush. After his outfit moved out to beach positions on December 7, 1941, self-appointed salvage artists had gone through the barracks: he lost two civilian suits, a tropical dinner outfit, a radio/Victrola and a hundred records, three expensive pairs of civilian shoes, and an assortment of other things, including his favorite pair of dice. When he was evacuated from Guadalcanal, he lost everything he owned except the fatigue uniform he wore and his toilet articles, including an A-1 portable typewriter. He was glad though now, because he didn't have to lug it all around or take care of it.

The two men plumped down their barracks bags in the dust and stood breathing heavily and wiping the sweat from their faces.

"Wilkinsson and Gettinger?" Johnny asked.

The two men nodded. "Wilkinsson," said the tall dark one. The short red-headed youth muttered "Gettinger."

"This is our truck," Johnny said. "You guys better report in when you get your breath."

Both men grunted sourly and continued to stand where they were, breathing heavily from the quarter-mile trip with the heavy cumbersome barracks bags. Johnny lit a cigaret.

The chief clerk stuck his head out the window. “All right, you two men,” he said. “Get in here and report. You can’t spend the morning out there.” Wilkinsson and Gettinger climbed up on the porch and went inside with tightened lips. After a moment, during which the chief clerk asked them their names, they came back out and sat down on the edge of the porch in the shade.

“Where we going?” the red-headed youth asked.

“Camp Campbell, Kentucky,” Johnny said. “26th Division.”

“Well, Jesus Christ,” commented Gettinger. “That outfit’s supposed to be getting ready to ship.”

Johnny nodded. “That’s what I heard.”

“These lousy cockbeaters,” said the dark saturnine Wilkinsson. “If they think they’re going to send me back overseas, they’re crazy.”

“You and me.” Gettinger shook his red head. “What the hell do they want from a man anyway? Were you in Surgery?”

“Yeah,” said Johnny. “That son of a bitch, O’Flagherty,” said Gettinger. He was referring to Captain O’Flagherty, in charge of convalescent surgery cases. “If he was overseas, he’d get his guts shot out in ten minutes.” Captain O’Flagherty was a huge Irishman with a caustic sarcasm for a voice and a sneering moustache.

“You know what he told me?” asked Gettinger. “O’Flagherty called me in and asked me if I could do Infantry duty. I told him no and he said: ‘What’s the matter with you, Gettinger? Don’t you like the army? You think you can goldbrick your way out of it? Well, you can’t. That’s why I’m here.’

“The son of a bitch,” repeated Gettinger. “He looked at my heel once and poked his finger into it until I hollered. Then he laughed and told me to quit acting, because it wouldn’t do me any good: I couldn’t get out.”

“Sure,” said Wilkinsson. He held up his right hand. The second finger was completely gone and the first joint of the third finger was missing. His index finger was completely stiff. “The lousy bastard. He told me I was better off than I was before I got hit. He said my fingers only got in my road anyway." The upper half of Wilkinsson's right ear was missing also.

"You know what I told him?" said Gettinger. "I asked him if he was a doctor in civilian life or if he learned to butcher in the army." Gettinger laughed harshly. "It made him mad; he said sure he was a doctor in civilian life. So I said: 'How did you manage to make a living? You're lucky the war came along.' He got madder'n hell and wrote me down to go back to duty, right then and there." Gettinger was becoming angry. "What right has a son of a bitch like that got to be where he is? What does he know about the goddamned war?"

"Take it easy, Red," said Wilkinsson with a sour grin.

"Look," said Gettinger angrily. He unlaced his right shoe and pulled off his sock. The heel of his naked foot was red and angry-looking. The flesh was twisted and raw with scar tissue. There was a hole in his heel that he could have stuck his little finger into. "I'll be a hell of a lot of good in the Infantry, won't I? Walking my fifteen to twenty-five miles per day? Balls," he said as he put his shoe and sock back on.

Wilkinsson laughed, "We all will," he said. "What's wrong with you?" he asked Johnny.

"I got a piece of mortar shrapnel in my left ankle," he said. "Right in the joint." These two men were strengthening his own opinion. They all had a raw deal in being sent back to the Infantry, let alone the possibility of going overseas again.

"Jap?"

"Yeah."

Wilkinsson gestured at his ear with his crippled hand. "That's what got me. And I got my right leg full of the same stuff," he said. "Where were you?"

"Guadalcanal," Johnny said.

"I was in Attu," said Wilkinsson.

They began to talk of their outfits: Wilkinson was in the 7th Division: The 7th had gone straight from desert training to the sub-zero beaches of Attu. With improper clothing and thinned blood they had made their initial landings through the icy surf and had crossed the frozen mountains in leather boots.

"There's two wards full of men in this hospital," said Wilkinsson, "who lost either one or both feet from having them frozen. And not another scratch on them." He spat angrily into the red dust.

Gettinger had been with the 32nd Division in New Guinea, the old Red Arrow, Hindenburg Line Division, made famous in the last war. A Jap .25 rifle bullet had torn off the butt of his right heel.

The chief clerk stuck his head out of the window. "All right, you two men," he said. "Get that equipment loaded in the back of the truck." Wilkinsson and Gettinger rose reluctantly. "Come on. Come on," said the chief clerk. "Move. A soldier's no good, without his equipment. You're supposed to be pulling out of here," he added with loud sarcasm.

"What does that bastard know about soldiers?" said Wilkinsson. "Does he think we're going off and leave it? What difference does it make whether we put it in now or later?"

Nobody answered.

They sat back down in the shade after throwing the bags into the truck. Johnny was thoughtfully cleaning his fingernails with a file he had taken from a small kit he carried in his pocket.

"Ah, this frigging hole," said Gettinger. "I'm glad to get out of it. Even if it does mean going back to duty." He looked off across the dusty red quadrangle of raw new brick that glared dryly in the bright sunlight,

"But I'll sure hate to leave Memphis," he added with a grin.

"Not me," said Wilkinsson. "I been in this hospital eight, nine months and I've been out of it five times: once on pass, and four times over the hill. I've spent the last two months in a lookup ward; Memphis don't mean nothing to me."

The three men looked strangely identical sitting on the porch edge: each with the summer uniform, each with the same five ribbons pinned in the same place: over the left pocket. All three wore the Purple Heart ribbon, although Johnny's had an Oak Leaf Cluster in the center of it. Each wore the Asiatic-Pacific Campaign ribbon with Bronze Stars, Johnny noticed that Wilkinsson wore an extra ribbon in addition to the five, one that he and Gettinger did not have. At first he could not place it, and then he recognized it for the Distinguished Service Cross. Blue with wide red stripes at the ends and thin white stripes between the red ones and the blue field.

"This is the first time I've been outside a building in two months," commented Wilkinsson. "But it ain't unusual: I been treated like a convict ever since I got here. When I put in for furlough, they wouldn't let me have it because I wasn't 'well enough.' And all the time the ward officer had me pulling fatigue details in the ward: sweeping up and mapping and cleaning the latrine. You're well enough to do that, but not to have a furlough."

He looked at Johnny and grinned malevolently. "So I took my own furlough," he said.

When they had waited forty-five minutes on the driver of the truck, the first lieutenant stuck his head out of the window. "What are you men sitting there for? Don't you know you're moving out? Set up off of there and get into that goddamned truck. The three of them rose. "Corporal," called the lieutenant from the window. "Come over here." Johnny walked over to the window and saluted and stood at attention. "Watch those two men, Corporal," said the lieutenant in a loud voice. "They'll try to take off on you. I don't want to hear of you reporting in to Campbell without them."

Johnny made a salute to the lieutenant, said "Yessir," to the warning, and walked back to the truck. "Okay," he said, "Let's climb in." Wilkinsson and Gettinger stared at him with narrowed eyes. As they climbed into the back of the truck and sat on their barracks bags, it was evident they had completely withdrawn from Johnny and shut him off. Johnny, as the non-com in charge, climbed into the cab. In the sun it was hot, and they sat irritably, sweating and waiting for the driver. It was another hour before he came strolling up.

He was wearing clean fatigues with big grease spots on the knees. He climbed into the truck, lit a cigaret, and stared boredly out across the dusty red quadrangle. "What a rotten hole," he said to nobody in particular.

"Come on," said Johnny irritably. "Let's get the hell out of this." He felt like ripping off his corporal's stripes. Because he was a corporal, these hospital bastards seemed to think that qualified him as a prison-chaser to ride herd on a bunch of men like an MP.

"Take it easy, Cawpr'l," drawled the driver sarcastically. "You'll get back into combat soon enough." But he started the motor and sent the truck lumbering out of the opening of the brick fortress toward town.

In the back end of the truck, Wilkinsson and Gettinger sat precariously on the barracks bags and bounced around heavily. The truckbed was filled with dust and particles of debris from a host of former rides. They sat in the hot sun and breathed the dust and cursed.

"That chickenshit corporal," said Wilkinsson. "You might know they'd stick him on us."

"Ah," said Gettinger disgustedly. "What is it makes a man a ass-kissing son of a bitch as soon as he gets a couple of stripes. It's a wonder they didn't issue him sidearms."

"Did you hear that lousy lieutenant?" growled Wilkinsson. "The goddamned Medical Administrative Corps. They learn military courtesy if they don't learn anything else. Them boys sure do a whole lot for this war. Every squinch-eyed bastard looking for a soft deal puts in for the Medical Administrative OCS."

Gettinger spat disgustedly at the omniscient dust. He was unable to think of an epithet strong enough.

They sat and jounced and coughed and tried to hatch up some plot by which they could get away from the corporal.

When the truck stopped in front of the railroad station, Johnny climbed out and got his bag out of the back. His officer's topcoat which he had bought at the same time he bought the forbidden uniforms, he carried slung over his shoulder. As he pulled his bag off the truck, he became aware again of the estranged looks with which the two men watched him. He cursed the lieutenant silently: leaders, officers and gentlemen. They sure knew how, by instinct, to frig up everything they put their fingers on.

They all went into the station, the other two lugging their cumbersome barracks bags, and Johnny went to find out how soon their train left. The driver took the truck on out into the stream of traffic, mentally calculating if he had time to run up to North Memphis and show his truck to his latest broad, without getting picked up or having his ass eaten out when he got back. He decided it was worth a chance. She would think he was a big shot to be running around in a truck all by himself.

"Hey, you guys," Johnny said, walking back to them from the information window. "Our train doesn't leave for an hour yet." He did not want to be at odds with these two; he was on the same side of the fence they were. He thought of himself as a soldier, not an MP.

"We might as well go uptown and get a couple of brews," he told them.They eyed him suspiciously for a moment, as if he were trying to pull some kind of fast one on them. Their faces had the furtive sullen look soldiers always direct upon inimical authority against which they are powerless. If there had been an officer in charge of the party, Johnny knew he would have looked at the officer in the same way. These men saw him standing between them and freedom, frustrating their desire. He was now Authority, with a Capital A. It made a bad taste in his mouth.

The three of them checked their baggage and sauntered out of the cathedral-like gloom of the station into the bright sun, looking for a beer joint. Walking up the street, unconsciously in step, they made a queer picture: tall Wilkinsson and short Gettinger with Johnny in the middle, a stair-step effect, all dressed alike and with the same ribbons. Wilkinsson and Gettinger both limped in the right leg, and Johnny, limping in the left leg, made a sort of rhythmical counterpoint to their main tempo.

It was early morning and they had to try several beer joints and walk quite a few blocks before they found one that was open. The beer joints in Memphis were enjoying a boom from the army and navy nearby, and they could plutocratically afford to remain closed until eleven or noon. Finally they found a place open and went in and sat down at a table in the cool mustiness. They had no passes, but even the most belligerent MP could hardly run them in for coming downtown to get a beer while waiting on a train. He might order them out and make them go back to the station, but he couldn't very well run them in.

Johnny ordered three beers and looked around the place. It was a typical dingy beer joint. There was no one there that early in the day except a couple of those whiskered old men one saw all through the South, loafing around and talking and doing little else. They sat at the very rear of the counter, drinking beer and talking to the barman.

While the barman was drawing the three beers, Wilkinsson tapped Johnny on the shoulder. "Don't order me no beer," he said sullenly. "I can't pay for it."

Johnny turned to look at Wilkinnson angrily. These guys were carrying a good thing too far.

"Neither one of us got any dough," Gettinger said. "We've both been red-lined for three months, and we haven't got paid a nickel."

"Take it easy," Johnny said, somewhat mollified. "I got plenty of dough. If I hadn't intended to pay for the beer, I'd have asked you if you had dough. I'm paying for it; if you don't want to drink it, I'll drink it myself."

Gettinger grinned. "Okay, Cawpr'l, okay."

Wilkinsson relaxed a little. "Okay," he said. "I just wanted to get it straight: I ain't bumming no beer off nobody." He implied not even a corporal, but he didn't say it.

By the time the barmen brought the glasses, they had warmed up enough to accept the beer without comment, "To the end of the war," Johnny said, and they clinked glasses and drank.

With the taste of the beer bitter in the back of his throat, Johnny watched Wilkinsson. To the end of the war. There was no end to the war. Worse than that, there was no beginning to the war. The war was not yet begun. Pearl Harbor was a song in the jukebox. People praised the Lord and passed the ammunition. But that was not a war. The Lord had nothing to do with ammunition or with the war. The German and the Jap were fighting a war, but the American—except for a few like Wilkinsson—only fought, fornicated, and fell back. They bought their monthly war bond, but still there was no war.

Wilkinsson was tall and very dark, but there was that sallow look about his face and long neck sticking up out of the cheap ill-fitting collar of his issue shirt that showed he had been sick a long time. His face was sharp and thin-looking, and there was a look of strong rancid bitterness about it. His mouth was twisted to one side and gave him a cynical sneer that never left his face. His eyes were dead, but occasionally a wide-eyed uncomprehending stare would come into them. At such times, the stare seemed startlingly out of place in so twisted and knowing a face.

Their antagonism toward Johnny was still strong, in an impersonal way, although the foray uptown after beer had assuaged them somewhat. Johnny knew that he had become, after the lieutenant's warning, a symbol—as were the lieutenant and the chief clerk—of the wartime home front army. He recalled a lieutenant who had come into his old company as a replacement; this lieutenant had been a home front soldier. But after a few quiet artful warnings from the members of his platoon, the lieutenant had dropped his military courtesy and discipline routine and become a soldier and a leader and an enlisted man's type of gentleman.

". . . sure do; them squinch-eyed little bastards are plenty good," Wilkinsson said. "They been training for this for a long time. They can drop a ninety-millimeter mortar shell on a dime. Our sixties and eighty-ones were so damned bad the only way we could put a Jap ninety out of action was to send a patrol to blow it up with grenades. Nobody knew anything but the riflemen, and all they knew was how to shoot. And every time we sent out a patrol like that, about half of them wouldn't come back."

"Ah," said Gettinger with sympathetic disgust. "It was the same way at Buna. We hung onto that place for days and couldn't even make an attack to clean it up. Just laid up there day after day, losing men. And then old Eichelberger comes up after the fighting's all over and *Life* magazine makes pictures of him aiming a rifle and peeking over the top of a trench. And there ain't a Jap within twenty miles. It's all part of the game."

"Part of the game hell," said Wilkinsson. "The Jap made a breakthrough on Attu. We had the last of them backed up in cul-de-sac, and they came down out of there in a suicide march. We was supposed to be waiting for daylight—with one sentry for security. They swept down from there like a wind from hell; they went through two or three companies before we finally got 'em. They swooped right into our rear area, bayoneting the wounded and killing and raising hell, and then when they used all their ammo, they blew themselves all over the place with their last grenade. You can't play war games with the Jap, because he don't know the rules."

"There ain't no rules," said Johnny.

"I know it. And there ain't no game."

Something about Wilkinsson's face disturbed Johnny. He was reminded of many things he had almost forgotten during his ten months in the hospital. Wilkinsson's face made him think of a boy named McCulloch from his old company, Johnny had run into McCulloch in a bar one night in Miami Beach while he was on his convalescent furlough staying at his brother's home. McCulloch had been stationed in Miami Beach for a month, ever since getting out of the hospital at Battle Creek. There was a startling similarity between the faces of Wilkinsson and McCulloch; and Johnny wondered what kind of a person Wilkinsson had been before the war. Mac had come from a small farm in Ohio.

McCulloch had been a sergeant in the old company, a squad leader, and he had seen his whole squad shot down all around him at almost the same instant. Johnny could still remember it. Mac had run screaming down the hill, yelling that his whole squad was dead and that he was dead too. Mac had lived with the men in his squad for over two years and he felt a strong sense of responsibility for them; he took his job as a squad leader seriously because he had the responsibility of so many lives; he had been looked upon by the officers as one of the best non-coms in the company. He and Johnny had been good friends, and Johnny remembered him as an intelligent sensitive very naive farmboy who didn't drink or whore around like the rest of them. He always had a happy good-natured grin on his face. When he had seen Mac in the bar, Johnny was shocked at the change in him.

". . . think it's a game," Gettinger said. "What I don't understand is these sons of bitches back here. You'd think they ran the goddam war. What right has a bastard like O'Flagherty got to talk to me like he does. If he's so hopped up on the war, whyn't he go overseas himself. Because ne's a frigging captain and I'm a buck-ass private, he sits back here on his big ass and tells me I'm a goldbrick, and explains the war to me. Whyn't he do something himself, the son of a bitch."

"He ain't the only one," said Johnny.

"I know it. They're damn near all like that."

"I was the happiest man in the world," said Wilkinsson with a humorless grin, "when I hit that Golden Gate. I didn't expect milk and honey, but I did expect at least common decency. But they don't even give you that. They drive you, from morning till night, one of these sons of bitches like O'Flagherty is always on your neck. They try to make you feel ashamed for being in the hospital, like you got wounded on purpose to get out of something."

"It ain't that so much," Gettinger said. "The guys in the army act like you were a damned fool for letting yourself get shoved into combat. And yet the goddamned civilians shake your hand and fall on your neck for a hero. One's as bad as the other. Then they all go home and forget there ever was a frigging war."

"I used to dream about coming back to the States," said Wilkinsson. "When I get back, I don't find anything I expect. The people talk about V for Victory and buying war bonds, work in the war plants and read the newspapers, but it's all like a movie they can turn off anytime they want. They don't know nothing about war and they don't want to know. I don't know how to explain it," he finished lamely and looked away from the table at the wall.

"V for Victory," snorted Gettinger. "No two-finger salute ain't going to win this war."

"I know what you mean," Johnny said to Wilkinsson. "It's in everything you see; the movies, the magazines, the books, the advertisements. And it ain't even about this war. It's about, something else altogether."

Johnny thought about his own return: the big ship, a Matson liner, unescorted out of New Zealand to the States; it docked at San Diego first, to put off sailors and marines. There were airfields on the edge of the water; there were big enormous planes taking off and landing; there were buildings and docks and oafs and ships and people. Everything was indication of the enormous strength and power, all converted to the prime use: the war. And tears had come into his eyes at being home and at the feel of this enormous source of energy flowing into one single channel out across the Pacific carrying hope and power and faith. But when he had passed through the front picture, like Alice through the looking glass, he had found a different world entirely; an indifferent world—strong, sweating, powerful, full-blasting; but it was uncaring, selfish power, indifferent to and unmoved by itself and what it was supposed to do.

". . . but they won't do that," said Wilkinsson.

"I wouldn't mind going back overseas so much, if I could go back to my old outfit."

The look upon Wilkinsson's face was very much like the look that had been on McCulloch's face when Johnny met him in the Miami Beach bar, and Johnny wondered suddenly if his face ever bad that same look that he saw upon their faces and upon the countless faces in the hospital. His mind went back to McCulloch sitting in the bar, and the conversation passed over his ears untapped.

Mac's face had lighted up when he saw Johnny. They felt very close, having been through so much together. Mac had been sitting alone, and when Johnny sat down beside him, they immediately started talking hungrily about the old company. The company had gone up to New Georgia after the 'Canal, and Mac began to tell Johnny. Mac had had a letter from Seaburt: Rosa was dead; Watson was dead; Berry had lost a leg; Cramm was dead; Horner had been blinded and had lost a hand from a short-fused grenade; Cooper was dead; Morello was dead, Mac went on sounding the knells indefinitely, Seaburt had said in his letter to Mac that there was only five men of the original old company left in the outfit.

Johnny thought of Wilkinsson's remark; what was the use of going back to your old outfit if the men you knew were gone? The outfit was the men in it, and not the number of the regiment.

Telling Johnny all these things across the table in the Miami Beach bar, Mac's face had lost its twisted acidulous look and tears had come into his eyes. They got drunk that night and Mac took Johnny up to see Quiller, who was also from the old company. Quiller was stationed at

Miami Beach too, but he had gotten married since coming back to the States, and he had partially achieved another world.

But as the three of them set on the floor in Quiller's little room (there was only one chair) while Quiller's wife had a board laid across the bed and was ironing, the feeling of the old company had come back to them. And they had recalled and smiled at things that were stories of the old company and its men. Quiller was glad to see them and he drank with them from the bottle they brought, but later when they left, Quiller stayed with his wife who was in her fifth month of pregnancy; Quiller was worried because his landlord would not allow children in the building, and Quiller would have to move as soon as his child was born. And there was no place to move.

Seeing Quiller's room (for which he paid $60 a month) and finding out about his having to move because of the baby offended both Mac and Johnny, and after they left they got drunker still. Mac had talked about Quiller's predicament, and he told Johnny that he had decided the only way for a man to live in the United States was to get a couple of .45s and take what he wanted and to hell with the rest. Johnny had disagreed with him and had told him to take it easy, that everything would work itself out, but he didn't believe it himself. Secretly, he was forced to think that Mac was right. Mac told him how he got busted to a private for going over the hill. He once had been proud of his sergeant's rating, but now he did not care; if he had to be in the army, he thought it better to be a private who did not have to be responsible for anybody's life but his own. Mac told Johnny, too, about how he and another fellow had stolen a car, just for a joyride over to Miami from the Beach. Mac had grinned and his eyes lighted up when he told the story. Mac had told Johnny he was not going back home after the war, that he could not stay around his family because the things he said and did shocked them, and he no longer liked to be with them. He was thinking about getting into the merchant marine, if he lived through the rest of the war. Johnny was puzzled and upset; Mac was vastly different from the good-natured responsible farmboy he had once known, but Johnny could think of no argument that would show Mac how and why he was wrong. Everything Mac said fitted the facts and was the truth. He could not blame Mac for having changed.

". . . plenty of men," Wilkinsson said. "And they ain't going to send this soldier back overseas. I figure I've done my part winning this war, and nobody like O'Flagherty can jump on me for being a goldbrick. A man can just stand so much."

Johnny pulled his mind away from the memory of Mac, but a residue of generalities remained. He was sick with hatred of war, hatred of the cause of war, hatred of the result of war. In combat you had little time to think. You fought and hated, but you did not think much. The thinking came later, after you came back home and passed below the superficial surface of the war. Then you could not help but think, you could not help but wonder. Why did a man have to suffer combat? What was he fighting *for*? Was it so he could be pictured in an advertisement as the reason (for some poor frigging civilian to buy a new refrigerator and a new automobile? Was it so the manufacturers could have a world market as he had heard people say? Surely not. Was his suffering to be displayed as the reason why there should be a porcelain commode in every home? Was that all that what he went through meant: a refrigerator in every kitchen? a commode in every bathroom? an automobile in every garage? It was an indignity Johnny could not swallow. It was a personal affront to every man who had been in combat. If that was all it was, it was not worth it.

When he had been carried back to the aid station after being hit he had noticed his own fingernails. They were cracked and broken and there was a roll of black dirt under each nail. The surface of each nail was covered with a gritty film of dried mud. While he was being carried out, he had stared at his fingernails and the personal affront of the sight of them had never left him. He could see them now as clearly as when he had first noticed them. He had spread his fingers gropingly and stared at them. They had felt heavy and queer and he had divined that to touch them together would be painful. His hands had dangled from his wrists helplessly, and he had been afraid to touch them to his body or to the stretcher on which he lay.

The memory of his own fingernails had become a symbol of the indignity he had had to suffer, only to find that that indignity was being used to sell post-war refrigerators and automobiles and commodes—even before the war was won, even before these things were made, *even while there was still a great chance that the war would be lost*! A raw scabrous hatred of civilians began to rise up in him. They did not understand the war or the men in it, and they did not want to understand. They only wanted to go on playing their little game: The reality was something they could not face, so they escaped it by reading advertisements, by buying war bonds, by making V signs with two fingers. Children, playing at children's games, because they could not face something they feared the thought of.

But Wilkinsson had faced it. Gettinger had faced it. McCulloch had faced it. He had faced it. It was in their eyes. Was O'Flagherty to deride them for it? Were the chief clerk and the first lieutenant to be allowed to play their little disciplinary games with them for it?

Johnny's fists clenched themselves in his lap. His jaw muscles tightened in frustrated anger. His hatred for the pompous self-righteous O'Flaghertys, caustic and domineering; his hatred for the chief clerks and first lieutenants who saw the war as a means of asserting their own obnoxious egos; his hatred for the smugly patriotic citizens who knew nothing and cared nothing about the real war; all of these rose high in him and burned so hotly that the sweat popped out upon his forehead. It was with a painfully deliberate, buttock-tightening effort that he forced himself to relax and refrain from smashing the beer glasses, the table, the whole bar.

He looked at his watch and saw it was almost time for the train. He deliberately finished his beer, his fourth, and looked at Wilkinsson and Gettinger. After Wilkinsson's last remark they had stopped talking, as if the talking itself had dwindled away at the futility of ever explaining. They drank their beer in silence, each lost in his own thoughts and oblivious to the others. Johnny did not break the silence for several moments. He sat and watched them, his jaw muscles twitching.

"Listen," he said suddenly. "You guys have been itching to figure out a way to get away from me so you can go over the hump without getting turned in before you get out of town." Both of them were jerked up out of their own thoughts by the harshness of Johnny's voice, and they stared at him, startled momentarily, "Well, I'm giving it to you," he went on. "You think I'm taking that looey's guff, you're crazy. I figure I've got a vacation coming myself, so you can leave any time you want. You don't have to worry about me turning you in, because I'll be over the hill myself."

His remark was unexpected, and it took the other two by surprise. They looked at him and then looked at each other. They began to grin.

"Well," said Wilkinsson, grinning malevolently, "you know how it is: You can't take chances with a non-com till you know what kind of guy he is, can you? Let's have another beer."

They ordered more beer and drinking it, began to plan how best to get out of town. Wilkinsson showed an amazingly accurate knowledge of roads and routes. Wilkinsson was going to Denver; Gettinger was going to a small town in Maine. Johnny had decided on the spur of the moment to go back to Endymion, where he had not been, and had had no inclination to be, since he had first joined the army.

"What are you guys going to do with your stuff?" Johnny asked.

"To hell with it," said Gettinger.

"Listen," said Johnny. "I've got plenty of money. I drew nine months' pay at one crack, last payday. Besides that, I've cleaned up a couple of games. Here's fifteen bucks apiece." The two men hesitated to take the money, "Go ahead," Johnny said. "If I needed it, I wouldn't give it to you. You'll need dough, if you want to keep from being picked up. I may never see either of you again. So if you never pay me back, okay; if you do, okay."

They took the money. "You better get your stuff and ship it in to Campbell," Johnny said, "It'll be there waiting for you when you do get there."

"Ah, to hell with it," growled Wilkinsson. "I've been red-lined for three months. Let 'em make out a statement of charges. Me and the army are about kits."

"That's right," said Gettinger.

Johnny shrugged. "Where can I get some liquor?" he asked.

Gettinger told him the name of a hotel and the name of the bell captain and to say that Robinson sent him. Johnny made a mental note.

After making their plans, they sat on in the bar until long after the train had left, drinking beer and talking. Johnny intended to go to Endymion by train. The other two would hitchhike. When they left the bar, they shook hands warmly, and split up, each going his own way.

Johnny got his bag from the station. On his way to the other station he took a cab and stopped at the hotel Gettinger had told him. He bought three quarts of bonded whiskey with the seal unbroken. He inspected the bottles for needling and, satisfied, paid the bell captain the thirty dollars he charged. Johnny packed the bottles in his bag with a sour grin. Not even an Armageddon could keep the American people from their prime function in life: making money.

He limped put across the high marble lobby with its potted plants. Wilkinsson was right: A man could only stand so much. Beyond that he could not go. When he had stood all he could take, he was forced to do something. Johnny stopped in the lobby and took the military tickets from his pocket. When he walked out toward his waiting cab, the torn pieces of the tickets fluttered in an eddy of air behind him. They floated to the floor. Later a hotel servant swept them up and deposited them in a waste can.

On French leave, Johnny Carter found himself in a booming wartime wasteland with vapid USO helpers: brainwashed civilians with unrealistic views about war and drunken, carousing, prevaricating soldiers (Johnny's membership in this group was prepaid). Johnny found a sexual partner on the train, no strings attached, as easily as Jones had compliant women in the Peabody Hotel.

This is the way it was, Jones defiantly declared. Maxwell Perkins had an inkling that Jones was giving a realistic picture of his world in late 1943, but he was unable to help Jones reshape his story. Perkins timidly believed the American public was not interested in Jones's subject and that civilians and military people would have been insulted by the presentations.

Perkins was probably wrong.

NIGHT TRAIN

ON THE ROAD, AUTUMN 1943

BY DECIDING TO GO AWOL, Johnny Carter was doing something unprecedented in his career as a soldier. It was the first time he had deliberately absented himself for any period longer than a few hours. He knew the unending repercussions that would come out of his action: busted to a private, dirty jobs, maybe a six months' jail sentence; like waves from a stone dropped into a quiet pool. But when he walked into the other station in Memphis, his jaw was set and his walk was pointed and resolute. He had made his decision and his plans; a man could only stand so much. He walked straight to the window and bought a ticket to Endymion.

He had an elder cousin in Endymion with whom he could stay for a while and he made up his mind to go there. He would have a much better chance of steering clear of MPs in Endymion than if he went to his brother in Miami Beach; the Beach was alive with MPs. Beyond Endymion he could not see, and he did not care to see. And so, because of chance or fate, he was determined to return to Endymion where he had been born. Had it not been for these circumstances, he would probably have never gone to that town again.

When he had his ticket he picked up his bag and stepped away from the window. With his ticket in his hand and a half hour to wait, his intense direction of purpose was ended for the moment, and he relaxed and looked around, orienting himself.

The station, bigger dirtier and older than the other, was terribly crowded. Swirls of people rushed this way at some train call and subsided to rush the other way upon discovering their train was not that one after all. All the waiting seats were filled: seam-faced old men and women, young girls in their teens with squalling babies in their inexperienced arms and wings or rank insignias pinned to their coat lapels, soldiers with legs in casts and crutches leaning against the seat beside them. Great hordes of soldiers rushed here and there, and back, frantic at wasting time that was so precious to them. Harried clerks rebelled against even pseudo-courtesy knowing they could quit tomorrow and become riveters or welders for twice or thrice the money.

Everything was rush and hurry; everything was sick with a war fever that no atabrine or sulfas or penicillin could cure. Johnny saw three decent-looking girls picked up in less than five minutes. Take what you can, the crowd seemed to scream from its red excited face. Soldiers with conspicuous bulges of whiskey bottles under their greatcoats wavered here and there grinning vaguely at crimson-lipped girls who were going to visit brothers or husbands or boyfriends. Sleep with me, the soldiers' faces seemed to say, sleep with me; I'm going to die in a month or two; sleep with me. Okay, came the unspoken answer from the girls, okay; what the hell; my old man's at a POE; he'll be shipped in another week. Life surged frantically, trying to jam twenty years into two months. Sex flared brightly, instinctively trying to recoup its losses to artillery shell and aerial bomb by more and quicker fornication. Sex, its laws and taboos for a long time broken and laughed at in private by the great majority of citizens, now flaunted itself in the open and thumbed its nose at society.

Johnny checked his bag and walked through this hysterical scene toward the nearest pair of MPs. As he came close to them, he stared pointedly at their feet. He had discovered that by doing this he could always make them self-conscious; self-conscious, they lost their sneering toughness of Authority.

"Jesus Christ!" he said to the biggest of the pair. "This place is a madhouse. Everybody's nuts."

The MP grinned. "You ain't kidding," he said. "We got to spend eight hours a day in this joint." He stared at Johnny's ribbons a little enviously; in 1943 ribbons were still unusual enough to cause some notice.

Johnny grinned sympathetically at the MP's remark. "Yeah," he said. "It's a big stinking deal."

"Where was you overseas?" the MP asked.

Johnny told him. After the MPs had seen his ribbons, Johnny put on his topcoat. He stood talking to the two MPs for a little while.

"Well, are them Japs tough?" asked the first MP, "or they just . . ." He broke off in the middle and stepped out into the aisle. "Hey, Mack," he bellowed toughly.

A private who was walking away from them turned around and pointed a finger at himself. "Me?"

"Yeh, you," sneered the MP. "Who the hell you think I meant? Come over here."

The private walked slowly to him.

"Let's see your pass, Mack," the MP said with a hard look at the private.

The private looked at him with resentment and began to fish in his hip pocket. Finally, he brought out a wallet and took a three-day pass out of it. The MP took the pass and examined it minutely. Then he looked at the private suspiciously.

"You didn't make this pass out yourself, did you?" he asked threateningly.

"Well, for Christ's sake," protested the private. "You can see it's signed, can't you?"

"Sure," sneered the MP. "But you could a signed it yourself."

"Well I didn't," said the private. "For Christ's sake. I haven't done nothing. What you jumping on me for?"

"Okay," said the MP with a belligerent nod. "Button up that collar and tighten your tie. You a sojer not a defense worker."

"You goddam MPs," said the private. "You put them brassards on, and you know nobody can do nothing." He finished buttoning his collar and tightening his tie and reached for his pass.

"Lissen you," said the MP, who had extended the pass but now drew it back; his voice was elaborately indifferent. "Don't give me none of your lip. Or I'll tear up this goddam pass and run you in."

The private looked at him for a moment. "Okay," he said. The MP handed him the pass. The private walked off muttering to himself.

"Tell me something," Johnny asked the MP genially. "What made you stop that guy?"

"Ah," said the big MP. "You can most always tell a guy who ain't got a pass. He'll try to give you the go by instead of walking right past you. You get to know it after a while."

"Oh," said Johnny with a nod of understanding.

Another soldier came up to the MP. "Where's the USO around this rat race?" he asked.

The MP pointed up the stairs to a tiny sign in one corner, and the soldier walked off toward it. Johnny watched him for a moment and then turned back to the MPs.

"You can always tell a ree-croot," said the second MP.

"I don't know why them guys want to go to the USO," said the first MP. "The coffee is rotten, and the doughnuts is just plain dough."

All three laughed heartily at this sally. Johnny stood and talked casually with them for several minutes. Then, his little stratagem completed, he walked away. His watch said he had twenty minutes more to wait. He decided to follow the other soldier to the USO. He walked up the steps toward the tiny sign, pleased with himself and inwardly laughing at the MPs and the excitement of breaking the law. He took off his topcoat and slung it over his arm. He could stay in that station for days and not be bothered by that pair of MPs.

The USO was crowded with soldiers drinking coffee, soldiers eating doughnuts, soldiers swallowing tiny cheese sandwiches. They all looked alike and they were dressed alike and they all gobbled doughnuts alike. There were four women behind the counter. Three of them were middle-aged and fat and gray-haired; the other was a young slim woman. Johnny watched them sweating and scurrying hurriedly about to see that all the boys got coffee and whatever else they had to offer.

Three Dear Moms and one Young Matron with lieutenant overseas, he thought. Dispensing good cheer measured out in coffee cups. Ministering to the lower classes. Three cheers for Dear Mom and the Old Homestead.

Johnny felt intensely irritated as he looked around the little room. The counter was covered with a thin sand of spilled sugar, was sticky with slopped coffee. The soldiers sat around at the tiny tables or leaned here and there against the wall. The women laughed and talked from behind their red faces and passed the coffee and doughnuts across the counter. It seemed as if on the two sides of the counter were two different worlds. The women handed down the coffee and doughnuts through a curtain of clouds beyond which they could not see into the nether world of the army. If they could have dissipated the obscuring clouds, they would not have done so. They supplied the coffee to the army, and insisted upon seeing the picture they wanted to see: happy young men with full bellies rushing off joyously to fight a war.

The soldiers, in their world, if they thought about it at all, saw only free coffee and doughnuts. The two worlds on different sides of the counter were so alien that neither could see into the other. The soldiers drank the coffee and ate the doughnuts because they were there and they were free, and thought no more about it unless it was to vaguely resent this disgusting cheerfulness. They went back to whatever miserable life they were living without being happily, or even unhappily, full.

It was wetly hot in the smell crowded room, and the soldiers between gulps of coffee wiped the sweat from their foreheads. When Johnny entered the room, it was with the intention of getting a cup of coffee. After watching the scene for several moments, he turned and started out. It would have been a personal degradation for him to accept a cup of coffee from these women and under these circumstances. The scene he saw made him intensely angry. If the coffee had been offered as coffee, it wouldn't have been so bad, but this coffee was intended to be more than simple prosaic coffee. This coffee was offered not only as a reason for fighting the war but as a reason for not being bitter about it. This coffee was like Salvation Army coffee, where the coffee is blessed of God and offered as a bait to salvation. This USO coffee, it seemed to him, was offered as a solution to the problems of the war and also of the post-war world by the women who shoveled it out, and by the advertisers was portrayed Dear Mom to sell bars, refrigerators, commodes, shoes, shirts, spectacles, liquor, houses, brassieres, radios, and menstruation cloths. This USO coffee was offered by Dear Mom with apparent pride as her contribution to "the war effort," Johnny could not stomach it.

As Johnny reached the door, one of the women trying futilely to serve half a dozen hands at once saw him and walked down the counter toward him. "Do you want something, Corporal?" she called. She seemed proud of her knowledge of rank. "Don't be bashful. Jump right in like everybody else." Her gray hair was beginning to look straggly, and a few drops of sweat stood out on her wrinkled forehead. Her face opened in a sweet motherly smile as Johnny turned back from the door.

"Don't you wish a cup of coffee?" she asked him.

Johnny looked at her for a moment. She seemed to be the living counterpart of the magazine advertisement. ("Gosh, Mom. Gee, Mom. This sure is a swell war, Mom. I wish I was home so I could play with old Towser, Mom.")

"No, thank you," Johnny said. "I don't want anything. I just came in to watch the fun."

The gray-haired woman looked puzzled. "Are you sure you don't want a cup of coffee?" she asked. "We've got some mighty fine coffee."

"No, thank you," Johnny said, looking into her face with dead eyes. "I never drink coffee: It rusts your stomach. Do you have any whiskey? I'd enjoy a drink of whiskey . . . I'd even take rum, seeing how hard whiskey is to get nowadays," he added.

The woman laughed a forced tinny laugh. "Now, now," she chided jokingly. "Why does a healthy young man like you want to drink whiskey? Have a cup of coffee instead, Corporal."

"Don't you have any whiskey?"

"Of course not," she said in an irritated voice. "We can't serve intoxicating drinks here. We do all we can to make the boys happy, but we don't want to aid them in ruining themselves."

"Oh," said Johnny. He stared at the woman solemnly. "I didn't mean to insult the USO. I've never been in a USO before, you see, so I didn't know. I just got back from Guadalcanal, and I've been in the hospital for ten months.

"Besides," he added modestly, "My first sergeant was a Regular Army soldier. He was neurotic. He made me swear an oath that I'd nearer go into a USO before he would sign my evacuation papers."

The gray-haired woman looked at him with puzzlement for a moment. She was not sure whether he was trying to ridicule her or not. At his mention of Guadalcanal, she immediately glanced at his left shirt pocket. The poor boy must have been through a lot of terrible experiences. She smiled at him again, at ease once more, and showing him she was not angry at what he had said to her.

"I saw your ribbons," she said, smiling. "Tell me what they mean. What's that one?" she asked, pointing to the Purple Heart.

Johnny stared at her for a moment with expressionless eyes set in a deadpan face. "Well-l-l," he said suddenly, in the expansive manner of a Rotarian explaining his button to a non-Rotarian, "that's the Purple Heart. You get that one for being wounded or killed. . . . I wasn't killed," he added; "I was only wounded."

The gray-haired woman laughed. "Where were you wounded?"

"I was wounded," he said after an expressionless pause, "in the leg. A terrible wound. They had to amputate my leg four inches above the knee," he said proudly. He leaned forward confidentially. "I'm wearing an artificial leg now," he said in a low voice.

"And this one," he said, pointing to the Pacific-Asiatic ribbon, "is the Congressional Medal of Honor. I got that for capturing a hundred and twenty-two Japs single-handed. Maybe you saw my picture in the paper? I'm the one that's going to make war bond tours for the rest of the war."

"No, no," said the gray-haired woman excitedly. "I didn't see it. What paper was it in?"

"Oh," he said with a magnanimous gesture. "It was in all the New York, Chicago, New Orleans, and Miami papers."

"Wait just a minute," said the gray-haired woman breathlessly. "I want the other girls to meet you. You're the first real hero we've had come into our little place."

"No, no, no," he protested. "Don't call them. I'm sort of shy about talking about myself. Besides, I have to go and endorse some soap advertisements. My train's about due in, and I have to find a shot of whiskey before I leave. I'll need some morale on the train."

Johnny walked to the door. A couple of soldiers who had been standing behind him grinned hugely. "You see?" Johnny said from the door. "If you'd had some whiskey, I'd have stayed and talked to the girls.

"The USO," he said, "ought to give the boys what they want. Whiskey and a nice young girl to spend the night with are much better for the morale than coffee and doughnuts." He turned and walked out of the place quickly before the woman had a chance to answer. Her eyes and mouth were open as she began to realize what he had said.

Johnny went over to the station restaurant and ordered a cup of coffee. He sneaked a shot of whiskey into the coffee from the half-pint bottle he always carried in his hip pocket. He felt a little ashamed of himself for deriding the old lady, and feeling ashamed made him more angry. A man bitches up his life in the goddamned war and then he is supposed to come home meekly and take his cup of coffee and his doughnut in the USO and be cheerful, happy, and satisfied. You were supposed to give your life, the only one you had, to straighten out some situation a lot of dimbrains had botched up twenty years before—just so they could go and do it all over again. He hadn't wanted to hurt her feelings; his mouth had just opened and the words came out. He was as surprised as she was. These people played games with their lives; they imagined a picture of themselves and played out the part they had imagined for themselves. And who had undertaken the vast job of providing for them the picture they felt called upon to mimic with its tremendous scope and far-reaching powerful implications? and for what? If Dear Mom was only kept busy at home, she wouldn't have time or energy to try living up to her archetype in the advertisements. These citizens could play out their mummery all their lives—at least until the deathbed scenes when the questions were asked; but you can't go on playing a game and imagining a picture when you're in combat. There the play is for keeps, and you learn it quick enough.

He sat in the restaurant amid the clank of dishes and the smell of rancid frying fat and drank his coffee and whiskey. The floor was sloppy and the counter wet and sticky. The waitresses yelled over his head, and the customers complained, paid, and left. He absorbed the panorama of the restaurant feeling mean and bitter. Everybody hated their jobs and everybody else. The restaurant seemed to be a parallel to his own life, a squalid reeking fetor. A pleasant picture. He gulped the reminder of his coffee and whiskey and got out of there quickly, intending to wait the remaining ten minutes at the track. It was not too great as stretch of the imagination to suppose that the old lady might call the MPs down on him. And he couldn't afford to be picked up now. He wandered out to the track where his train would come in and stood there, his fists jammed deep in his pockets, staring at nothing with a bitter scowl on his face.

At the track, there were a number of people already lined up waiting for the train. Some of them looked like they had been waiting for hours. When the train pulled into the track, the line lengthened behind Johnny until he could not see the end of it. Everyone had waited quietly though nervously, but as soon as the train stopped, the line broke. There was a sudden wave of frenzied excitement as everyone in the line rushed the various vestibules. The agitation possessed all the people waiting, tensing their muscles and heightening their nervous perception.

Johnny was near one of the vestibules and bag in hand, his body moving without his conscious command, he grabbed the handhold and jumped with nervous quickness almost before the train had stopped. He was the first one in that vestibule, and as he entered the day coach, he could hear a bedlam of noise at the place where he entered as a crowd of people tried to force their way past other people. For a moment, he felt a sense of degradation at having allowed himself to charge and jostle like one of a herd of frightened cattle. The impulse had been almost hypnotic, a fear, a feeling that he must get on the train. And yet none of them would have been any the worse if they had not gotten on. It was humiliating. Like a bunch of wild animals. They all seemed as if they were afraid of the thought of having to do nothing but sit for a couple of hours, as if they were afraid to death to be alone with their own minds.

He grinned to himself and selected one of the few empty seats. If he didn't get on first, somebody would beat him to it. The coach was almost full when it pulled in, and the passengers going on through Memphis already had their seats. They sat looking out of the windows at the yelling pushing throng with disdainful amusement and contempt at such antics. Johnny looked once at the young woman sitting beside him and then looked away; there was nothing worth having there. The young woman was pasty-faced, and her skin was greasy with old sweat; her eyes looked exhausted. She had evidently been riding a long time. She wore a captain's bars pinned to her coat, and she was holding a dirty uncomfortable-looking little baby. Probably she had been to see her husband, Johnny thought. This war sure was hard on the kids.

By the time the train pulled out of Memphis, Johnny was already tired of sitting. Looking around to see if the train MPs were near, he opened his bag and extracted one of the three quarts of whiskey in it and slid the bottle into the pocket of his topcoat and hung the coat over his arm. He grinned wryly, thinking that the suitcase contained everything he owned in the world and still had room for three quarts. Asking the young woman to watch his seat for him, he started making his way to the lounge car carrying the topcoat. The aisles were full of standing passengers and each rest room was so crowded with people who had no place to sit that it was next to impossible to get into one to use the toilet. The three Pullman cars were not quite so crowded. In the last one, four soldiers were playing poker. One of them, seeing Johnny's ribbons, called to him; he was invited to sit in. The four of them, all overseas men and all drunk, were going to Indianapolis to report for duty. They had come from the hospital in Temple, Texas, and they had been playing poker all day, fifty-cent ante and a dollar to open on jacks or better.

Johnny played for an hour and won back the thirty he had loaned to Wilkinsson and Red, plus another ten. He quit and started back to the lounge car. They had drunk some of the whiskey, and the quart was over half-empty. He still had the half-pint bottle in his pocket and he calculated mentally, figuring he had enough to do the trick. He passionlessly intended to pick up a woman, preferably one with a Pullman berth, and he would need the whiskey. It all depended on how much the unknown wench liked to drink. If he needed more, he could always go back and get it out of the bag.

The lounge car was crowded and smoke filled. All the seats were taken, and extra passengers, mostly soldiers, were standing in all the available space. Johnny stood inside the door and looked around. The liquor he had drunk, on top of the beer, was beginning to make his head blurry; he felt a comforting relaxation stealing through his arms and legs; his lungs were free and seemed far away from him, as if it were someone else breathing this stale smoke-filled air into his lungs instead of himself. He looked around the bar until he saw a woman who seemed to fit what he wanted, a sophisticated-looking woman of about thirty-five who was sitting by a window next to a wizened old woman. There was no man with her, and Johnny watched her for a few moments, but she did not speak to the old woman. The setup seemed perfect.

He walked over to them and grinned at the younger woman. He had been like the actor who walks out upon the stage. The brief pause of orientation, the deep breath of the plunge, and suddenly he was completely another person. He was no longer Johnny Carter as he knew Johnny Carter. He was the man he divined this woman would like to see.

"Pardon me," he said. "I'm a hero just back from the Pacific and I've got a bum leg. May I sit on your lap?"

The woman looked up at him coldly and she did not speak. Then, in spite of herself, she smiled.

"I don't think you'd find my lap very comfortable; my knees are rather bony." He felt she had accepted him. It was the gay boyish smile that did it. The gay boyish smile always worked for a starter. All he had to do now was play the tedious game through to completion. Of course, the completion didn't always follow from the beginning, but usually it did.

"I don't think your knees are bony," he said gently, grinning. "They appear very rounded and beautiful to me. And I'm sure of all the laps I've seen, I think I'd rather sit on that one than any."

"You have a very glib tongue, Corporal," the woman countered, smiling. "To be honest, I'm the one that would be uncomfortable. You're too husky-looking. But maybe there's room for you between us." As she spoke she glanced pointedly at the old woman, who looked back at her reprovingly but inched over so there was room enough for Johnny to squeeze in between them.

"What's wrong with your leg, Corporal?" the woman asked as he sat down. "Were you wounded?"

"Twice," Johnny grinned and nodded. "You may call me Johnny. I'm off duty now."

"All right, Johnny, and my name is Carroll. Were you wounded very badly? Or maybe you'd rather not talk about it."

"No, I don't mind talking about it," he said. "I love to talk about it. But it's not very exciting. It really was nothing. I got shot in the leg with a dum-dum bullet. I went into enemy territory after a wounded major who was crying piteously for aid and carried him back to safety where the medics could give him plasma and save his life. I got hit on the way back, but that didn't stop me because I knew that poor wounded major was vital to our winning the battle. If I got crippled or lost a leg, or even died, it didn't matter, so long as I got that major back to where he could help direct and win the battle. That's all there was to it. That's not heroic or exciting. Just plain run of the mill newspaper stuff." He made a deprecating gesture and looked at the woman very humbly.

The woman's eyes twinkled. "Why I think that's wonderful," she exclaimed. "Didn't you get a medal for such a magnificent deed?"

Johnny made a disparaging face. "Well, yes," he said, "I did get a couple. But I was lucky: Most of the guys don't have an influential major to recommend them. But you know how it is. Medals don't really mean anything. Of course, they're nice to show to your grandchildren, but they don't mean much to us fighting men. We know there's a great job to be done, and we just try to do our bit.

"You know anything about these ribbons?"

"No," she smiled seriously. "I really know nothing at all about them, but I've always wanted to learn what they meant; it makes one feel stupid not to know the various ribbons when all the boys are wearing them. Will you explain them to me?"

"Of course," Johnny assented magnanimously, "of course. Now this one is the Distinguished Service Cross; I got that for saving the poor wounded major. I would have gotten the Congressional Medal of Honor, but I lost my nerve. I didn't get killed and I don't know how to write songs. After the dum-dum broke my leg, I let them carry me back to the hospital when I really should have stayed and fought some more. I'm really a coward at heart."

The woman laughed softly. "That's queer," she said innocently. "I thought that purple one with the two white bands at the ends was the Purple Heart."

Johnny looked at her for a moment and then grinned.

"Aha," he cried. "Sabotage rears its ugly head. Are you going to believe me, a returned hero, or are you going to believe what you read in some silly propagandist magazine?"

The woman's smile spread. "Why of course I believe *you,*" she protested. "How could you ever doubt that? But didn't you get the Purple Heart for being wounded?"

"Sure," he said. "I got it, but us real soldiers never like to wear a ribbon so many people have got. The Purple Heart's a dime a dozen."

"What does it look like?" she persisted.

"What, the Purple Heart? It's green, a green ribbon with a little red heart printed in the center of the ribbon. That's why they call it the Purple Heart, because it's green. . . . I tried to hock my Purple Heart in Memphis, and you know what the guy in the hockshop offered me? Six bits. He took me in the back room and showed me a whole drawer full of medals from the last war. All kinds of medals, and Purple Hearts galore."

A tall staff sergeant who was standing near the seat laughed out loud. Johnny looked up at him and grinned. "That really happened," he said.

"I don't doubt it a bit," retorted the staff sergeant.

"Seventy-five cents?" The woman was shocked. "You're kidding me. Surely they're worth more than that."

"Well, I don't know," Johnny said. "The general who pinned it on me at the hospital told me they cost twenty-seven-fifty apiece, but I'm inclined to think he was quoting inflation prices. Supply and demand, you know." The tall dark staff sergeant laughed explosively.

"Here, Mack," Johnny said, pulling the bottle out of his topcoat, "have a drink."

The staff sergeant took the bottle and examined it, grinning.

"To the end of the war," Johnny said softly as the staff sergeant uncorked the bottle. The staff sergeant stopped in the act of raising the bottle to his lips and gazed at Johnny for a second. Then he dipped the bottle. "By God, I'll drink to that," he said.

After he drank, he handed back the bottle. Johnny took it and stared at it, thinking he needed one, too. His record was beginning to run down. If he was to keep the gay boyish grin from drooping, he'd need several. The wit was being drilled against the rock of sobriety, and the gay boyish humor was wilting: His smiling muscles were getting tired. He took a deep drink from the bottle.

"That's a nice toast," the woman Carroll said to him, "I've never heard that before. It's so simple, you'd think I would have."

"No," said Johnny. "I guess it's too simple for most people. They like high-sounding oratory with their liquor. We used to toast each other in the New Zealand hospital with that one; there was a bunch of guys from my outfit there together. All of us expected to go back up to the 'Canal." He paused. Christ only knew where the rest were now; only two of them had come back to the States. What the hell was he crying on *her* shoulder for? "I never drink to anything else myself."

"Does it have some special significance?" the woman asked.

Johnny surveyed her ironically. "Yes," he said. "It does. It signifies about forty men in my company. They all got killed. That's what the toast means: to the end of killing guys like them and like me. . . . Here," he said. "Have a drink."

The woman took the bottle from him and examined it closely, her eyes lowered to hide her embarrassment. She felt like an insensitive fool; for the first time, she had had a glimpse underneath the surface they wore. It was not a pleasant sight, and she wanted to avoid that part of the conversation, to steer it back to the light mood of a few minutes ago; tearing her hair with unhappy soldiers was no way to spend a holiday from her own unhappiness. She was intruding into something where she had no place or understanding, and she wanted to keep it out of her life. The staff sergeant also wore a Purple Heart ribbon and there was an odd look on his face, too. It seemed there were wounds for which there were no wound stripes or Purple Hearts.

"I can't drink whiskey straight," she said. "But I'll order a round of old-fashioneds if you want one."

"Sure," Johnny said, "I can drink anything. We're not very high class about our drinking in the army. After you get used to drinking Aqua Velva and torpedo juice, straight whiskey tastes pretty good."

"Do you want one?" she asked the staff sergeant.

"I've never refused one yet," he said.

The woman kept buying drinks, and as they got drunker, the light mood of before returned to them. They talked and laughed above the buzz and hubbub of the smoking car. The woman was expensively dressed in a British tweed suit and a violet sweater of Indian cashmere, and she carried a pair of soft French kid gloves. Her marriage rings were diamonds set in platinum; she wore a star sapphire on her right hand. She had an air of poise and authority that bespoke an environment of wealth and richness. Johnny watched her and sighed deeply; life was wonderful. He could feel a flood of lights as the liquor rose in him.

The porter returned and requested obsequiously if the lady wanted another drink. Johnny had not noticed the porter coming around to see if anyone else wanted another drink. Not unless he was called. This gal must *really* be Mrs Rich Bitch, he thought. He hoped she wasn't so Rich Bitch that she had to watch her reputation.

"I don't want any more," Johnny said. "I'm going to have all I can take care of to drink this whiskey."

"Then we won't have anymore, George," she told the porter.

"Sure," said Johnny. "We can't get drunk in uniform and bring disrepute upon the armed services. How did you know his name was George?"

"All porters are named George," she said. "That's an unwritten law of the railroad."

"Well, well," he sighed. "I used to know a bartender named George. . . . Come, let us leave this macabre place, this sink of iniquity. I am becoming depressed watching all these foolish people fritter away their lives eating and drinking and laughing hollow laughter. I would rather be alone. Well, almost alone."

"Did you buy this lousy seat?" he asked her.

"Good God, no! I wouldn't ride on a train if I had to sit up all night. I've got a berth in the second car up."

"Do you mean to tell me you've been sitting here and taking this seat from some poor person who paid to ride in this bloody club car when you've got a berth? For shame. How the hell did you manage to get a berth? You must have had a reservation in for months."

"Don't be silly," she said. "You can get a berth any time you want one, provided you know who to see and have the pull. They always keep some berths back for the right people."

Johnny sighed. "I thought I knew my way around. Well, let's go. I'm bored with this low-class place. Let us adjourn to your berth and drink up my whiskey; whiskey is good for the soul. And then the sarge here can have your seat. He's been standing up all night. Can you get some setups around here?" He looked at the woman, his blood rising in his ears. That was the pay-off. The buildup was always okay with the gay boyish grin, but you could never be sure till the pay-off. And you always had to cover your self-consciousness with banter.

The woman looked at him and smiled like a purring cat. The liquor made pinpoints of fire in her dark eyes. She had been expecting it for some time; she was surprised he hadn't brought it up before. A woman could hold a man in the palm of her hand—if the man really wanted her—even a wild soldier like this, and make him nervous and bashful as an adolescent, "I'd rather drink than eat. I love the way liquor spreads out over your body and gives it such a mellow glow. It makes me all relaxed and sleepy. I get excited as hell when I drink. I just can't get enough when I'm drinking."

"Well," said Johnny. "Well, well. What in hell are we waiting for? I can't ever get enough."

"Listen, Johnny. We can't go to my berth together. I'll go ahead and order some setups. You wait ten minutes before you come. It's the second car up, lower five. And don't forget the whiskey."

Johnny nodded and watched the woman get up and leave. Well, well, he thought. Old lucky pants; you never can tell what you'll run into till you try. "Looks like you hit the jackpot," grinned the staff sergeant as he sat down in the woman's vacated seat. "Yeah," said Johnny. He winked at the staff sergeant. "Here, have another drink. I've got ten minutes yet." The sergeant took the bottle. "Where were you?" he asked. "Guadalcanal," said Johnny laconically. "You?" "Africa," said the sergeant. "I was standing a full field inspection at the Battle of Kasserine Pass." Johnny snorted; "I heard about that," he said. They had another drink. At her car, the woman told the porter what she wanted and gave him a good tip. She got into her berth and began to undress. Her eyes were bright with anticipation. What would they say at home if they could see her now? Picking up a strange soldier on a train and taking him to her berth? She laughed a low excited laugh. An enlisted soldier! But he was clean-cut and decent-looking in a wild sort of way. This was the perfect adventure: no strings, no social alliances, not long enough to be tiresome or boring, like marriage. She finished undressing and lay on the top of the covers, waiting for the soldier.

The next morning at five Johnny was dressed and waiting for the train to pull into Evansville. He stood in the day coach where he had left his bag the night before and looked out through the grimy window at the lightening dark. The weary-looking captain's wife was gone, and someone else was asleep in his seat. He didn't mind. He had left the woman Carroll without waking her to say goodby. He did not even know her last name. It didn't bother him. He had gotten what he wanted. Both had had a night of sex and liquor without any strings of sentiment, just what they wanted, he told himself, but he was not as pleased as he thought he would be. He was at a low ebb, very tired from the night's orgy, and he was still a little drunk. He shouldered into his topcoat as the train began to pull into Evansville.

He stood with his hands jammed in the topcoat pockets, watching the lights flash past, each light an asterisk of indication above the life of some house or some street, all clustered together like ants and their eggs under a big rock for protection and so seeing nothing and knowing nothing of all the vast life that goes on beyond and outside the rock. All around him the people in the car were asleep and he felt that strange sense of fascination and of wonder that a man feels when he alone is out and the world about him sleeps. He turned away slowly from the Hollywood technique of city-life-at-a-glance and watched the sleeping people in the car. The people slept. The people slept because they would get their techniques at the movies fresh out of the can because then it would be romantic and thrilling and not like now when in the flesh city-life-at-a-glance only bored them and they would rather sleep. They would rather sleep. They would rather sleep because their imaginations and their susceptibilities needed the hypodermic shot in the arm that only melodramatic plots fresh out of the can and trumpeting city-life-at-a-glance could give. Their life was a can and their ego was a lid and they were shut into the ego-can by the ego-lid and the only way they could get out was to climb out into fresh-out-of-the-can. His mind felt the wonder of prodigy at being awake and looking down at the sleeping people each in his can, each in his ego-can, while he watched the technique of city-life-at-a-glance in marquee asterisk lights. Rich men who wanted to be poor and simple farmboys; wives who wanted to be single women; unmarried women who wanted to be married women; waitresses who wanted to be chorus girls; movie stars who wanted to be waitresses; soldiers who hated the army; 4-Fs who hated hating the army. Everybody who hated being everybody and envied being somebody. And all because the ego can shut off everything beyond and outside of the rock and like an improperly canned can of peaches acquire the mold and fester and sourness of being in the can beneath the rock. And because of all of this the Hollywood technique of city-life-at-a-glance made each canned celluloid life a prodigious affair of nothing-at-all-under-the-screen. Two-dimensional life and each embryo that did not know it was an embryo slept in its can as city-life-at-a-glance-in-the-flesh flashed past.

Johnny snorted. He shook his head. He had almost fallen asleep standing in the aisle. He looked again out of the window at the lights of Evansville and felt he had dreamed. He lit a cigaret and tried to recapture the vague memory of what he had dreamt. It seemed he had dreamt about himself and the woman of last night, but he could not remember the dream, and the vague memory faded away and was gone. He felt irritated that he could not remember it, because it seemed to be something important.

The memory of the dream, or whatever it was, recalled the woman to his mind. He felt suddenly that she would be disgusted and remorseful when she woke. The thought of this irritated him. She had certainly gotten what she wanted. He had. Exactly what he wanted. In spite of that, he felt a rising irritation and dissatisfaction. There was nothing for the woman to feel remorseful about, and yet he was sure she would. It had been natural and he had enjoyed it. So why in hell should he feel irritated and dissatisfied?

He had spent ten months in the hospital in Memphis and it had been that same sort of thing: A perpetual bout of drinking and bedding, and he had been peaceful. But now his mind refused to be peaceful. The peace and relief of his body became only exhaustion and tiredness under the influence of his still racing mind. Hence the irritation and dissatisfaction, a feeling of something missing, like a missing heel from a shoe will throw the whole body out of balance. The irritation grew and he became angry at himself for not being peaceful, angry at the people for sleeping like cattle while he was angry at them.

The conductor came through the car hog-calling the name of the city. The car that had a moment before seemed asleep except for himself leaped into a sudden savage life. People jumped from sleep into quick movement like sprinters at the gun. Before Johnny had time to straighten himself and reach up for his bag, a stream of bodies was already moving past him, pushing him against the seat. He stood that way, an island buffeted by the river of bodies flowing toward the vestibule, until his growing anger boiled over into action. Powerfully, he pushed his body back from the seat and reached up to the luggage rack. He jerked his heavy black suitcase down from the rack into the moving stream of bodies. The blunt insouciant end of the bag collided forcefully with the squirming bottom of a shrewish young woman who was in the act of attempting to push past him. The force of the blow pushed her sharply off balance. She fell against the seat opposite and sprawled across a technical sergeant who was sitting in that seat, her face buried in his lap. The technical sergeant, who with his buddies had been imbibing of the dubious good cheer of a bottle of cheap rum, looked down at his lap with amiable amazement. Then he looked up at the ceiling with wide eyes to see if there was a hole in it. Punching the backs of his two buddies seated in front of him, he breathed, “Manna. Manna. And I never b’lieved that stuff about Moses and the power of prayer.”

The woman got to her feet unaided; none of them offered to help her up. She turned to Johnny with an indignant and hurt expression on her face; it was obvious that he had assaulted her, had offended her sacred right, as a woman, to be protected. He grinned at her maliciously over his shoulder and cocked an insolent eyebrow. “I beg your pardon, madam,” he said, “if I have hurt your feelings.” He looked pointedly at her resilient bottom. “Perhaps the next time you’ll take it a little easier.” He shoved his bag in front of him and stepped in front of the woman with deliberate rudeness. The tech sergeant and his two buddies broke into uproarious sarcastic laughter. The goddam little bitch, he thought; somebody’s wife or somebody’s mother. All you had to do was be born a woman and you had life handed to you on a silver platter. The women possessed what the men wanted, and they capitalized on it and flaunted it at every occasion. He detected something of the same feeling in the laughter of the three soldiers. They were getting even with the woman for being a woman. It was a hell of a situation, and they would get no boot-licking from him.

As Johnny climbed off the train, the fresh air of early morning smote him in the face, climbing from the noisy shoving badly lighted car was like climbing down into another world, a strange quiet pleasantly smelling world that he had been away from so long he had forgotten it existed. It was cool, and he drank the coolness in like a long drought of water. He walked away from the station and hailed a cab to take him out to the edge of town. He had decided to hitchhike from Evansville to Endymion.

He paid the cab and watched it disappear down the long concrete highway back to town, leaving him alone in a world that slept. He set his bag down and stood in the autumn chill of early morning waiting for a ride, a lonely figure that stood out sharply and rebelliously against a backdrop of shanty filling stations and short order hash houses.

It was cold with a penetrating chill of early morning. He hunched his neck down inside the collar of the officer's topcoat and stood still by the side of the road . . . Waiting for a car that would stop and give him a ride.

The stories in To the End of the War *are presented here as interrelated stories, similar to Sherwood Anderson's* Winesburg, Ohio. *This story, "Back Home in Endymion," is yoked to the next one, "Johnny Meets Sandy." To put them together makes the story too long. Let the two be.*

Wilson (Will) Carpenter is Johnny's friend from childhood and had escaped a domineering mother just as Jones did. Will is suspected of being gay, but Johnny will have nothing to do with this gossip, defending Will as an artist.

Jones cleverly presents our first glimpses of Sandy through Fanny's eyes, not Johnny's, for he was soon to be bedazzled by outlier Sandy.

BACK HOME IN ENDYMION

THE CARTER MANSION, NOVEMBER 1943

IN THE TWO DAYS HE had been home Johnny had already become a source of considerable annoyance to both his cousin Erskine and Erskine's wife, Fanny. Erskine, who had been as far as Fort Dix in the last war and understood about war, could not find it in him to condone or to explain young Johnny's actions because of having been in a war.

Erskine was forty-four or -five and Fanny was thirty-nine and a half, or as she would explain it to herself: something under forty. Erskine was the son of Johnny's father's eldest brother, and both he and his wife were considerably removed by years and outlook from their cousin. Although they had sent Johnny an invitation to visit them several months before, they had not really expected him to accept it, and in the intervening months they had nearly forgotten about the invitation. They were surprised when Johnny showed up unexpectedly, and the surprise took on an additionally unpleasant cast when they found that he was AWOL. They had expected, if he came at all, that he would come up for a three-day pass or at most a ten-day furlough. When they learned that he had spent his convalescent furlough with Tom in Miami, they felt that he was only using his visit to them as a means of evading military authorities while he was over the hill, and they did not like this aspect of the situation. They were right in feeling that he was using them, of course—to a certain extent—and when he freely admitted his reason for visiting them, they were more upset.

They were proud of him, however. Johnny was one of the first boys to come home after having been wounded in combat. They were proud of him, and they naturally wanted him to meet people and associate with their numerous friends. The second evening he was home they had a sort of little open house to which Erskine's business friends were invited.

Erskine had taken a degree in law at the University. However, being a lawyer was more or less a side issue; Erskine ran a branch insurance and had a chattel mortgage and loan business. He used his law as a sort of lever for his other businesses. Having these businesses, a good part of his work was entertaining business associates and friends who could aid him in extending and furthering his influence. It was both a lucrative and very pleasant way of conducting business.

The old Carter home with its large high-ceilinged rooms was enlivened by this party Erskine and Fanny gave for Johnny. The only blot on the whole evening was due to the guest of honor, who was inclined to be asocial and uncivil with a sort of sarcastic humor, and who got so drunk early in the evening that he had to be stacked on the shelf, letting the open house get along as best it could without his presence. Both Erskine and Fanny, who were inclined toward a little indecorous drinking themselves at times, if the occasion warranted, were astonished at the prodigious amount of all kinds of liquor that Johnny drank.

The whole situation was not to Erskine's liking, and he expected the worst. Johnny seemed sure to make a public spectacle of himself, and he made no bones about telling anybody who asked that he was over the hill.

Now Fanny sat wearily at the table in the sunroom of the over-big Carter house wondering what to do with him. Johnny had phoned her from next door and informed her that he was at Wilson's. In three days, she was already at her wit's end. She had suspected that Johnny would be different from the boy she had known, but she had not realized or even, guessed at the magnitude or the direction of the change. It had not taken her long to discover it however. She liked Johnny personally, and as it was her duty to like him, because he was a part of the Carter family she had adopted by marrying Erskine. The Carter family was her family, and she had been taught, partly by her parents as a child (she was a Southerner) and partly by Erskine after she was married, a pride in family that amounted to a religion. As Erskine's wife, she felt the same fierce unbending pride for all the Carter family, good or bad, living or dead. Fanny, like her spouse, felt deeply the fact that her name was Carter, and she felt deeply the responsibility of the name and that as a Carter she had a certain position to live up to. Some of the Carters may have been bad, Erskine would say, but they were always bad in a good sort of way. Then, too, Fanny liked Johnny with the feeling of maternity that women usually feel toward the wayward sons. For some inexplicable reason, the black sheep seem to hold a higher place in the hearts of their mothers and all the other womenfolk of their families. And Johnny was already catalogued as a black sheep.

In the two days he had been home, he had hardly drawn a sober breath. Fanny had had no experience with returned-from-overseas soldiers, nor had she heard much talk about them in the Endymion gossip mart, for Johnny was one of the first to come home. She had read, though, a number of articles by both male and female war correspondents and statesmen which stated that the young men who were fighting the war were not taking it any more to heart than they would have taken an unpleasant job in the next county, that they were all very stable young men, down to earth, feet on the ground, who would return to their old lives easily by casting off their war experiences like a locust casts off its dead shell; in other words they were not losing their perspective of American life and their place in it. Fanny believed the articles faithfully. Consequently, she could not figure out what had come over Johnny, could not understand what made him change so radically. There was a wild light that came into his eyes at times which Fanny could only attribute to some quirk, of bad blood.

Erskine had suggested forcefully that Johnny take it easy around Endymion, because he, Erskine, had built the family name up to its former position of respect from which Johnny's father had previously dragged it down, and because the townspeople were too prone to say like father like son.

That Johnny would laugh at Erskine's advice was a shocking thing. He was over twenty years Erskine's junior, and he did not seem to care about family, or he surely would not have done such a thing as laugh. Fanny could not see that he cared about anything. He would not listen to what either of them said; he went his own way regardless of advice or of how many people he might hurt.

Fanny did not know what to do, and Johnny and Erskine were fast approaching a crisis. She got up from the chair and walked up and down the room in indecision. Fanny was a member of the Endymion Underground. This unsung unofficial organization was composed of the wives of various businessmen of the more respected types. Of course, the Endymion Underground had its various factions who were out to subtly dig and cut the throats of the enemy factions; and of course, these factions were continually breaking up to form new factions. But each woman was always a member of one faction or other, so that when she or her man got in trouble (usually it was the man), the woman could turn to her underground faction for aid. When a husband got in some kind of business or personal trouble, the wife would go to the phone and, via this secret weapon, organize a resistance. The other wives would put pressure to bear upon their own husbands, using the various methods at which they were so deft, and the troubled husband would suddenly find his troubles evaporated. He would come home patting himself proudly on the back and tell his wife the good news, and the wife would go to the phone and give the all-clear signal to the rest of the Endymion Underground.

Fanny continued her indecisive walking. This did not seem to be a job for the underground. She could see no one else to turn to then but Sandy Marion. Sandy Marion did not play at politics with the rest of the underground factions, but the wives secretly considered her their expert on children's affairs. She seemed especially to have a way with the children of whom the mothers seemed to have lost all contact.

Fanny went to the phone, picked it up, and asked for a number.

"Hello?" she said anxiously into the phone. "Hello? Is that you,

Sandy? This is Fanny . . . I've got something bothering me and I was wondering if you would help me out. . . .

"Well, young Johnny is here; Joe's boy. He's in the army and he's been in the hospital since he got back: from overseas. . . .

"Yes. Guadalcanal. . . . Well, I know how all the kids in town like you and how you've fiddled around with them. And I wonder if I could bring Johnny down to see you. Just like it was a social call, you know. . . . I thought you might do something with him. . . .

"Oh, no. I wouldn't do that. I didn't know you had a guest. . . . When did he get in to town; I hadn't heard a word about it. . . .Yesterday? . . . Well, maybe it would be a good thing if they got together, both being overseas and all. . . . I always liked George. I hate to hear about his leg. . . .

"To be honest with you, Sandy. I don't know what to do with him, really. He won't listen to anything Erskine and I say to him. He's been drunk ever since he got here. We just can't handle him; honestly, he's a problem. It's nothing on the surface. It's something I can't just put my finger on. He just looks at you, you know? I'm terribly worried, and I'm afraid he and Erskine are going to have trouble. I really wouldn't be surprised to see them come to blows. Seriously, I . . . I'd like to bring him down this afternoon. . . . I know it's an imposition, but it might be good for George. Surely. . . .

"He's over next door at Wilson Carpenter's now. Could I bring him and Wilson down this afternoon? . . . In about an hour or so, yes. Thanks a lot, Sandy."

Fanny put the phone back and sat looking out the window, waiting for Johnny and Wilson to come in. She felt as if a great load had been lifted from her mind. There was some intangible thing about Sandy that inspired great confidence. Fanny considered herself one of Sandy's best friends, although Sandy had become an enigma to all the women of Endymion. Sandy was eccentric, to say the least. But Fanny liked her. Sandy had been one of the leading women in Endymion for a number of years, and then she had just suddenly dropped out of everything. She had been a wonderful bridge player, but now she never played anymore. She had run the Country Club for a couple of years and then she had quit that. She never played golf anymore, and she never even went out to the Club. She went to a few of the dances at the Caribou and she went down to the Caribou Club's Grille to eat now and then with Eddie. But outside of that, she might as well not have been in the town. She preferred to stay home, she said, and read.

Sandy never drank at all, the way the rest of the crowd did. Sometimes the crowd would spend the whole night down at the Caribou Grille and then end up at somebody's house for breakfast. Sandy and Eddie would go occasionally, and Eddie would drink like everybody else, but Sandy would just sit, and maybe talk a little. She'd stay until the end of the night's party and yet she never did anything. She'd take them all down to her house and cook a huge breakfast, and yet she never ran around anymore or made calls or spent much time with the other women. And half of the time, she would disconnect her phone and not even try to answer it. This last was not even explainable.

Fanny couldn't figure her out at all. She and Eddie were always running off somewhere for a vacation before the war. To Europe or to the Bahamas or Mexico. Fanny, who was a native of Texas, could never see anything in going to a dirty filthy place like Mexico. And sometimes Sandy would take her car and go off for months at a time alone, leaving poor Eddie to take care of himself the best way he could. Leaving him to eat his meals out or cook them himself and with nobody but himself living in the house for months at a time. And yet Eddie never seemed to mind; he took it all in his stride and even seemed to like being alone. If Fanny or any of the other women she knew did things like that, their husbands would kick them out in a minute.

Yet people always liked Sandy, liked her immensely. When she gave them the chance. She was always the life of any party; she always made people feel like they were having an exceptional time. People seemed drawn to her, and yet she hardly ever said a word. She'd just sit, and smile, and when someone asked her, she'd talk, but she didn't talk much and seemed reluctant to talk the little she did. For months now, she hadn't gone out to any parties at the Country Club or the Caribou; if

Eddie went anywhere, he went by himself. It was a terrible way to treat Eddie. Fanny considered Sandy and Eddie a strange couple. She could not imagine spending so much time by herself. It would drive her mad.

Yet a lot of the young ones hung out down there. There was something about her that seemed to attract people, but for the life of her Fanny could not figure out what it was.

Fanny got up and mixed herself a quick drink and drank it. She had got so she usually needed a toddy in the afternoon, especially now that Johnny was here to worry her.

She had the glass washed and put away when Johnny came in with Wilson, and she told them about going down to Sandy's.

"She called up and wants me to bring you down," Fanny said.

Johnny, in the kitchen mixing himself a drink, grinned to himself. "I've done all my social duties today," he said. "I need some time to catch up on my drinking."

Wilson Carpenter grinned a slow easy grin; he felt a strange affection for Johnny's sarcasm. Wilson sat down in a wicker chair, looking out of place in his private's uniform.

"She's a very fine person," Fanny said, wishing Johnny would not drink so much so soon. "And she's very influential. Eddie is one of the biggest men in Endymion. And Sandy has several influential friends. She's got famous friends all over the country. A couple of writers come and stay with her." Fanny racked her brains to find something that would make some impression on Johnny.

"No thanks," said Johnny. "I know those. Women with no brains to speak of and too goddam much time on their hands. They review books. I'd rather stay here and talk to Will. I have no desire to meet the president of the Endymion Literary Guild."

"Oh, she's nothing like that," said Fanny, taking another tack, and not mentioning that she belonged to the Tuesday Literary Guild herself. "She's really a queer character. You might get a kick out of her. She's got a fellow visiting her who lost a leg on Attu. You could talk to him."

For the first time, Johnny showed a little interest. "Who is he?" he asked, coming out of the kitchen. "Is he from Endymion?" Before Fanny could answer, he turned to Wilson who was sitting easily in his chair, enjoying the conversation. "I'll go up and get that thing and show it to you, Will," Johnny said. "It explains how a lot of the guys I've met feel about the whole thing." Without waiting for Fanny to answer his question, Johnny turned and went upstairs, leaving his drink sitting on the table. Fanny decided to wait until he came back down. Johnny upset her with his abrupt manner, and she felt indignant, but she decided to say nothing about it, because he would only look at her in that expressionless way. She debated asking Wilson what he thought of Johnny, but before she could speak, Johnny was back, down with a paper in his hand. He handed it to Will, who began to read it.

"What about this guy?" Johnny asked her.

Fanny told him about George Schwartz who had just come to stay at Sandy's. George was from Vincennes, Sandy's home. He was a couple of years younger than Sandy and had gone to high school with her. They were old friends. George was engaged to Sandy's sister, Riley. It had struck Fanny that George was awfully old for the Infantry.

Johnny snorted. "If a man's got two legs and two arms, he's fit for the Infantry. Anybody that can carry a pack and rifle is an Infantryman. If he can't carry them, they give him a carbine and make him a runner. Unless he raises so much hell they transfer him to get rid of him." Johnny looked at Fanny for a moment, intending to say more, but he decided he might as well quit wasting his breath. The ways of the Infantry and the army were the same as another world to Fanny. He looked over at Will and winked sourly at him.

Fanny looked at Wilson, wondering what he was reading. She waited for Johnny to offer some explanation. When he didn't, her curiosity got the better of her.

"What's the paper you brought down?"

Johnny looked at her for a moment with his dull flat expression. "It's nothing, much," he said.

"It's a poem," Wilson said in his deep rich voice, looking up. He handed the paper back to Johnny. "I like it," he said. "I don't know anything about poetry."

"Neither do I," Johnny put in with a laugh. Wilson smiled. "But whether it's good poetry or not, the thought ought to be given to people. Did you ever try to have it published?"

"Tom did," Johnny said. "When I was on furlough. He sent three of them to *Esquire*, but they turned them down."

"Did you write it?" asked Fanny.

"Yeah," said Johnny.

"May I see it?"

"Sure," he said, "If you want to." He handed her the poem. He looked at Will. "That's the way it is," he said. "I just fiddle around with the stuff for fun, but someday somebody ought to write it up. There is too much crap out about this war, and people are beginning to believe it." He shrugged. "I don't know. It's all such a bitched-up mess."

"I know," said Will, with an understanding smile. "I can't put it into words, either." Johnny grinned suddenly. Wilson's long supple fingers lay relaxed on the arms of his chair. He seemed calm and steady beside the erratic Johnny.

Fanny handed the poem back to Johnny. "It's very nice," she said. "Are you going to go down to Sandy's with me?"

Johnny looked at her and grinned again. He folded the paper and jammed it into his hip pocket. "What do you say, Will?" he asked. "You want to go along and watch the hero show off? I'd just as soon stay here."

"I'd like to go," Will said. "I've heard all kinds of strange stories about Sandy Marion, but I've never met her, I'd like to see what she's like."

"Has she got any liquor, Fanny?" Johnny asked, grinning.

"I imagine so," said Fanny, not seeing the joke. "Eddie drinks," she went on. "He's a good host. They've probably got plenty of liquor." She paused. "If George Schwartz is anything like you," she added, "they'll need a lot of it." She laughed her low throaty Southern laugh, trying not to show her anxiety over Johnny. Wilson politely laughed with her; Johnny only flashed a taut grin.

He downed his drink without taking the glass away from his mouth. "Let's go, then," he said. "Let's get the show on the road. I don't suppose we should begrudge Sandy a chance to do something for the returned heroes."

Fanny breathed an inward sigh of relief. She felt for some reason that if she could just get him down to Sandy's, everything would be all right. She rose and went quickly to the door, and Wilson followed her. Johnny turned to the kitchen to rinse out his glass.

As Johnny went out the door, Wilson, tall and straight, so straight he looked to leaning over backward, was standing beside the car door waiting for him. Seeing him standing there in the sunlight, in the uniform that looked so out of place on him, Johnny's throat constricted affectionately. As kids, he and Will had been out from the same mould, although for different reasons. They had both been lonely youngsters, set apart from the other kids in town, and they had formed a sort of alliance and friendship.

Now Will had developed from the skinny terribly self-conscious boy of then. He had become tall and filled out. His voice was deep and rich and easy, filled with some inner self-confidence he had not had the last time Johnny had seen him. He had a tremendous poise that seemed to say he was capable of taking almost any situation in his stride. He was self-contained and relaxed and easy. He had a strong belief in himself; he knew what he wanted to do and knew he could do it once this war was out of the way. The thought of a person with Will's sensibilities and talent being drafted into the army sent a deep hatred coursing through Johnny. Like any great artist, Will was good at one thing and one thing only; he could only be a complete loss as far as the army was concerned. There were some men who just weren't born to fight—if any of them were. Johnny laughed at the thought of Wilson Carpenter playing piano in a GI band.

"I ran into Edith Wainwright yesterday," Johnny said when Will had climbed into the car after him. "That's how I found out you were home."

"Oh, did you?" Will laughed easily. "How's she getting along? She had a baby, I heard."

"Yeah," said Johnny. "She invited me down to see it."

In high school, Edith Wainwright had been the nearest thing Wilson Carpenter had ever had to a girlfriend. She and Will had been the child prodigies of the town. Edith had a wonderful soprano voice, and the band director and her voice teacher had prophesied great things of her.

"Did you go?" Will asked.

"No," Johnny said, "She was too fat, and besides, she insisted on telling me about how she was trying to sing and work on her voice but couldn't, on account of washing diapers and feeding the kid. I told her I better not come with her, because little babies always made me want to bash their heads against the wall."

"My God!" Will exclaimed, laughing. "You're a crazy bastard. What did she say to that?"

Johnny grinned his tight grin. "She didn't say much of anything. I think it scared her a little." His eyes twinkled mischievously. "I shouldn't have said that, I suppose, but she was so damned smug and she got on my nerves. She was supercilious and matronly, you know? This 'I've-got-a-man-look-at-me-now-I-can-relax' stuff."

Will laughed and shook his head with mock disapproval. He was pleased with the way Johnny had developed from the skinny kid who was always in a fight. There was an impelling drive about him that made people look instinctively to him for the first move. He generated and threw off nervous energy like a dynamo. Will figured Johnny was the kind of man who would have made a *good* officer. But that kind of man never became officers, unless they started out as officers, and few of them did.

Edith Wainwright had stopped Johnny on the street to welcome him home. She asked him how he liked the army, asked him how he liked being home, asked him if he was going to be discharged and, if not, if he was going back overseas, told him he probably had the time of his life fighting the Japs, and proceeded to talk about herself, her baby, her singing, and why she wasn't. Johnny's answers were either not noted or unsatisfying or puzzling to Edith.

"I hear Wilson Carpenter's back in town," Edith said, elevating her eyebrows with a knowing look. "Have you seen him?"

"No," said Johnny. "I haven't yet."

"I don't blame you," Edith said with a sweet self-righteous look.

"There was always something funny about old sis, even in high school. He was so girlish."

"I didn't mean I wasn't going to see him," Johnny said. "I intend to see him as soon as I get the chance. I didn't know you disliked Will."

"Oh, I don't dislike him," said Edith hastily. "He's a very fine pianist, as small towns go. And I guess he's nice. But he's so effeminate that it disgusts me."

The smug self-righteous look on her face did not completely cover the avidity in her eyes. Johnny watched her and felt a swift red of anger rising in him.

"You mean you think he's a queer, a homosexual?" he asked easily.

Edith was shocked. "Why, no! Of course not," she exclaimed. "I never said any such thing."

"You implied it," said Johnny flatly. He was mad. "It looks to me as if your sex life is suffering from lack of satisfaction. Half the people who are accused of being queer are done so to provide food for somebody else's mental perversion, which is never guessed at, let alone discussed. What you like to see as Will's effeminacy is really almost perfect coordination. Will has practiced coordination so much it's become a part of him. He reminds me more of a panther than a woman."

Edith's little face was white, and her mouth pinched up into little wrinkles.

Johnny relented. "Of course, you probably never thought about it. You just listened to what other people said and picked it up. You ought to think more before you go around implying things like that."

Edith's composure had been badly mangled, but she managed to go on talking for a while and then invited Johnny up to see her baby, which kept her from continuing with her voice.

In the car, Fanny drove without hearing the voices of the boys. She was thinking she must remember to ask Sandy for her recipe for making cherry chiffon pie with canned fruit. She also wanted to stop at O'Mara's and get some of those new winter sausages that Agnes Camelot had told her about. Pork was getting scarcer every day.

An important date for James Jones was November 3, 1943, when he met Lowney Handy, wrote A.B.C. Whipple in Life, *May 7, 1951. Whipple speculated: "If this meeting had not taken place,* From Here to Eternity *would not have been written at all." Perhaps this is true; Lowney and Harry Handy did help Jones. He could have continued to study at New York University, where he would have met many writers. He could have studied with G.I. Bill support at the University of Illinois where there were several creative writing teachers and* Accent, *a well-known little magazine. He remained with Lowney for years.*

The conversations of Johnny, George, and Will are the real strengths of this story, but Sandy is seen as a sympathetic woman who was interested in helping servicemen with problems. Johnny was enchanted by her.

JOHNNY MEETS SANDY

THE MARION HOME, AUTUMN 1943

"HOW'S THE PLAYING COMING ALONG, Will?" Johnny asked after a pause.

Will waved his hand in a dismissing gesture. "You know how it is, in the army," he said easily. "I never have any time to practice. The only piano around is in the Service Club, and it's badly out of tune; it's a gift from somebody that didn't want it anymore. And somebody's always playing the jukebox. Or else a bunch of guys come up and hang around the piano and want me to play popular numbers for them. What can you do? You can't turn them down. My fingers are stiff now from not getting enough practice."

Will smiled and glanced at his long fingers, inspecting them. He had spent the morning in the church at the organ. He was alone and playing for his own amusement and enjoyment. He had played the organ in his mother's church since he had been in the eighth grade. The morning had left him a little depressed. He had finally had to quit, his fingering was so bad.

"I played in a band and orchestra in Miami Beach. But I quit that; I couldn't stand it. You know how a GI band is. After I quit that, I got into this ASTP thing." Wilson laughed. "That's the biggest hoax of the war.

I had to get into the Engineering part of it. They aren't really trying to teach anybody anything. You have to have a Master's Degree to get into either the Psychology or the Languages. You know how many young men who got drafted out of mid-year in college are going to have a Master's Degree. Nobody tries anymore. We all go to classes and play tick-tack-toe or just sit. The instructors are worse than the students: Everybody's just putting in time. Nobody expects to learn anything or teach anything.

"I'm going to get out of that as soon as I go back from furlough. If they won't let me quit, I'll get myself flunked out and go back to being a clerk, typist, I guess. At least I'm still in the Air Corps. Why in God's name did you transfer out of the Air Corps into the Infantry?"

Johnny grinned and shrugged. "Hell, I don't know. I suppose you could say I was looking for adventure, I guess. I was just a punk kid who believed all the crap he read in books. I wanted to be a soldier in the old British tradition of Kipling and P. C. Wren. Comradeship and the Regiment-Against-the-World-Stuff. There was none of that at Hickam Field, and I thought I could find it in the Infantry."

"Did you find it?" Wilson grinned.

"Sure. Like hell. They don't make that kind of soldier anymore. I doubt if they ever did, except in some romantic writer's mind."

"This ASTP thing," Will went on, "is terrible." Will felt he had struck a topic that Johnny did not like to talk about, and he tactfully swung away from Johnny's acrid embarrassment. "It's a graft racket of some kind; I wish I knew just what. I think it's a means of finding work for a lot of colonels and majors who got political commissions and are useless for anything else. It's a terrible mess, and it's going to crack pretty soon. They'll turn these thousands of guys back to straight duty and probably stick them in the Infantry. That's the way the rumour has it. They're the cream of the brains of the enlisted ranks, and they'll all get shoved right into Combat Infantry. It's too big a stink to last much longer, and they'll have to find something to do with all those men. I'm getting out while I can still get back into the Air Corps; I have no desire to be a slogging Infantryman. It'll bust pretty soon, and there'll be hell to pay for somebody. A situation like that makes soldiers wonder what in hell this war is, a war for freedom or a way to provide employment for a bunch of future generals."

"Yeah," said Johnny. "I know what you mean. It's the same way overseas." It was a strange thing, Johnny found, to be riding in the back of "Aunt" Fanny's car with Wilson Carpenter and talking about the army. It was strange to hear familiar terms and expressions of bitterness coming from the mouth of Wilson Carpenter. Always before, his life in the army and the war and his life in Endymion had been two complete compartments, but now he was seeing them merge and become one. Even smug, self-centered, hateful little Endymion was being caught up by the great maelstrom. It brought home to Johnny the fact that nowhere in the world anymore, was there a place safe from the invading hatred and blood-lust and bitterness. He had felt somehow that when he came here to Endymion he could swing into a world from which the war and death and army politics were absent, could have a short breather in which he could forget about wearing a uniform and taking orders from some senator's lawyer's son, from the rah-rah ROTC boys who needed a sergeant to always tell them what to do. He should have known better. Even Wilson Carpenter who played the piano well enough to make a concert tour with a group of professional singers before the war, even he was inextricably bound into this thing, even he felt the slow bite of the acid of hate.

Wilson's mention of the rumours and the gripes brought back pictures into Johnny's mind teeming with men, bitter men who griped, not because the custom was to gripe but because if they didn't let out their hatred that way they would turn upon themselves and bite themselves like rattlesnakes and die of their own venom; unhappy men who lived by rumour because they had no other force to tie their lives to. Johnny remembered suddenly that he was a soldier in uniform, and that he was over-the-hill, and that in time he must go back.

"I've been doing a little composing, Johnny," Wilson told him. "Nothing much. Just setting some poems I like to music. But I'm feeling my way around, in the dark sort of. Maybe when this silly war is over, I'll be able to do something. I've seen some things in the past two years that I'd like to be able to say in music."

Johnny watched Wilson light a cigaret. As kids, there had been a quality about Wilson that had always made Johnny feel loutish and uncouth, made him feel big and brutish and dumb, though actually he had been no bigger or stronger than Will. The feeling was still there. Johnny felt as if his fingers were all thumbs beside the superb coordination of Will's body. He envied Will his relaxed and easy-going poise. He envied Will his outward calm. There was some inner conviction in Will that gave him an ability to take things as they came Johnny could feel the calm power that radiated from Will's personality.

He and Will had lived side by side as children. They had been seated next to each other in almost every class in school, clear through high school. As far back as Johnny could remember, Wilson's mother had dominated Wilson's life with an iron-clad hand. He could still hear, her sharp insistent voice calling, "Will-l-l-l-*son*! You come home now. You have to practice." He actually believed they could hear her a block away. Even as a small boy, a frown would pucker Will's little pug-dog face, and he would say reluctantly, "Gee, I gotta go home. I'd sure like to stay and play some more, but I gotta do my practicing." And he would trudge off home, his feet dragging, his hands jammed into his pockets. Wilson had never rebelled or fought back. He had always done what his mother told him; he was a "good son." But Johnny knew there was more to it than that. The same situation of the mother's dominance of the son occurred hundreds of times in every generation in every town. And almost invariably, it was a symbol for the failure of the young man who was dominated. The mother tied the boy to her apron strings, and the boy could never fight loose, from the moment he learned about sex, he turned his knowledge and twisted it around his mother; he fell in love with his mother, and—even like Stendhal—dreamed about sleeping with her and being her lover. He measured other women, as he grew older, alongside the yardstick of his mother, and none of them ever quite measured up. That was common knowledge, everyday psychology, known by laymen who never heard of the Oedipus complex. And yet the mothers continued to bind their sons with apron strings, in order to receive the pure kind of love their husbands could not give them, and never was there a surer recipe for failure. It made homosexuals, it made misfits who could not adjust to life, and still the mothers continued their ravenous eating of their young.

It was supposed to make great artists of men, but Johnny knew that such a superstition was untrue. A man could not become great at anything unless he found some way to combat the absorption of his soul. Most men did it by fighting and by rebellion, and by the time they had fought free, their freedom was lost in their own rebellion. But Wilson had never needed to fight free. Somewhere along the line as a child, he had learned some inner secret, had learned to tap some hidden wellspring of strength that other men did not know about. Wilson had found some way to be mentally free of his mother's dominance, and so he could afford to ignore his physical dominance. It was this same source of spiritual knowledge that puzzled Johnny. He could feel its presence, but he could never grasp it.

Johnny shook his head and lit a cigaret, himself, noticing how awkwardly he did it compared to Will.

"I've got a Negro friend down at camp," Will was saying, "Who's doing some fine work. He's from Terre Haute; I met him over a piano and we got to talking about Terre Haute. He's really got a lot of talent. I'd like for you to meet him. He's already finished a concerto since I've known him. His ear is so fine he doesn't even need a piano to compose. He does it on paper right out of his head. I've been trying that some and I'm getting on to it. If I can do that, I'll be able to work no matter where I am. I'll need that knowledge, because I expect to be sent overseas as soon as I get myself kicked out of ASTP. My Negro friend has been helping me. We work together a lot."

Wilson laughed. "I almost got beat up by a couple of guys who were in my barracks, because I ran around with this Negro boy. They told me I couldn't associate with him, and that if I didn't quit being friendly to him, they'd beat me up." He laughed again, pleasantly.

Johnny's face tightened up and became taut. Wilson was surprised to see how such subtle changes of expression could make his face into a diabolic mask. "What did you do?" Johnny asked in a flat voice.

"Nothing," said Will. "I just talked to them. I told them in as calm a voice as I could muster that I'd kill them both if they ever laid a finger on me or the Negro. I wouldn't of course; I wouldn't know what to do but run if they started to beat me up. But my bluff worked; I impressed them enough so that they've left me alone. You wouldn't think sane, intelligent men would act that way, would you?"

"No," said Johnny. "Nobody could be intelligent and feel like that."

"Well, they're supposed to be intelligent," Will said quietly. "They seem to be pretty smart. I suppose they just don't think much."

Fanny pulled the car into Sandy's driveway, and they got out. Johnny's face remained taut and his eyes cold and hard. Wilson had never seen him look like that before, and he was sorry he had ever mentioned the affair. He wondered what Johnny was thinking to make his face look so.

Actually, Johnny was not thinking anything. Several visions were in his mind, swirlingly mingled together so that he couldn't have sorted one from the other. One memory was a scene from a novel by Jim Tully, a scene which told in brutal photographic words of the lynching and burning of a Negro. Another was a scene he had himself witnessed in Honolulu; three MPs beating a helpless drunken soldier unmercifully with their loaded sticks. The other memory he had also seen; three American Infantrymen, carrying a sick and helpless Jap prisoner, stripped naked, carrying him back to the rear. They carried him face down; the Jap was sick with dysentery and the excreta dribbled from him in a yellow stream; every time the three soldiers came near a rock in their path, they would bounce the Jap viciously against it either on his chest or on his face or perhaps his crotch. If Johnny had been asked to voice his thought, he would have mumbled something about it being an inhuman perverse thing that made strong men, powerful in number, enjoy oppressing and injuring a helpless defenseless man, all of which would have sounded rather trite and platitudinous to a listener.

Fanny led them to the front door where she knocked several times. Sandy came and let them in. She took them through the house to the sunroom where George Schwartz sat sullen and defensively in a deep chair, his right pants leg pinned up and his crutches leaning against the wall behind him. On the floor of the room were two large cardboard boxes filled with books, wrapping paper, and cut cord lying in disarray around them.

"You'll have to excuse the way things look, Fanny," Sandy said, with what might have been a touch of irony. "I just got some books in today from Indianapolis. George and I have been giving them the once-over." She moved a stack of books from the divan to make room and set them haphazardly in a corner. Johnny and Wilson sat down on the vacated divan near George's chair. Johnny was half lost in his own chain of thoughts begun by Wilson's remark about the Negro, and Wilson seemed his usual easy self, but both of them partially felt that feeling of awkwardness that belongs to just-arrived guests who as yet don't know what to do with themselves or what to say.

The room was a small one with a low ceiling that made it seem smaller than it was, in comparison to the larger and higher-ceilinged other rooms. It had the effect of a hidden private alcove. There was one big easy chair, an antique love-seat, and a big couch-bed covered with a green and cream plaid that looked soft and comfortably mussable. There were small windows along two sides, and the other two were covered with shelves of books. Bookcases had been built in over the couch to form a tiny canopy at the head which concealed two fluorescent reading lamps. The other wall was covered with bookshelves to the low ceiling, leaving only room for the door into the next room. It was a comfortable, lived-in room, a hodge-podge with no pretension toward "style" or "period." It was a room people walked into and made themselves at home, at the same time feeling self-conscious about doing so.

Fanny leaned over the boxes sitting in the center of the floor and inspected book titles without much interest.

"Oh, that's all right, Sandy," she answered in her rough friendly Southerner's voice. Fanny had seen Sandy's books before; the whole house was filled with them as this room. Sandy's mania for books was a frequent topic whenever her name came up at a party. It was always mentioned that Sandy probably had as many books as the Endymion Carnegie Library. Fanny could never get over her amazement at the thought of so many books. It wasn't natural to spend so much money for books.

"Do you want a drink?" Sandy asked them. "I've been trying to keep George off the liquor. He's been hitting the bottle too much, but I don't guess one more will hurt him." Sandy winked at George and laughed.

"Yes, by God!" said George with a surly grin. "I've been trying to get a drink all day. If you people hadn't come down here, I probably never would've got one." George's voice was heavy with jocularity, as if he were making an effort that didn't quite take. His grin, too, was heavy and seemed about to fall apart from its own weight. There was a false belligerence in his manner.

George was long-boned and big. His head was long and meaty and thin-lipped. His hands were large and heavy. He seemed to radiate physical strength, but there were circles under his eyes and he moved the stump of his leg, amputated just below the knee, gingerly, as if it hurt him and he was still feeling around, trying to get used to its being gone. He was a fine specimen of the American athlete, and so made a rather sad sight, like a pianist minus his hands.

Johnny assented, and Wilson also, to Johnny's surprise, accepted a drink. Sandy rose and went into the kitchen to mix them. Johnny, knowing how disgusted and embarrassed he felt when some fool tried to be sympathetic about his own limp, tuned to George and began to talk, trying hard to ignore George's missing leg. He and George felt a sense of intimacy from which the others were excluded, and they talked about combat using terms and phrases that the others, even Wilson, did not understand.

Abstractedly, Johnny was surprised by Sandy Marion. He had expected some heavily literary female with gray or even white hair and horse-like hips, a woman frustrated by her own life who had turned to being a littérateur. Sandy was nothing like these. She looked startlingly young, and her long loose hair was black as coal with only a single gray hair here and there. Her body was that of a young woman of twenty-five. But even more startling, there was some youthfulness of spirit about her that made her seem to be enjoying with relish all the world of experience that a young person suddenly discovers is at his command. She seemed to be more contemporary of the two young men than of Fanny and George.

She came back with four drinks, handed them around without taking one herself, and sat down on the end of the large couch-like bed beside Fanny.

"Did George tell you about his leg?" she asked quietly. "Kirby's going to do a story on it for him. Do you remember Kirby Atkinson?" She looked at Johnny and Will with a quick smile. Johnny remembered Kirby vaguely as a tall, gangling boy several years older than himself who never talked much; he nodded to her question, wondering if she had called attention to George's leg on purpose. The remark should have been out of place, but oddly enough, when she said it, everything became less strained; the tension of trying to ignore George's missing leg relaxed.

"He's a fine musician." Wilson said in his rich pleasing voice. "I didn't know he was writing."

"Is Kirby Atkinson a writer?" Fanny asked with surprise.

Sandy smiled. "Well, he's struggling at it. If he isn't, he's having a lot of fun."

"Why don't you show Sandy your poem?" Fanny asked Johnny. "Johnny's a writer, too," she told Sandy.

"I'm not a writer," Johnny said quickly. Fanny sounded like a kid who had the biggest agate on the block.

"I'd like to see it," Sandy said. "If you want to show it." She looked at Johnny's perpetually dour face. No one would have taken him for another would-be writer. It was an amazing thing how so many of these boys in the war turned to something like that for expression. Sandy had seen it a number of times. When a man was bound up externally so that he had no release for his individuality, he would always turn to some form of art for release. She remembered a remark Maugham had made in one of his recent anthologies, about the great amount of poetry that had come out of the last war as a result of the moral shock of the war. She was more inclined to think it because the men who wrote it were unhappy and had no other way of getting rid of it.

"I liked it," Will said, "when I read it. Why don't you show it to them? It's on the war, too."

"Sure," said George roughly. "Let's see it." George acquired a quick interest upon finding the poem was on the war.

Feeling foolish and inwardly cursing Fanny, Johnny pulled the poem out of his pocket and began to read it, wasting no time on preliminaries.

"*The White and The Black.*
See this picture:
A hotel room
In a Southern city,
And in the room a soldier sits.
He sits relaxed—and happy—
In a saddened fashion.
His shirt is off;
The blond hairs upon his chest
Glisten
With a salty dew of Southern heat.
His shoes are off;
His stockinged feet are cocked
Upon the window sill.
The fan drones with the weariness
Of never-ending energy,
A sound unheard through repetition.
A scotch and soda sits,
Smoking with coldness,
Upon the ashstand at his elbow.
A cigaret smoulders away its life
Waiting on his pleasure.
The upholstered rocking chair
Rolls gently with contentment.
The soldier is at peace—
A saddened peace—
But still a peace.

He has much money in his pocket,
And a three-day pass lies on the dresser.
The soldier sits
And rocks
And thinks
And stares out of his hotel room window
High above the tiny Lilliputians
Who rush about their daily business
With a zest that is amusing
To the soldier.
For the soldier
(Though he is but twenty-one)
Is old and tired.
He's fresh from overseas,
And the ribbons on his shirt
That is hanging neatly in the closet
Speak of battles, wounds, and fighting.
And as he stares out across the city
To the greenness of the farms beyond,
He sees America—
That abstraction he's been fighting for—
Spread out before him.
And perhaps it is the scotch
That flows pleasantly through his muscles,
But every sound and smell and sight
Is pregnant . . .
With America.
And the soldier sits
And rocks
And thinks
And, in thinking, wonders
And, in wondering,
Feels happy—
Yet unhappy,

Feels proud—
Yet feels ashamed.
The scotch has freed his brain,
And the thoughts he thinks are never thoughts
But misty moods,
Impressions.

Have you seen the picture?
Then feel the thoughts
That are not thoughts:

This is America,
This is the life I've lived.
It is inconceivable
To me
That this life might someday be gone;
That trains,
That buses,
That this hotel,
Will someday not exist,
And being non-existent
Also unremembered;
That I,
My friends,
The life I know,
Might someday
Be the reason for the speculation
Of historians,
For the vast energetic diggings
Of bearded and be-spectacled professors.
But Rome fell—
And, in falling, believed
Beyond any doubt whatever
That it would never fall.

* * *

This city is America,
And in being America,
And part and parcel of America,
Is foolish, asinine, and wrong—
And yet is wise, magnificent, and right.
And while these people read
The newspapers and magazines
That tell how many thousand men have died
Today
And tell stories of the mighty heroes
Of freedom
And of Democracy,
My gang, my friends, my fellow drunks and cocksmen
Are cursing them, Democracy, and freedom—
And are dying for them
And the things they curse.
While my friends are dying cursing God,
These people go to movies of
Nurses in Bataan—
And cry.
I saw that movie,
And I laughed—
I could not help myself—
And these people of America
Who were sitting near enough to hear,
Stared at me with hurt looks
In their eyes
And made me laugh the more.
These people of America
Knit sweaters
And 'Do Their Bit'
By going to the USO.
They volunteer for Red Cross work,

And all the time my friends
Are dying
With curses in their mouths.
They live in the white;
We live in the black.
I; I am a mutation,
A lucky one.
I am back inside the white,
But my soul's still in the black.
I am both
But neither.
And still the buses run—
The USO—
The ARC—
I am of the black
And anxious mothers say:
'Keep our sons clean.
They should not drink
Or be allowed to patronize the whores.' "

After he finished reading, Johnny sat for a moment staring at the papers in his hand. He ran his tongue over his teeth pensively, then with an abrupt movement refolded the papers and jammed them back into his hip pocket.

"That's good, now isn't it," Fanny said to nobody in particular.

Johnny took another drink from his glass and stared at Fanny over the rim of it without expression. George stirred his body and shifted the stump of his leg reflectively. His eyes were moist and he stared at Johnny with a crooked grin.

"That fits me, too," he said in his rough voice. "That fits me, too. People don't understand that part of it. It's like a different life."

Sandy felt she must say something, although Johnny did not appear to care whether she commented on the poem or not. Nevertheless, she felt he was watching her to see what she would say. The emotional effect the poem had had on both Johnny and George was obvious; it had nothing to do with good or bad poetry. It was a part of their lives that they had seen and understood in the poem.

"I liked it," she said sincerely. "You gave me an insight into soldiers that I'd never had before. And more important, I got an emotion out of it. That's the main purpose of poetry. Of course, I know you and George, but if I was touched emotionally without knowing either of you fellows—and without having shared your experience—then your poem has been effective. It's good, because it's effective—and that's the only purpose of poetry, at least to me."

Johnny took his eyes away from Fanny and looked at Sandy. He grinned suddenly with embarrassment. Sandy smiled kindly. "It seems to me too much emphasis has been placed on tradition and the subtle perfection of craft, without giving due credit to poetry's real purpose: the creation of emotion in a reader and the giving of an insight into an experience of life that he has never had before. You don't have to worry about meter or imagery, if your poetry is true to your experience and strikes some responsive chord of emotion in the reader. I think the poetic days of rose gardens and big full moons are about gone."

Johnny shook his head. "I just fool around with it," he said.

"Don't let people tell you it must rhyme or have meter—or else sound like Whitman. If it's something you feel inside, that's what's important.

"If you'd let me, I'd like to make a copy of it to send to Kirby. I think he'd like to read it."

Johnny shrugged. "Okay," he said. "Sure." He got the poem out of his pocket and handed it to her. She laid it on a small table beside the bed.

"How would you all like another drink?" she asked. Her answer was three nods. Everybody seemed to have settled into a semi-introspective relaxation.

"Sandy," Fanny asked, "are you and Eddie going to the Thanksgiving Dance Wednesday?"

Sandy gave her a quick warning frown, but Fanny either did not see it or did not get it.

Fanny looked at Sandy.

"Yes, we're going," Sandy said, unable to avoid the question. "We've already reserved a table. My sister, Riley, is coming down from Chicago. She and George are going with us."

"Wow, goddam it, Sandy," George burst out. "I'm not going to any goddam dance. We've argued the whole thing out before." He raised the stump of his leg gingerly and shifted his buttocks irritably in the chair. "I don't give a goddam whether Riley comes down here from Chicago or not. I'm not going to any goddamned dance." George's big husky frame bristled stolidly with his angry determination. He laughed harshly. "I'd be a hell of a lot of use at a dance, wouldn't I? The one-armed paperhanger."

Fanny suddenly realized what Sandy meant by the warning frown. There had been talk of trouble between George and Riley since George had come home minus a leg. Fanny blushed quietly and wondered when she'd learn to keep her big mouth shut.

"All right, George," said Sandy soothingly. "You don't have to go if you don't want to. Nobody's going to force you." In spite of the soothing tone of her voice, there was as much evidence of strong will about Sandy as there was about George. "I don't care what you do. But you're only putting it off. Eventually, you're going to have to start going out in public. The longer you wait to do it, the harder it's going to be. You can't spend your whole life hiding in a house without ever going out."

George raised his stump and shifted again, angrily. "I'm not going," he bellowed clumsily. "I'll be goddamned if I'll go to a goddamned dance with a leg off and on crutches." Wilson looked at him and softly stroked the knee of his trousers with his long fingers. How would you do that? What minors and crescendos would one use to portray this? Moke Jones would know. What mathematical strings of notes could you use to show a man who shifted and squirmed and twisted, trying to feel a leg that was no longer there? The concerto of the man with one leg. There were songs that needed to be sung, songs the world needed to hear. Moke Jones who was a Negro would understand how to compose a song of a man without his leg to stand on.

Fanny sat still, feeling embarrassed, and wishing people had enough manners to keep their personal troubles private.

"What do you say we have that other drink, Sandy?" Johnny asked. "How about it, George?" Johnny turned his cold eyes on Sandy, and she felt their apathetic stare penetrate her.

"Sure," George said with a morose grin. "I'm beginning to need another." He settled back in his chair and took a long drink that finished his present one.

Sandy smiled quickly and rose from the bed. Fanny followed her out into the kitchen.

"You know," Johnny said to George. "It's a funny thing. Talking about writing made me think. I used to read all the books about war I could get my hands on. All those novels that came out after the last war. I read all of them and every one of them made me itch to get into a war. Even *All Quiet on the Western Front* seemed romantic to me. When I was a kid, I'd almost cry when I'd think there wouldn't be a war for me to fight in when I grew up." He laughed sourly. "Can you feature that?"

George laughed with him.

In the kitchen, Fanny watched Sandy go about mixing the drinks with a swift economy of movement that bespoke much knowledge and practice. It always amazed Fanny that someone who didn't drink at all could make so many different drinks and cocktails, so well.

"I'm sorry about George," she began lamely. Sandy laughed. "Forget it," she said. "We go on like that all the time. It's the best thing in the world to get him over the first stile. Yelling at me sort of takes the edge off."

"I suppose so," Fanny said, "but I feel as if I caused all the trouble."

"No," Sandy said. "I've been talking up his going to the dance ever since he came. It's only natural for him to be like that. He's always been a fine athlete, and this is something strange to him. But he'll have to learn to get over it. I know how to handle him."

"Did you see that look Johnny gave you?" Fanny asked fretfully. "That's what I meant over the phone. You can talk to him all day long and he'll just sit and stare at you like that. Or else laugh."

"What do you want him to do?" Sandy asked her.

"Well, I don't know," Fanny said. "But he ought to he more . . ." Her voice faded away into perplexity.

"Listen, Fanny," Sandy said. "If you'll only leave him alone and see which way he falls, you'll be doing yourself more good, and him, too. Save your energy and stop worrying yourself into a stew."

Sandy set the drinks on a tray. "I'm going to get George to that dance," she said, "if I have to hog tie him and drag him. I'm going to call up most everybody who will be there and ask them to come over to our table and talk to George and have a drink with him. I want you to do me a favor. You bring Erskine over to our table for a while, will you? And tell everybody you see down there to come over and say hello to George. Okay?"

"Yes," said Fanny. "Of course."

"Is Johnny going to the dance with you and Erskine?"

"I don't know," Fanny said. "I never know what he'll do."

"Well," said Sandy, "if he comes to the dance with you and Erskine, send him over to my table. He and George can talk and get drunk together and I'll see that he gets home all right, so you won't have to worry."

"You know I'm not against drinking, Sandy," Fanny explained. "But when people just drink themselves into a stupor and pass out, it's time something was done to keep them from it."

"What would you suggest?" asked Sandy blandly.

"Well, I don't know," Fanny said. "You know about his father, don't you?"

"Not very much," Sandy said. "Nothing except that he drank and shot himself."

"Well, if Johnny doesn't stop drinking so much, he'll end up just like his father. Erskine and I have held up the Carter reputation after Joe tried his best to tear it down. We're respected people in Endymion, and now, if Johnny goes on like he has been, I don't know what Erskine will do. He can't stand very much more. Why, honestly, Sandy, right now the boy is absent without leave! And he doesn't make any bones about telling it to just anyone, either!"

Sandy looked at her for a moment, wondering what could make so many people so afraid of so many things. "Well, I don't know very much about the army," she said. "But I do know people don't just become drunkards and commit suicide, simply because their fathers did. You're building this whole thing up in your mind too much. You and Erskine will go along living your lives in this town. Whether the boy gets drunk and passes out or not. That won't make one whit of difference to your friends or alter your lives or Erskine's business. Surely, Fanny, you can see that?"

"You don't know this town like I do," Fanny said.

"Quit worrying about yourself for a minute and think about the boy. He's much worse-off than you or Erskine will ever be. And he needs more thought than your reputation. If he wants to get drunk, let him. Get drunk with him. Let him do what he wants. He's hunting for something, for all you know he may have to go back overseas."

"Oh, he won't go back overseas," Fanny said. "Besides, you don't understand."

"Come on," Sandy said. "Let's go back in the other room. Remember what I said about the dance."

The three men were talking earnestly about the army when Sandy and Fanny entered the little room. Sandy handed the drinks around and she and Fanny sat down on the bed. They listened to the soldiers talk for a while; Sandy quietly, Fanny nervously.

"I've really got to go, Sandy," Fanny said. She collected her purse and car keys. "I've got to get home and cook dinner. Erskine will expect dinner ready for him when he gets home." Fanny reminded herself to stop off at O'Mara's and pick up some of those sausages.

"You stay here and enjoy yourself," she said to Johnny. "You'll want to talk to George."

"Okay," said Johnny dryly. "Thanks."

"You'll be home for dinner?" Fanny asked him.

"No," Johnny said. "I think I'll go down to the Caribou and eat me a steak. I've got a bottle down there." The Caribou Club Grille specialized in steaks, and it was about the only place in town to get one now.

"You really ought to be home for dinner," Fanny said tentatively. "Erskine likes to have you there for dinner, you know."

"Why?" Johnny said. "What difference does it make? It doesn't make the food taste any better if I'm there. Erskine's appetite doesn't depend on me."

"No," Fanny agreed, "but Erskine doesn't get to see you very often."

"He sees me all he wants," Johnny said.

"Well," said Fanny dubiously, still feeling that Johnny's place was at home for dinner. "After all, you're a Carter, too, you know."

Johnny grinned at her. "Yes," he said. "That's right." Fanny gave up, although she still felt his place was home at dinner time. Sandy saw her to the door, and Fanny remembered to ask her for the chiffon pie recipe. "Have you got any more poetry?" Will asked Johnny when Sandy and Fanny went out.

"Yeah," Johnny said with a grin. "I got a bunch of them stuck around. I lose track of them after a while." He paused to take a drink.

"You see, Will," he explained, "I'm not like you are. I've got no talent, no training. I just fiddle around for my own amusement. I get an idea sometimes and I put it down on paper to get it out of my mind. Hell! I haven't got any ambitions or delusions about being a poet."

Wilson nodded. He was inclined to skeptical of Johnny's words, but he said nothing.

"About the only thing I ever found them any good for was with women," Johnny went on with another grin. "I bet I've made twenty women I couldn't have made otherwise, just by reading them some of these poems of mine." George and Wilson laughed. "I've got one I call *Dirge to a Reluctant Virgin*," Johnny said grinning. "It's infallible. Works every time. Most women think there's something wonderful and romantic about a guy who is a poet. If they find out you write, and you can prove it by showing them some, they'll push you over and beat you to the ground."

"You're a character," Will said, laughing. "That's the one line *Esquire* overlooked. Who ever heard of a poet who wrote poems just to make women."

Johnny's eyes took on a light of irony. "You'd be surprised," he said. "Didn't Rossetti bury his poems with his lover and then have to dig them up when he couldn't remember them? If the truth were known, most poets wrote their greatest masterpieces—whether they were love poems or not—just to impress some dame. If they didn't continue to do it, they probably started out that way.

"Anyway that's not why I write them. I just said that was the only use I ever found for them."

George listened to the conversation with wry enjoyment, although a little self-consciously. Women was a topic George had taught himself to put aside. Twice he had been out on pass since his last operation. Both times he had been downtown in Salt Lake City; both times he had been with buddies; both times he had been drunk. But he had not been drunk enough either time to have the guts to pick up a woman. The buddies he was with both times had found themselves women, and George had gone back to the hospital alone. He decided he would not again to go town with fellows who had all their parts.

Sandy came back and stood in the doorway, looking down at them. She made a graceful figure leaning against the door jamb.

"Come on, you guys," she said, smiling. "Let's adjourn this meeting to the kitchen. The kitchen is the hearthstone of this house. I've got to clean those books up." She led them through the next room into the living room and into the kitchen. George hoisted himself out of his chair awkwardly, and Johnny handed him his crutches.

Johnny followed him into the next room, carrying George's drink and his own. A man on crutches was an awkward, ungainly thing. Johnny felt a little low, watching George, and he wondered how George would in the end adjust himself. The army was a long chain of succeeding links, each stronger and more binding than the last. There were no weakest links in this long chain of circumstances, at the end of which, for George, was the amazing experience of having no right leg to walk on. He wondered how strange such a vision must have seemed to George as he was being drafted into the first binding section of the chain. George was extricating himself from the very last link, for him, and Johnny wondered what would be at the end of his own succession of links. He shrugged the thought away, deciding he was becoming a little drunk. That was the way to do it. Getting drunk would always fix it up. The end of the chain of drinks could be foreseen: a bed where you could relax into sleep. And in the pursuit of that succession of links, you could forget the greater, more binding chain. You knew where you were going then. No questions asked or needed.

In the kitchen, Sandy sat them in the sturdy kitchen chairs around the table with its red-and-white checkered cloth. She fixed a cushion in one chair for George. "Make yourself at home," she said. She opened one of the low cupboard doors. "Here's the liquor cabinet," she said to Johnny and Will. "The ice cubes are in the refrigerator, and if you run out of soda, there're several cases more in the garage. If you want a sandwich, help yourself to what there is. If there's anything else you want and can't find, just holler. I've got things to do." With that, she smiled brightly and left them.

Johnny began mixing drinks for the three of them.

"Not for me," Will said. "No more, thanks." Johnny looked at George. George nodded.

"Is she always like that?" Johnny asked curiously.

George grinned. "Yeah," he said. "That's why I came down here. I couldn't stand it up home with my mother. Three days there, and I was ready to go back to the hospital."

Johnny laughed. "*Nothing* could be that bad."

"It is," George said. "Yeah, Sandy's always like that. She just turns the house over to you and lets you do what you want. She'll go off upstairs and read and fool around, do whatever it is she does. Maybe she'll come back and sit and talk awhile. Eddie's the same way. When I was going to college, I'd bring down the whole football squad. Eddie'd walk in home from work and there'd be a mob of guys in the kitchen, eating and drinking, and Sandy cooking fried chicken. He'd never bat an eye, just sit down and start drinking with us." George laughed a misty reminiscent laugh. "By Christ! We used to have some fun back in those days. The guys on the squad thought they were wonderful; they'd always dedicate one touchdown to Sandy and Eddie.

"Eddie played on the State team," George said, conferring a great compliment. "You wouldn't think a little runt like him would last five minutes.

"They're a couple of mighty swell people. But don't let her fool you any. She can be tougher than hell when she wants. The first bloody nose I got in my life I got from Sandy Pruitt in grade school."

Johnny joined in his laugh, thinking that George would probably end up at the dance.

"How old do you think I am?" George said.

"Thirty-two or -three," Will said, deliberately lowering it.

"Thirty-eight," George said.

"Yeah," said Johnny, "Fanny told me she thought you seemed a little old for the Infantry."

George laughed gratingly. "Did you explain the army to her?"

Johnny grinned. "Yeah," he said. "I told her. She knows all about it now. Understands it all; just like the rest of the PFCs."

The kitchen was a gaily decorated place. The curtains over the small square windows matched the red and white check of the tablecloth, and the shelves of the china cabinets were covered with shelf paper of the same checked design. There were concealed fluorescent lamps above the windows behind the curtains turned them on before she left because it was getting dusk, outside, and they gave out a diffused gay light. The three soldiers sat in the room and talked, and some of the unobtrusive happiness, the serene gaiety that permeated the room crept into their minds. The bitter "gripes" became less bitter jokes. Johnny and George became drunker, and the combat and the army faded away from them in this room that was the antithesis of all army barracks and bivouacs. They laughed and felt very fine.

"When you were talking about war books," Will said, "you made me think of something. Why is it that they always sound romantic to someone who hasn't had the experience? Even now when I think of combat, I think of it with a sort of thrill of adventure. Even though I know it isn't." He got up from the table and rinsed his glass, stood it bottom up on the side of the sink.

"I don't read much," George said, "but you know what I think? I think a man has to go through a war before he can understand it—even in books." George squirmed on his chair. "Hand me them crutches, Johnny. I got to go to the can." Johnny stepped after them, and George swung himself awkwardly into the other room. A twinge went through Wilson and he looked at Johnny quickly. A man so helpless he couldn't even go to the toilet privately and with dignity, without help or a pair of wooden sticks. Johnny was looking down at the table, rolling his cigaret around the lip of the ashtray.

"That's nothing, Will," he said without looking up, "There was a guy next to me in the hospital in the New Hebrides who had both hands off. He had to be fed by the wardboys, and when the food dribbled down his chin, they wiped his chin off for him. He was a grown man about George's age. When he went to the can, he had to have somebody unbutton his pants and wipe his ass for him." Johnny seemed to have divined Will's thought.

"Both hands," said Will thoughtfully. "What could he do?"

"He could go to the movies and laugh," Johnny said.

Will watched Johnny's face tighten up. "He was a nice guy," Johnny said. "Had three kids."

"It seems to me," Johnny said as George came back, "that if the reader don't get the author's point, then it's the author's fault. When you write a book, it's your job to get across to people what you've got to say."

"They got too much propaganda stuffing their heads," George said. He sat down awkwardly, and Johnny took his crutches, leaned them against the wall.

"That's partly it," Johnny said. "Take Wilson. He knows how rotten the army is. Cutthroat and full of graft. How monotonous and inefficient and chickenshit it is. He know all that, but he's never been overseas. So he gets the idea it's different overseas. Adventurous. He figures it will magically change if he gets overseas. Most of the guys in the States hate the army, but they figure if they could get overseas it would be different. When they do, they find it's just the same as here—except more people get killed."

"You may be right about most fellows," Wilson said, "but you're dead wrong about me. I just said it *seemed* adventurous. If I never get overseas, it'll be too soon. I'll forego punching my typewriter at the enemy just to selfishly get out and go ahead with my own work."

Johnny got up to mix himself and George another drink. "Well," he said, "I'd sure like to see somebody come out with a book on this war that would cut the romance out of it; I've got two nephews aged seven and three. . . . It seems the more terrible and realistic they make war seem, the better people like it. This Great Crusade stuff, coupled with the dissatisfaction of their daily lives, always gets them. Most people would rather be crusading against some poor son of a bitch than live like peaceful hermits. It makes them feel superior; people are always crusading against something or other."

"You know," George said in a surprised voice. "That's what Sandy and Eddie are, in a way." He was pleased at his own thought. "They're peaceful hermits, right in the middle of a town. They live their own lives and never bother anybody. But if somebody wants what they've got to offer, they give it and help all they can. If you don't want it, they leave you alone and just keep on going their own way."

"Yeah, I guess," Johnny said. He had not heard. He was staring down at his glass, thinking.

Jones's agent Maxwell Aley wrote Jones on March 25 1945: "The Red Cross attack will probably run into trouble with any publisher. It sounds to exaggerated to be convincing. Defeats itself." Lowney scrawled on that page of the letter: "disagree. handle it better. refer to what Millie told us and question why we never see an auditing or a statement like a bank—No corporation laws to stop swindling on a mammoth, scale. don't say name but imply all you will."

Jones apparently did some revisions of this section before mailing the final draft to Perkins, but the name remained. Jones and his surrogate Johnny did not worship sacred cows.

SURELY NOT THE RED CROSS

AT THE CARIBOU CLUB GRILLE, ENDYMION, AUTUMN 1943

CLIFF MERRITT INTRODUCED HIM TO the strange girl, Sylvia Greening, a Red Cross Recreation Worker. Shortly after Cliff left the table.

"Surely not the Red Cross," Johnny said in mock surprise. "You look much too lovely and intelligent."

"What's wrong with the Red Cross?" the girl asked, coloring slightly. Her voice was not angry.

"Nothing particularly," Johnny answered. "Except that I don't like it. It could be I'm prejudiced; I may have read too many magazine articles written by Red Cross girls who have been overseas helping our boys. I'm allergic to such concentrated goodness. Actually, I've had no dealings with the Red Cross.

"I'll take that back," he added. "The Red Cross did give me a pack of cigarets in New Zealand. I had to sit through a sociological interrogation that lasted half an hour and covered everything from my birthmarks to my ambitions in life before I got them. But they did give them to me." Of course, this was not strictly the truth. Johnny had had more than one pack of cigarets from the Red Cross. After he got back to the States, he had made friends with one of the civilian girls who did the secretarial work for the Red Cross in the hospital, and he had got all the cigarets he wanted.

"I take it you don't think so much of the Red Cross," the strange girl said, not unkindly.

Johnny stared at her obdurately. "Frankly no, I don't," he said. "I've been in the army almost five years, and the only Red Cross outfit I've seen that was worth a damn was the one my brother runs."

At this remark, the girl perked up her ears, and her slightly condescending attitude of before took on more interest. "Oh," she said in a significant tone, as if his brother being in the Red Cross changed him into another person. "Is your brother in the Red Cross?"

"Yes," he said. "He's a field director."

"Is he really?" she said in a surprised tone.

"Sure," he said. "I told him to stay the hell out but he wouldn't listen to me."

"Why are you so set against the Red Cross?" she asked, "Or are you just set against everything?"

"That's it," Johnny said. "I'm like the Chicago *Tribune*; I'm an agin-er."

"No, seriously."

"Well, in my own personal experience, I've never seen the Red Cross do anything worth a damn—except collect money."

"Perhaps there are other people in the world," said the girl sarcastically.

"I was just coming to that. Among all the guys I've met in the army, in combat and in the hospital afterwards, the Red Cross is a joke."

"Well, there are millions of people in the service, you know," she said.

Johnny agreed. "So I read in the papers. I'll grant you that much. And then again, I think the guys I've met are a pretty good cross-section of these millions you speak about—except for officers, of course. I don't know whether they like the Red Cross or not; I imagine they do since they can at least date the Red Cross girls." The girl started to speak, but he made a motion with his hand and continued. "Besides that, I'm inclined to think the Red Cross is just a gravytrain. For the big shots, I mean. It's possible I'm wrong; but there's a lot of money donated to the Red Cross in this country. Why is it nobody ever sees an annual statement from the Red Cross? The world has a right to ask for an accounting, I guess, since everybody is a stockholder, haven't they? Why don't they publish an account of funds received and funds spent like any other business? You never see a bank or corporation that doesn't publish an annual statement, do you?—unless they're crooked. Where does the money go? How is it spent? And did you ever notice that all the really big jobs in the Red Cross are political appointments? and that some politician appoints somebody to the jobs?"

The girl was almost swept under by this tirade. "Oh, I'm sure they do publish a statement," she said. "Someplace."

"Have you ever seen one? I never have." Johnny did not pay much attention to what he was saying. He felt a vague desire to antagonize this girl, to make her angry. It was not quite a conscious desire, or he would have realized that he resented the girl because she was attractive and because, as a Red Cross worker, she was in the officer class, and so immediately out of bounds for him. "I don't mean the little guys when I say that," he went on. "It's the big shots I mean. The little guys in the Red Cross are all right; they work hard and they're conscientious. The only bone I have to pick with them is that ninety-nine percent of them are dumber than hell and don't know the first thing about people or how to handle them—in spite of their psychology and sociology majors.

"Now. What were you going to say?"

The girl smiled. "There's not much for me *to* say, is there? Except that I disagree with you completely. For one thing, Red Cross girls are not hired to date the enlisted men."

"They're not *hired* to date the officers, either," Johnny put in.

"They're hired to provide them with recreation," she continued. "That's what they're hired for, and that's what their official designation is: Recreational Workers."

"What if you don't like quoits or croquet? I never saw anything so goofy as a bunch of battle-weary Infantrymen tossing rings at a stick."

"There are a lot of other things they provide beside those," the girl said, laughing in spite of herself.

"Oh, yes," Johnny grinned. "Excuse me. I forgot about the movies."

A scene from They Shall Inherit the Laughter *not printed in* To the End of the War *shows Jones developing the background for George's reactions in the ironic conclusion of "Air Raid":*

On Attu, May 29, 1943: The Jap concussion grenade hit George's leg; it exploded, blinding him, deafening him, shocking his nervous system into disintegration.

Oh, Christ, he sobbed. Oh, Jesus Christ. The dirty bastards blew my leg off. Oh, Christ, Oh, Jesus, Jesus Christ.

I'm hit, George, Smitty said. They're all dead but us.

A bunch of Japs came into the camp, prodding the bodies, bayoneting those who weren't dead yet. They stopped in front of Smitty. They struck him deliberately five times until Smitty finally writhed on the ground, screamed once: You yellow bastards! and lay still. They must have decided George was dead, because they went on and left him. He looked dead, all covered with blood and mud and his leg mangled, just hanging by a thin strip of flesh.

I want a bath, Riley, he kept saying to the medic. Don't let me die dirty.

AIR RAID

SANDY'S SISTER, RILEY, ARRIVED IN midafternoon. In the golden, soft breathing autumn afternoon she drove her conservatively maroon Buick roadster up onto the Marion driveway and tooted the horn as a signal of her arrival. Jimmy, her nine-year-old son, peered owlishly over the top of the dashboard at the garage. He was on a vacation from a private boys' school, an exclusive one, and happy that his mother had brought him along on this trip. He always had more fun at this aunt's house than he ever had anywhere else. He had secretly packed four of his smaller board games in his suitcase; there was always somebody to play the games with him here, provided that there were games present. So he had taken care of that contingency.

As Riley stopped the car, Sandy came to the back door with greetings. Sandy was not in the mood for receiving guests, but she was able to make her smile seem as cheerful as ever.

Young Jimmy hopped out of the car and ran across the front yard to climb up onto the three-foot stump of a tree. After climbing it, he stood atop the flat tableland in his blue single-breasted suit, arms akimbo, his tie fluttering in the mild breeze, the master of all he surveyed.

"Come here, Jimmy," his mother called primly. "Carry in the bags like a gentleman should." Without argument or comment Jimmy climbed down from his throne and walked to the car. "And tuck in your tie, darling," amended Riley, as she brushed a speck from his knickerbocker trousers.

"Where's George?" Jimmy asked Sandy, peering at her from within his little old man's face, and concealing his excitement almost as well as a grownup. "Is George here?"

"He's not up yet, Jim." Sandy led them into the house, carrying two of the larger bags.

"Let him do it," Riley said. "I want him to learn how to behave properly."

"I don't mind," Sandy smiled. "These big ones are a little heavy for him. How's Chicago?"

Chicago was fine, but colder. Riley proceeded to explain how nice it was to get away from Chicago for a while, although she'd go mad in the dullness of a small town if she stayed away for over a week. It was nice to get away from business and the office for a while, too.

Eddie and George, sleeping the well-earned sleep of the hangover, were awakened in their respective beds by the dissonant blasting of the car horn. By the time they had almost gotten back to sleep, Sandy called to them to come down.

"Riley's here," she said. "Come to take a week with us. Get up, you morons, and come on down." After she called, she went back in the kitchen to talk to Riley about George, while young Jimmy was in the downstairs guest bedroom putting away things should not exist for them—although exist they did, and Riley failed to realize that children are perceptive to the moods and emotions of their grownups, even if they are only present after the completion of the quarrels.

For this orientation confab, Eddie assumed his customary Sunday position in spite of guests, which was to stretch himself out luxuriously on his back in the center of the thick rug. He relaxed and remained silent with closed eyes.

The main topic, of course, was George, and Riley was confidently solicitous in her inquiry, in her efforts to close the gap of open water and bring the drifting boat against the sturdily founded dock. George did not accept the proper part in the mooring process.

"How are things going at the hospital?" Riley asked with kindly interest. "Not worth a goddam," George said. "What the medics know is a deep dark secret. And they intend to keep it a secret because they don't want anybody to know how goddam dumb they are." He laughed abruptly.

This was not the answer Riley expected. "Will you have to have any more operations?" she asked with composure.

"Probably," said George sullenly. "Probably several. They say there's another piece of bone has to come out. The last three operations I've had have been the 'final' one. This one will be the final one, too."

"Why, I didn't know they were as bad as all that," Riley smiled indulgently. "I'd understood the army had the very best doctors."

Riley's open indulgence irked George and he laughed harshly. "Sure," he said. "The army has all the best food, too. Just try and eat it. There's a helluva lot more to the army than you people read in the newspapers and magazines."

Riley was non-plussed but not enough to lose her poise. "Oh, I think we get a pretty fair picture of how things are, back here," she said with sweet composure. She felt it best to overlook George's breach of courtesy, although he ought to know that talking rudely would do no good to anybody. It was unlike George to be nasty about things, and complaining. He had always been the type of man who took things as they came and turned them to his own use. It was one of his traits that she most admired.

"Yeah?" said George truculently. "I know a guy who got court-martialed and is doing six months, for refusing to have a minor operation. I wonder if you folks back here ever heard about that one? And there's plenty more I could mention." George was a little frightened by his own vehemence; he had no desire to talk to Riley like this. He loved her—more than anything, but she made him squirm by her calm assurance with something she didn't know anything about. Why didn't she get off the army and drop it?

"No," Riley said. "I haven't heard about it, but I imagine the man did something meriting punishment if he was court-martialed. Even the army can't be as injust as all that," she laughed lightly.

George looked at her with quick anger. "That's what too many people think," he said slowly, in an effort to control his sudden anger. "You ought to do six months in the army. Then give me your opinion. . . . Let's forget the army," he said shortly.

"All right," said Riley genially. She refused to show that George had hurt her. "You'll get over it in time," she smiled sympathetically.

"I hope not," George said.

It was better to discuss another subject for a while, Riley thought. He really couldn't be blamed for being biased in his position; at the same time, that was not an excuse for being openly rude. A bitter discourteous husband would certainly not fit in with her plan. George would have to be made over into a gentleman once more.

"What are you wearing to the dance?" Sandy switched to banalities hopefully.

Under his closed lids, Eddie let his eyes run over George's face. He knew that stubborn, more a sullen look that Riley was having trouble with. It would take a lot more than a conversation to rehabilitate George. He had spent all last night with that wild look of sullen reproach. Eddie's head ached, and he hoped this battle of undercurrent forces so thinly gilded over with conversation would let up now. He had that old feeling of being in a locked meeting: both sides fighting, both sides demanding, neither willing to concede one inch to the other. If he'd been in one labor-capital meeting like that, he'd been in a thousand, always trying to be the mediator. This was Sunday!

No, he thought, George wouldn't get over it very soon. And it was a bad thing; it was that bitter frustration and lack of being understood that made fellows go criminal. It was a pity that that sense of protest could not be retained and the bitterness lost. But if one went, the other followed. How many thousands of men had come home from the last war, feeling like George? They stayed bitter just long enough to cause heartache at home, and then they changed. How many came home saying: "By God, this world is screwed up, and I, for one, am going to see that it is changed"? There must have been millions. But when the bitterness left them "in time," the sense of protest and injustice went toe. Too bad, Eddie thought, too very bad. And now they all, except perhaps a very few, now they all went to American Legion conventions, they got drunk, they gave the "little woman" the slip for a "cutie." We'll put over your reforms, the Legion told them, so they joined up. And in a year, the reformer ideas died of their own lack of power. Instead, they get drunk; they went back into the old game of business: "Let the other guy look out for himself." It was a pity that men always seemed to forget oppression so easily. The Legion, like the unions, got one or two big "executive type" men guiding the reins, and all its political power was used to swing votes for this or that, but never for what the men had originally intended, and the men were too busy getting drunk with "cutie" to bother about it. It seemed that any big organization always always got a "potential capitalist" at the head of it. Those were the kind of men that always headed everything, whether the CIO or General Motors. They had the will and the energy; the dreamer seldom had the energy to make it stick. And if he did, there were always too many forces to break him down.

You "hope not" now, George, Eddie thought; but there'll come a day when you'll have a paunch and you'll slap all the vets on the back and talk about your old outfit as if it was heaven, paradise lost. Leave it up to the younger generation to change the world. You'll forget what you told me last night; you'll forget your indignant anger when you were ordered to dump a shipload of fine hams in the California ocean, useless destruction of food your own company would have been glad to have; you'll forget how you were refused passes and furlough for a whole year, after you got on the shit list for offering suggestions; you'll forget all those things, George, because you won't be oppressed anymore. You'll forget the vomiting hell of combat, the fear, the death, the privation. You'll forget it all, George, and join the Legion—or whatever they call the vets organization after this war. Poor George. You'll work and maybe make money.

Eddie felt sad and wished he could get out of this place for a while to rest his aching head.

A man needs to find his work, he mused, rubbing his temples. He thanked God he had found his work. A man's work is more than the money he makes out of it; he needs to feel it is good, that it helps the things he believes in. Or else the satisfaction is not there. And all the Georges coming home would forget their work needed that.

I told Sandy before she invited you down that I wasn't going. And I'm not."

"Don't be silly," Riley said soothingly. "I remember you as a man who went his own way and didn't care what anybody thought."

"Yeah?" said George defensively. "Well, I still am. And my way is to not go to no goddamned dance. I'm not going out where people are supposed to dance and sit on my can like a damn fool."

"Really, George," Sandy said, trying to rectify her error. "You don't know our dances. Most people go to them and never stir from their chairs in the Grille. They go to drink and have a good time, not to dance."

"Look, darling," Riley said. "People like you; you're a hero to them. They don't think anything about your leg. You're acting more adolescent than Jimmy."

This remark offended George's dignity. He remembered Riley as a woman who understood him and who wanted to help him. Her letters had certainly never sounded like this.

Eddie listened silently while the two women strove to mollify George and finally succeeded in quieting him. He remembered George's remarks last night. The women of America, like those of France, had always been the power behind the men, although the American women were much more subtle about it. Eddie was aware of how little he would ever have accomplished had it not been for Sandy's strength behind him. But the women were going to find it much harder to manage these strangers who came home to them from the war. It might be a good thing, or it might not. But there was going to be a great gulf that would have to be bridged, and it would probably require more patience than most women were used to exerting.

"You're going to have to learn to live in the world, darling," Riley was saying with the calm self-assurance of one who has already learned. "There will be lots of fellows worse off than you. I have my life to think of, too, you know. You are going to have to meet my friends. You can't always be self-conscious about your leg. Nobody likes a man who pities himself." Riley spoke kindly and with what to her was sincere understanding. After the abatement of her first gust of emotion, she was genuinely taken aback by the change in George. She was glad she was not inclined to be emotional like Sandy and jump right into things.

Eddie with a feeling of discomfiture was remembering that that was what they had told them after the last war: There were always plenty worse off than you were. But it hadn't helped much. And nobody ever found the man that somebody else was not worse off than. When you called upon a man's pride to shame him into keeping his mouth shut, you still didn't take away the source of the trouble; indeed you may have made it worse. When they came home after the last one, they had lived in chicken coops and abandoned shacks, city jails, old boxcars—there was no place for them—and always they were told to remember that there was someone worse off yet than they. The real hero, they were told, the men who had really been there just couldn't bear to discuss it. So, it naturally followed, anyone who bitched just hadn't been there and didn't deserve consideration. There was a tremendous power of vote behind so many voices, but it had been successfully hushed in various ways. Would it be the same after this one? Eddie wondered.

However, love triumphed here, helped by the fact that young Jimmy came back in the house to be near George. And the conversation was dropped, and once more there was peace. It'll all work out, Riley thought, looking at George with young Jimmy staring up at him adoringly.

"Listen, darling," Sandy said to Riley. "You folks would like to be alone, I know. Eddie and I will drive out and see the man at the farm and find out when he is going to butcher again. Maybe we can get you some ham and tenderloin to take back to Chicago with you. I imagine it's pretty short up there."

"It certainly is," Riley laughed. "Food's the only thing I envy about you country gentlemen down here. You might ask about eggs, too, if you'd like."

They left George and Riley standing in the door with their arms around each other's waist with the small figure of little Jimmy standing beside them.

"That makes a wonderful picture," Eddie said slowly. "Perfectly stylized and complete—on the surface. But there are always so many unacknowledged undercurrents that nobody recognizes."

"It's that way in every family though," Sandy said. "I'm sorry I pulled such boners, like mentioning the dance. It's better if we're away. And I knew you wanted to get out and get some air. I wonder where it all will end?"

"I guess it won't end," Sandy answered her own question. "It will go on and on, always getting a little better, then sliding back a little. But oh, sometimes I wish I could . . ." Her voice trailed off.

"That's right," Eddie agreed with her first statement. "This war is only a catalyst that works on the usual forces people are subject to, and heightens them. Its total effect on an individual may be better or worse than without it. But those forces are what have to be kept in mind; it is on them that the work must be put." He told her his own tale of last night, shaking his head a little ruefully.

Back at the house, Riley sent Jimmy outdoors again—to play. Then she sprang her plan. "I've been thinking about it a long time," she said delightedly. "And I've figured out the best plan in the world for us. As soon as you're discharged, you come into my office. We'll make a swell business partnership. I've got a grand business, especially now, and between us we can run it perfectly. It's the perfect answer to your problems."

George was not delighted. "I can't do that," he said earnestly. "Don't you see, honey? I'm a contractor. I don't know anything about real estate. I like contracting building, not selling houses. I like to work with things, not just sell stuff to people. Besides, that's your business. You built it and made it. How would it look for me to just meekly take over and work for you."

"But you wouldn't be working for me," Riley protested. "You'd be a partner. The kind of partner anybody'd want in their business. You see, you'd be an addition. Nobody can appraise a house as well as a person who builds them."

"Yes, but it would amount to working for you. That's the way everybody would see it. I don't want to be called Mr. Riley Stafford."

"Oh, you're being silly. You sound like a melodrama."

"I'm not being silly," George said with an earnest frown, trying to make Riley understand. "And anyway, I don't want to live in Chicago. I want to live where there's more trees and air and not miles of streets. If I take this job in Vincennes I've been offered, I'll have enough dough to buy a farm in a few years. I want a farm to live on."

"We can buy one now," Riley said. "We could live in the suburbs and commute into town to work. I've got a deal for a perfect place, one that you'd love, near Glencoe. I'm willing to adjust in every way."

"Jesus Christ!" George said. "What the hell? You don't have to adjust to me. All you have to do is marry me. I don't need sympathy," he added belligerently.

Riley refused to become angry. This was not only important to her; it was also important to George. "But you must consider my life, too, darling. I've got my own circle of friends and business acquaintances. I don't want to give them up. I don't want to subordinate my whole personality to your whims."

"When a woman really loves a man, that's what she wants to do," George persisted.

Leaning on his crutches, he took Riley into his arms again and kissed her. Riley was a little weary with the whole thing; emotion would not substitute for common sense.

"But it's silly," she said, squirming free of the embrace. Even Riley's squirming was done with assurance and poise. "A woman has a right to her own life as much as a man. Besides, I've got the business, the necessary connections for success, the capital to work from. It's silly not to use it; it isn't good business, even. Just to throw it all away because you are worried about what people will say. No businessman would disregard all those assets."

"All right, goddam it," George said, "then I'm not a good businessman. My self-respect is more important to me. I need to do things for myself, not have you do them for me. Besides, you got all those assets from the Stafford family," he said, trying not to be irritable. "If you hadn't been married to big Jim, you wouldn't be where you are. I can't just step into Jim Stafford's donation and take it over."

"What difference does it make where it comes from?" Riley asked. "Besides, you're not going to be a lackey. Why, with your prestige as a veteran after the war, and having been wounded and all that, why you'll be the biggest asset in the deal."

"Sure," George said with a laugh. "But if I wanted to trade on having a leg off, I could sell pencils. You know, the guy with a hat that sits on the corner. It's the same damn thing."

"Oh, George!" Riley said in a hurt voice.

George shrugged disconsolately. "You just don't understand."

"I understand rightly enough. You think I should just throw everything I like to the four winds and follow you wherever you see fit to go. You . . . Oh, never mind. We'll talk about it later. Here comes Jimmy. And besides, I'm tired. I've had a hard trip. I'm going in and lie down for a while."

Reluctantly, George watched her go into her room. He sat down in the big chair wondering what the hell?

"Where's mother?" Jimmy asked.

"She's taking a nap," George said.

"Listen, George," said Jimmy with great seriousness. "I've got a keen game. If I can get it out, will you play it with me?"

"Yeah," George said. "Yeah. Sure."

"Oh, boy! Swell!" Jimmy went cautiously into the guest room to sneak out the game. George rubbed his head with his fingertips reflectively.

George looked up when young Jimmy reentered the living room. He carried a large board something like a dart board; his eyes were shining with amused excitement. In his other hand, he held a small rectangular cardboard box. He laid the board flat on the rug.

"We'll play this one, George," Jimmy said enthusiastically. "This is about the best game I have. I'll explain it to you." George smiled and leaned closer while Jimmy explained the technical processes of the game.

The game was called "Bombsight," or "Air Raid," or something of that sort. George had not been in any air raids, but he remembered how the Mitchell bombers had pasted hell out of Holtz Bay. The board was covered with thin cork, and on the cork was drawn in color a miniature city with docks, ships, factories, airfields, dumps, and railroads all marked prominently in red. The small box was the "bombsight." It had two eyeholes in one end and a mirror in the other, set at an angle to reflect horizontal vision downward. At the mirror end were four holes through the box; in each resided a wooden bomb with celluloid tailfins and a steel point like a dart. Each dart was held in place with a little wooden pin which, when pulled, allowed the bomb to fall upon the city below.

"This is a swell game," Jimmy said, after his detailed explanation. "Of course, you're not moving like a plane. You have to stand still, because this bombsight doesn't allow for forward movement like a real bombsight. But it's the same idea." He leaned over the board, sighting through the eyeholes; then he straightened again and grinned. "This can be Berlin, or Tokyo's better. And you're one bomber and I'm another. . . . And we try to beat each other hitting vital installations. And we have to make good, because we only get one chance in this raid because we've got so far to fly back to a base, like General Doolittle's raid. Here, you make your pass first."

George took the game and leaned forward from his chair to sight.

"You have to hit the vital installations," Jimmy said, "because they are military targets, and if you don't hit them, you don't cause much damage and only just kill a few civilians. There's one ammunition dump. If you hit that, you can really blow things up. But it's away off by itself and if you miss it, you don't hit anything else."

George let one of the bombs fall.

"No good," Jimmy said. "I've always wanted to be a bombardier," he confided to George. "Being a bombardier must be the most fun in the army. You fly over and let those old bombs fall and watch them spread out all over. A bombardier has the most fun, I bet."

"Yes," George said. "Yes, I guess. You stick to the Air Corps. Don't ever get in the Infantry."

"Oh, I like the Infantry," Jimmy said quickly. "The Infantry is what wins the battles," he parroted. "The Infantry takes the land and holds it. I can't decide whether I'd rather be in the Infantry or a bombardier."

George made a hit on one of the ships in the blue cork harbor.

"Swell!" Jimmy said.

"I was aiming at the airport," George said.

"It doesn't matter," Jimmy said. "Any hit counts. This game is really fun."

"Yes," George said. "It sure is." He handed Jimmy the box.

"You know, George," Jimmy said, sighting through the box, "I'd like to go overseas." George did not answer.

"I've got a Thompson gun at home," Jimmy said, releasing his first bomb, it struck the airport. "A hit!" He prepared to loose the next bomb.

"It's just a wooden gun," he explained, "but it looks like a real one off a ways; it's got a pistol grip with notches for your fingers, like a real one. When we play, I'm the captain, because I've got the Thompson gun—on account of that captain in the Philippines."

"Is that right?" George said.

"Yeah," Jimmy said. He released another bomb. It fell into the cork sea. "Aw, missed. I'm gonna try for the railroad station. Did you ever have a Thompson gun?"

"No," George said. Then he added: "I knew a staff sergeant who had one."

"I thought only officers had them," Jimmy said. "What happened to him?"

"He got shot," George said.

"Killed in action?" Jimmy said.

"Yes," George said.

"Did you see him get shot?"

"Yes."

"I'll bet it's terribly exciting, isn't it, sometimes?" Jimmy said.

"Yes," George said. "I guess you could say it was."

Jimmy frowned. He laid the bombsight on the table. "Well, I got the railroad station, but I missed the ammunition dump. I only used one bomb on it. Not so good, but I still beat you."

"That's right," George said. "Now I'll have to pay off when we get to the base."

Jimmy smiled briefly and then frowned again. "I think I'll go outside and play a while," he said. "You sort of have to use your imagination with this game. We play war at school a lot. Someday I'm going to buy a real Thompson gun. I like things where it's really true like the true thing."

"Yes," George said. "But the real thing never pans out quite like you think."

Jimmy was not listening. "I think I'll go outdoors for a while," he said.

"Okay," George said. "I'll tell your mother when she wakes up."

Jimmy went out, and George picked up the child's bomb-sight, wondering what city the board had been drawn from, if any. This must be the way it looked to the brass when they planned it all out.

Johnny and another troubled serviceman in Sandy's orbit, Ensign Al Garnnon, escape Endymion for a toot in Evansville, Indiana. Johnny had participated through nonstop orgies in Memphis. The two merry-makers added Freedie, a former Flying Tiger in China, who was also ready for a wild time.

Jones had probably read in the library at Schofield Barracks or from Lowney's collection Sinclair Lewis's Elmer Gantry, *a satirical novel about a hypocritical revival preacher. To his understanding of Lewis's art, Jones seems to add firsthand knowledge about wartime religious revivals. Jones in this story adds to the drunken spree of the musketeers the sermon of a revival preacher who is a warmonger. The sermon was interrupted by Freedie, as embittered and vocal as Johnny.*

WILD FESTIVITY IN EVANSVILLE

EVANSVILLE, INDIANA, AUTUMN 1943

IN EVANSVILLE, AS IN EVERY city in the country, the hotel business and its associate industries were booming. Men and women far from home, and with no place else to go, flocked to the larger hotels, and after as goodly a fashion as possible set up temporary substitutes for the homes they missed. A man who stayed at one of the large hotels often enough to become known to clerks and hotel detectives felt a thrill of pleasure at being addressed by name in the midst of hordes of other servicemen. He felt he was truly coming home again. A man who had just spent from a week to a month in the barren squalor of nameless men in nameless barracks wanted pomp, lavishness, and individual recognition; and to hell with the cost. With an eye on the business and a hand on the register, cash, or guest, hotel managers to the best of their abilities strove to fulfill this desire. They instructed detectives, porters, maids, barmen, clerks, to note faces, to remember names. It was hard on the hired help, submerged in breakers of khaki, but they did their best.

Where before the hotels had enforced at least a pretention of rigid respectability, because of customers' reputations, they now turned a lidded eye upon any but the most riotous goings-on. The customer was always right, and now the clientele had changed to those who laid no claim to rigorous respectability and cared not if everybody knew it.

In Evansville the Hotel Roquefort was the tops. It was a world within a world, completely self-sufficient except for one thing, its customers' money. Without ever stepping outside its doors, a man could live for months, even years, and still have everything his heart desired, including fresh air. Within its walls, a man could buy anything and everything, from condoms to wedding rings. Sufficient unto the day is the money thereof.

And soldiers flipped the dice and sweated out the cards.

Those who won went gloriously to the Roquefort; those who didn't went to a lesser hotel or to a tourist cabin, if lucky, and if not, stayed in camp till next payday. One month's pay equaled approximately a weekend pass at the Roquefort. Two months' pay, yours and one of the losers, equaled a weekend plus a three-day pass. And, so on up. Some of the very lucky were able to spend every weekend in the month plus a three-day within the bounteous walls of the Roquefort, forgetting the war, the army, the wife; everything a man in the army, navy, or marines needs to forget.

In the Hotel Roquefort was the Rendezvous, the bar of the century. Soft indirect lighting, soft deep cushions covered with soft maroon leather, sweetly soft piped music from invisible speakers—nothing as shockingly low class as a jukebox would be thought of here, beautiful murals of soft tropic scenes—such scenes that the men back from the Pacific commented upon them with a whistle of amazement, soft-voiced polite very friendly barmen, soft-voiced polite not quite so friendly waitresses. All the conveniences and graciousnesses of which civilization is capable. A loud rushing place, but loud and rushing in a soft pleasing way. The antithesis of PX 3.2 beer gardens, the antithesis of hard barren unadorned bunks and walls. Here, a man could be a soldier as the movies portrayed soldiers! Here, men from Breckenridge or Campbell, or any other camp within range of a weekend pass, could meet men they knew from Breckenridge or Campbell, or whatever camp, and they could form a closer comradeship because they were meeting old friends in a new rich world, so alien to their daily lives. And here, battle-weary men from convalescent hospitals could proceed with drinking their way back to health.

Through this world, Al and Johnny moved with a familiarity bred of practice. And as they moved from bar to grille to lobby to dining room to luxuriant latrine, their old friendship grew deeper and ripened with their understanding of each other and of the Hotel Roquefort.

"This is my hangout," Al said, in the Rendezvous. "When home gets too much to stand, and Rose too much to lay, I retire to the Roquefort for some headcheese. About half my leave, every time I'm home. Home is strange, but the old Roquefort is familiar, and I can breathe easily here."

Johnny grinned his understanding. It was a world that was familiar to him also, a world in which he, too, moved with the ease of long association. The particulars were different in Evansville, but it was the same wild festivity, every night a New Year's Eve, that he had lived for ten months in Memphis.

"They say the Jew who opened this hotel picked Roquefort for a name because it was such a high-sounding French word. Later on, he found out it meant cheese. So now the joint specialized in all sorts of cheeses."

The three of them at the table laughed. The third man, who had just recounted the familiar legend, was a well-built blond-headed youth, a staff sergeant in the Air Corps. He wore a nest of ribbons, many of them with Clusters. On his left sleeve the Air Corps patch and on his right the red white and blue shield with the five-pointed star and the many-pointed star of China. He was a former Flying Tiger and was now recuperating from malaria and a compound leg fracture in the local general hospital. He called himself the King of the Rendezvous Bar. His wide face was good looking until he smiled. Smiling, his eyes squinted up and nasty lines formed under them. He was possessed of a great bitterness, and his humour was peculiarly pungent.

"Come on," he said jitterishly. "Let's get out of this tropic beauty. I can't stand it. Makes me homesick."

"What's the matter, Freedie?" Johnny asked. "You getting sober?"

"Almost," Freedie said. "Almost. It's terrible. These Evansville broads are too educated. They should do a hitch in China. Every time I try to drink one of them groggy enough to lay, I pass out first."

Johnny and Al laughed with enjoyment. More comical than what he said was his way of saying it with lugubrious sarcasm, a very thinly skinned hatred. Where he had come from, where he was going, they did not know; neither did they know who or what he was. Nothing, except that he was a staff sergeant in the Air Corps, at present in sickbay, and formerly a Flying Tiger. Their paths had crossed in the Roquefort lobby and they had joined forces for a while, no questions asked or expected.

"Come on," Freedie said. "Come on. Let's go. Let's leave this den of depravity. It's ruining my morals watching what I can't get in on."

"Where'll we go?" said. "Too early to start another party."

"Go for a walk," Freedie said. "Anywhere. But get out a here."

They finished their drinks. In the Rendezvous, people passed and repassed, people drank, laughed, made dates, broke dates, got drunk. For Johnny and Al, it was a break, a pleasant lull. For Freedie, it was merely a distasteful period to be endured until a new party started. Last night, Sunday night, had been a big party. Tonight would be another. Right now Johnny and Al were relaxing, but Freedie seemed incapable of it. He looked enviously and with hatred at each woman who passed the table. Last night, he had spent more time in the bathroom with more women than any of them, but now that was forgotten and he resented each woman he saw because he had not slept with her.

The big double room with two double beds Al had gotten through his acquaintance with the chief hotel detective had been a replica of the Grand Central Station. He and Johnny had invited people up, those invited others, and the others still others. Introductions were a time-wasting formality. The word got around that Room 507 on the fifth floor was going strong, and the room became a clearinghouse for everybody. The main party settled down to Al and Johnny, the chief detective who stopped in every ten or fifteen minutes for another drink, three unknown women, and Freedie, who had appeared from nowhere with two of the women.

Freedie had abandoned his own room for this one where there were more people, more noise, more liquor, and more love-making. He was just shortly back from China, and he had more money than he could throw away, although he still made the attempt, flinging it about with curses rather than smiles. He liked having lots of people around him, although he bitterly despised all of them individually.

The rest of the shifting crowd was considered as transient. Later, after midnight, the crowd overflowed the room into the hall, and the crowd in the hall brought other people. The bottles overflowed off of the two dressers into the corners of the floor and from the corners spread out to meet each other until the two double beds became one island in the sea of bottles. Everybody seemed to bring a new one. Bellboys brought bottles of chaser and stayed to drink. The beds became the combined coatracks and petting places. For more strenuous love-making the bathroom was pressed into service. When a man had a woman drunk enough or hot enough, he took her to the bathroom, if it wasn't already locked and in use. It was uncomfortable but private, and most of the women had scruples about privacy with their copulation. In the haze of smoke and alcohol, the harsher lines on the faces were obscured, and every woman became beautiful. It was almost possible for the uniformed men to believe the women's scruples were sincere.

At eight o'clock in the morning when the firing ceased, Al and Johnny found themselves alone in the sea of bottles and cigaret butts with only Freedie, the China staff sergeant, left. He was passed out on the coatrack after having practically monopolized the bathroom all night. They sent out for a pack of cards and played two-handed stud at a dollar ante until Freedie came to. Then they played three-handed and drank until they all fell asleep. In the afternoon they awoke, showered, and adjourned to the Roquefort Grille Room for breakfast. By that time, the arrangement had become permanent, and plans were made to use the big room as a sitting room and Freedie's room (a secret among the three) up on the next floor was to be the "bed" room. A man's finesse could be used to much better advantage in a bed than in a tile bathroom, no matter how expensive, with a poor choice between the commode, the bathtub, or standing up.

After the three of them finished their drinks, they sauntered out into the outside world that still existed, beyond the jurisdiction of the Hotel Roquefort. Freedie carried a full pint bottle in his hip pocket under his blouse. It was a bottle that had been refilled from other bottles many times.

"He's a good soldier," Freedie told them, patting the bottle, "He rates a dozen Purple Hearts. He's been killed in action more times than any other soldier on earth!" Since it was now Monday, the bars were open, and they stopped at several for reinforcement. One drink to a bar. While they sat to the drinks, Freedie quietly cursed every woman he saw for being a woman and for not coming over and offering herself to him; he cursed all the civilian men for being 4F; he cursed all the uniformed men for being damned fools.

Pasted up in the windows of all the stores along the streets they followed were large placards. More and more frequently as the three men walked along, Freedie stopped to read these placards. After a while he was moving in short jerks from one store window to the next, stopping at each and reading the announcements upon the placards with great intensity. Johnny and Al watched his antics with unconcealed amusement.

The placards which Freedie examined with such deep interest were announcements of the presence of a noted evangelist. The manner of their printing had obviously been intended to excite attention. At the top of the placard in large red letters was proclaimed the single word "REVIVAL!" with each letter vividly underscored in red and followed by a large bold red exclamation mark. Beneath this was the picture of a man with a long upper lip and wearing glasses. The picture was labeled in black: "THOMAS M POSTELWAITE" and beneath this caption in smaller print: "NATIONALLY KNOWN EVANGELIST AND ORATOR. APPEARING CURRENTLY AT THE GEORGE WASHINGTON HIGH SCHOOL AUDITORIUM. WILL PREACH NIGHTLY FOR ONE WEEK BEGINNING MONDAY" and it gave the date. Said the poster: "THE GENERAL TEXT Of REV. POSTELWAITE'S SERMONS IS: WHAT GOD HAS AGAINST EVANSVILLE." Then it went on to say that each evening's individual text would be different.

Finally, the poster ended with the reminder in red: "ALL INVITED. COME BRING OTHERS."

In the center of the various posters in black letters almost as large as the red "REVIVAL" at the top were sentences of expostulation. These varied on different posters. "GET RIGHT WITH GOD." "THE SAVIOR WANTS YOU!" This one was accompanied by a drawing copied from the Uncle Sam recruiting poster. "HAVE YOU MADE YOUR PEACE?" "HAVE YOU GOT SOUL INSURANCE?" "ARE YOU PREPARED TO MEET *DEATH*?" "GOD IS COMING!"

Freedie examined each of these for several blocks. Finally, he clapped his hands and shouted.

"Hurray," he said. "Come here, you guys. Come here. I've finally found two alike." Al and Johnny walked over to where he stood. The sentence he pointed out read: "ARE YOU AFRAID TO DIE? WHY?"

"I knew I could do it." Freedie smiled, and his eyes squinted up into those peculiar lines. "I knew if I kept at it I could find two of them that were the same. I saw one back that said the same as this one." He resembled a small boy who had just inherited a bicycle.

"Come on," Freedie said. "This calls for a drink."

They walked to the end of the block where there was another bar. At the corner strung up over the street was a huge cloth sign that wavered back and forth in the mild wind. The words printed in eighteen-inch letters read: "JESUS. COMING SOON." At the ends of the sign were small letters which referred to the visit to Evansville of Rev. Postelwaite.

"Coming attractions," Johnny said.

"Just look at that," Freedie said in awe. "This guy Postelwaite must be a cousin of Aimee. That ought a be good. You know? 'What God Has Against Evansville.' "

When they came out of the bar, Freedie stopped and looked up at the sign again.

"You know what?" he said. "I've got a lot against Evansville myself. What you say we go hear what God has against it. He may agree with some of my ideas." He paused for a moment and made up his mind. "Come on. Let's go. It really ought a be good. Anything for a laugh

Friedenberger. That's me. Besides, the dames who go to them revivals are really something. We can pick some of them up afterwards. Jesus!! Boy, you can't beat a gal who's just had her soul saved at a revival."

"What the hell," Al said. "Who wants to listen to that crap?"

"I do," Freedie declared solemnly. "It's very enlightening. Come on. No kidding. You want a learn what you're fightin for? Well, come on out to the George Washington High School and listen." Freedie whistled shrilly at a cruising cab.

Johnny grinned and winked at Al and started for the cab. "Okay," he said. "I'll try anything once."

Freedie gave the address and the cabbie looked at him. The cabbie asked for the address a second time, and Freedie stared at him belligerently.

"Well? What's a matter?" he asked litigiously. "Dincha ever see a sojer go to church?" The cabbie shrugged and drove on.

When the cab pulled up to the brilliantly lighted high school, Johnny reached for the door handle, but Freedie grabbed his arm.

"Wait a minute," Freedie said. He hauled out his bottle. "Take a shot of this first. You may need it." All three of them drank, and Freedie offered the cabbie a drink. He took it.

They walked inside the high school building and removed their hats. A big burly usher with a heavy dark beard closely shaven pointed the way for them. They were met at the door of the auditorium by a white-haired old man with a white moustache that covered all but the tip of his lower lip. He smiled at them pleasantly with the tip of his lower lip and shook hands elaborately with each of them before leading them to seats halfway down the aisle. From the doors they had entered, the aisle ran straight down to the small stage at the back of the hall. The room was long and both sides of the aisle were crowded with seats. The seats were crowded with people, most of them middle-aged or old but with a fair sprinkling of young people. As the old man led them to the seat, the people turned to stare at them. They all smiled their welcome and nodded with pleasure at the three uniformed men. There were only two other uniforms in the large auditorium. Rev. Thomas M Postelwaite stopped his address for a moment and held out an open palm of welcome toward the three men and smiled at them benevolently. Freedie made a slight bow in return.

"You watch," Freedie whispered. "This is goin a be rare."

The three of them sat down with Freedie in the middle. After the old man had left them and gone back to the door, Freedie whispered, "You guys lean over and pick up your hymnbooks." As the other two leaned over to pluck hymnals from where they resided on the end seat in the row, Freedie hauled out his bottle and sneaked a drink.

Rev. Thomas M Postelwaite was continuing his address. Behind him was a large placard set upon an easel that read: "SUBJECT TONIGHT: THE PRESENT WAR, TEMPERANCE, AND THE VALUE AND NECESSITY OF SALVATION."

Rev. Postelwaite was taking the entrance of the three servicemen as a supplemental text. He was a short slim man with a small paunch, a high forehead, and gold-rimmed glasses. He looked to be about thirty-five. His long upper lip quivered with intensity as he spoke.

"It does my heart good, dear people," he said, spreading an open palm toward the three men, "it gives me a measure of hope for all humanity when I see young men in uniform enter into meetings like ours. And don't mistake me. There are a lot of such young men. I have seen them all over the nation. They are brave young men, fighting for their country, and we are all proud of them."

Rev. Postelwaite paused for breath, and Freedie grinned, shook his shoulders up and down rapidly in the fashion of a belly-laugh, and winked at Al.

"We are proud of them," Rev. Postelwaite went on, "very proud of them, for fighting for their country. They are brave and courageous warriors. But we are even more proud of them because they have not forsaken the religion and faith of their fathers."

"Hear, hear," said Freedie loudly. There was a momentary hush, and several people turned to look at the three servicemen; some of them smiled. Freedie was enjoying himself. Johnny and Al both grinned without self-consciousness.

Johnny was reminded suddenly of a newsreel he had seen, in which

General MacArthur had spoken to a group of Australian statesmen. At the General's remark about returning to Bataan, all the Australian statesmen had shouted, "Hear, hear!" Now that he noticed it, Rev. Postelwaite had the same mannerism that General MacArthur possessed, a slight, dramatic bobbing and jerking of the head to punctuate his remarks. Johnny was highly amused at this similarity. No wonder, he thought, that all the novelty companies made plaster of paris busts of General MacArthur to sell in all the ten-cent stores.

". . . but such young men are in a minority, my friends," Rev. Postelwaite was saying. "Such young men as these are few in our armed forces. Who among us has not seen the nation's young men carousing in drunken orgies? rolling in the filth of the gutters? parading shamelessly their carnal lusts?" At each question mark, Rev. Postelwaite jerked his head dramatically at his audience. At the end of the sentence, he spread his arms to his audience, and his long upper lip quivered. He paused for a dramatic moment.

Freedie shook his head sorrowfully and clicked his tongue against his teeth. Rev. Postelwaite brought one of his upraised arms down into a fist that pounded upon his altar. "But I say to you, my brethren; I say to you: Our Father is a loving Father, but He is also a just God. He is a vengeful God—and a terrible God when His wrath is roused. It has been written that for those who sin, there is the everlasting agony of Hell. It has been so written and so it shall be. The Eye of God is forever upon us, noting and recording unmercifully the blackness that lies in the soul, ferreting out with Supreme Intelligence those tiny black thoughts of evil that lurk in us and are kept hidden from all the world but ourselves. And when the Day of Judgment comes, no such mark shall escape unpunished."

Johnny grinned at Freedie obliquely. "Well?" he asked. "You heard enough? Man can't live by dogma alone. I'm gettin thirsty."

Freedie scraped one forefinger along the other in a gesture of shame. "Not yet," he said. "Wait till they start bein saved."

"From the way it looks now," Johnny said, "it'll be in the morning."

". . . but one God, and He gave His Only-Begotten Son to be sacrificed. For Himself? Nay, my brethren; no, no. For us. For you and for me.

For these young men in uniform, so many of whom are sinking into the downward path. Young men who are free to drink, free to associate with evil persons. Look about you in your own city, my friends. Look about you." Rev. Postelwaite paused and jerked his head at his audience. He raised his fist to the ceiling.

"What do you see, my friends? You see liquor sold in the open with no more shame than if it were fruit and grain that come from God's Own trees and fields. You see our government turning a closed eye upon the sale of liquor to people who are not capable of saying no to its temptation."

"Amen," said Freedie in a loud voice. In the pause, several other people murmured a soft "Amen."

Rev. Postelwaite raised his arm to continue. During the harangue against vice that followed this action, the Amens that were spoken in the pauses became louder and less reverent, as the speech progressed the listeners became more excited. Johnny noticed that Freedie ceased to grin and began to fidget irritably. Once or twice, Johnny disgustedly suggested leaving, but Freedie either did not hear or else paid no attention. He became gradually more and more agitated. Johnny thought suddenly of his old battalion chaplain, young, mild, bespectacled, he remembered how the chaplain had knelt by Shelley, how he had gone on all around the hill, kneeling by the men who were dying.

"And why do you think this war has come down upon us like a scourge?" Rev. Postelwaite asked. "Because of politics? because of profiteering? because of unfair treaties and weak alliances?" At each question mark, Rev. Postelwaite jerked his head at his audience as punctuation. He raised his arms to his audience. "Hey, not so, my brothers. This war has come upon us as Divine Retribution. This war is a scourge, the Scourge of God. Men upon the earth have lost the Fear of God, and *all* must pay for it. Men have strayed from the Arms of God, into the soft caressing arms of sin.

"It is our sacred duty, yours and mine, to bring them back into the Fold. Just as it is the duty of our nation, our people, to bring the world back into the Fold, our duty to search out the lost lambs and return them to their Master. Our young men and women in the armed forces are losing sight of this Divine Ideal of this war, are losing faith in us and in God. We must bring them back. Someday Armageddon will arise, and the Faithful will be called. The rest will descend to Everlasting Hellfire. It is our Divine Commission to save these poor sinners from the Eternal Hell they are courting. Do we let our children play with matches and with fire?"

Rev. Postelwaite paused for a moment, and several of the listeners cried enthusiastic Amens. Rev. Postelwaite raised his arm to continue.

"Stop!" said Freedie in a loud voice. He stood up, his arm raised above his head like an MP stopping traffic. The movement was so fast and unexpected that neither Al nor Johnny could have stopped him. Freedie's face was livid. He was dragging air into his lungs in great whoops. Rev. Postelwaite stood with his arm still raised, struck, dumb, a look of confused wonder upon his face.

"You think Armageddon's coming? You got the guts to say that after this war there's goin to be another like it, only worse? And you don't even want to stop it! You should a been in this war, and then see what you say. Armageddon! You think the guys who get drunk and whore around are goin to go to everlasting hell? Them guys you talkin about just come from hell. I drink; I whore around. *I'm* not ashamed of it. Did you ever lay in a goddam slit trench and listen to bombs whistling down on you? Did you ever try to forget it afterwards?" Freedie's words tumbled out on the heels of each other in his effort to get them said. He closed his hand and stabbed at Rev. Postelwaite with his forefinger.

"No. You stay home and talk about salvation. You think God gives a damn what happens to Evansville? or New York? or Washington? or Berlin? You think God sits up in heaven with a little black book and marks off hits and errors like a baseball score? You think God's spendin his time watchin you and your little shows? You think He's goin to give you a gold Heavenly Medal of Honor when you walk up? Guess again, Mister.

"Let me tell you somethin: You *talk* about hell, you guess at what hell is. Come and ask me sometime. I don't have to guess. I'll *tell* you what it is. I've been there. I've lived there for three years. No hell devised could be any worse than that one. You think *I'll* go to hell when *I* die? I've *been* to hell. I'm already dead.

"You think God don't count that? You think this war is punishment? Have you been punished? Sure, God took away your gasoline, didn't He? You're plain nuts. You think God could be such a son of a bitch to bring a war like this down on anybody, even a rat? You don't know *this* war, Mister. You better guess again, or learn what you're preachin about.

"*I'll* tell you who caused this goddam war. It's people like you. Poor dumb bastards who shut their eyes to every goddam thing but them and their souls. You think prayin and bein saved is goin to make this world better? Tell that to a Jap while he's cuttin your nuts out. Tell that to a Nazi while he's rapin your daughter. Tell that to the oil companies and steel companies while they're sendin oil and steel to Argentina for the Germans and rakin in the dough hand over fist. Tell that to the guys who are sellin equipment to the Japs in China. Americans. Sure, right now while you're talkin. Dumb bastards like you are the kind the big boys like. You so busy prayin and savin your soul, you forget about the doggies who are gettin their heads blown off. You so busy prayin, you forget the world you live in, you say it's 'Evil' and let it go at that. You bitch about the doggies drinkin and whorin. They ain't doin no harm; they ain't causin no wars. They're the guys that's in it. Your soul! You don't know what a soul is. And now you kin yell Amen."

Freedie's neck was bulging with pent-up rage and hate. His breath was coming great whoops between words. As he spoke, he shook his fist at Rev. Postelwaite. The white-haired old man was on his way, hotfooting it down the aisle followed by two ushers. The ushers towered over the old man like skyscrapers over a hashhouse.

"Wait'll this war's over," Freedie raged. "Then the truth'll come out. Only then nobody'll give a damn. But guys like me. It's over and done with then. You ain't lost nothing. You think God causes wars? Look at yourself. What has God got against Evansville? Nothing but the damn fool sons of bitches that live there. And the ones that travel around and preach to them to make a living. How many hundred thousand you got stuck away in the bank? Hunh? How many?"

Al and Johnny were on their feet when the two big men grabbed Freedie roughly.

"Take it easy, Mack," Al said in an ominous voice.

"Lay a hand on him, and you won't have no tabernacle left," Johnny said. "Get him out. Take him outside. But you hit him and, by God, we'll tear your goddam house apart. If we can't do it alone, there'll be a hundred guys here as soon as I yell."

The man whose fingers were sunk into the soft spot at the base of Freedie's neck looked at Johnny's deadpan face and icy eyes and moved his hand down and crooked it around Freedie's elbow.

"Go ahead," Johnny urged. "Take him out. We'll help you get him out. But don't lay a finger on him."

The four of them hustled Freedie up the aisle toward the door. Freedie squirmed around and shouted back at Rev. Postelwaite, shaking his trembling fist over Johnny's shoulder.

"You think prayin can save the goddam world?" he screamed. "Go tell it to the Marines. See what they say. You goddam hypocritical son of a bitch. The only thing can save the world is the men in it. And they'd rather save their goddam souls. Save your soul, you son of a bitch, save your soul. When you get to your hell, remember me. I've already been there. You won't see me, you lousy son of a bitch."

Rev. Postelwaite's congregation was staring at the crazed soldier with wide eyes, as if someone had poured cold water over them. Rev. Postelwaite was standing by his pulpit, his arms hanging loosely. There was a sad look on his face, mingled with an uncompromising sternness. The four men got Freedie outside, and Johnny took his bottle and gave him a drink. Johnny and Al exchanged a swift glance, and Al shook his head; but Freedie did not notice. They walked him along the street and Johnny gave him another drink. Freedie's face was tightened up and the lines beneath his eyes stood out sharply. He was clenching and unclenching his fists. He was crying.

"Well," said Johnny. "I guess that wound up the revival meeting for tonight."

"Son of a bitch," Freedie sobbed. "Dirty Jesus monger son of a bitch.

He can talk about hell. Guys livin in hell right now and he talks about salvation. Dirty sky-pilot son of a bitch."

Finally, they got him quieted.

They walked him around for some time before they decided to go back to the Hotel Roquefort. By the time they entered the Rendezvous, Freedie had control of himself again. He stared obdurately at all the women who passed them.

"Ahhh," he said disgustedly. "We could of had a lot of fun, if I hadn't of blew up. You ought to see them when the preacher asks if they want to be saved. It's almost as good as a holy roller meeting. They all get down there together and pray, and the preacher blesses them. When they get up, they're saved, and that makes them different people."

Freedie drained his glass. "When's the big show goin to start?" he asked Al. "It's nine o'clock already. . . . If I hadn't of blown up, we could of picked up some honeys down there after the meeting was over. I had a couple in the crowd picked out. Boy, listen, there's nothing hotter in the world than a gal who's just been saved. You can't even keep 'em on the bed."

They ordered more drinks, and Freedie glowered at the waitress as she brought the drinks. She had a nice figure, and Freedie cursed her softly as she walked away from the table. A tall beautifully built young woman walked past them just after the waitress left. The girl was dark-haired and dressed in a red dress of some thin, light-absorbing material and a black bolero jacket of the same cloth. Her skirt fitted her hips very clingingly, and the edges of her panties made visible ridges in the skirt, passing just under her buttocks and fading out of sight. Freedie ogled her sullenly. The woman stopped just beyond their table and looked around the room over the tops of the heads.

Freedie cursed for a moment and then called to her. "Hey," he said without rising. "Come on over and have a drink." He flashed his likeable grin at her as she turned to look at him. The girl stared at him coldly with lifted eyebrows and made a little moue of distaste. She lifted her shoulder slightly and turned on her heel and walked across the room. She selected one of the empty tables clear across the room.

Freedie looked at his watch. "I'll give her ten minutes to soften up before I go over," he said. "That stuff's for me tonight. When you guys be ready to start?"

Al shrugged. "We'll get the next one that come in," he said.

Johnny shook his head. "I got a date with that redhead you had in the bathroom all night," he said to Freedie. He looked at his watch. "Half an hour."

"Okay," Freedie said. He toyed with his drink and looked down into it reflectively. "You want to know why I blew my top?"

"It doesn't make any difference," Johnny said. "Forget it."

"I know," Freedie said, "but that's not what I mean." He tilted his glass and rolled the bottom around and around in a circle. "You want to know something? I'll tell you something that'll knock your hat off. You guys think the Flying Tigers is a wonderful outfit? It ain't wonderful. It's rotten. Except for the guys; the guys are the best bunch in the world. If it wasn't for the guys, a man would be ashamed to be in it.

"You want to know something?" he said, staring at them penetratingly. "I'll tell you something. You know Milton Caniff's *Terry and the Pirates* comic strip? Well, all the guys in the Air Corps swear by Caniff, especially in China. That guy knows more about the Air Corps than any man in it.

"Well, he's got a character in the strip he calls 'Silk.' That girl actually exists. God only knows how Caniff learned about her. 'Silk' ain't her real name, of course, but she's Chinese. Well, that gal is worse than Mata Hari in the last war. That gal is one of the ringleaders in the biggest graft scandal in this war. The list of names would stagger you." Freedie lit a cigaret sourly.

"You think I'm kidding? You remember what I told you and watch the papers. There'll be a court-martial list as long as your arm come out on that deal someday. Both Americans and Chinese. It'll be hushed up in the papers, because there's plenty of big men in on it. Them guys'll get out of it, because no government ever court-martials itself; only the little guys.

"Listen: This gal 'Silk' goes over to Japan and she gets a list of things the Japs need in the way of small arms and stuff like ammunition and grenades, and she gets a list of places where the small outfits need it. Then she comes back to China. Pretty soon orders go down over the hump for equipment to be sent up. They send up ships loaded to the gills, but those ships never land, and we never see the equipment. A couple of weeks later, we get reports that the Japanese in such and such a sector are using American rifles and grenades; our guys find dead Japs with American packs and entrenching tools and canteens and ammo belts and knives. They find a lot of American knives on dead Japs, and they find 'em in sectors where none of our men have been captured. Why, they've even found the Japs using American fieldpieces. And our artillery ain't lost any.

"Listen: Before I went overseas, they gave us guys indoctrination talks. Guys who had been there. They told us they'd just as soon kill a Chinese coolie as a Jap. One guy was educated in China but when he got to Burma and around in there and found out how 'ignorant and dumb' they were, he said he hated them so much he'd just as soon kill them as Japs. There's something screwy in that setup. Why do they have guys like that give indoctrination lectures like that to guys who are just going to China? China's supposed to be our ally. I've seen them pack coolies on trains to send 'em off for training under armed guards. The coolies didn't want to go. After they are shipped away from home, they just sit down and die off like flies.

"The Chinese Army has orders not to fight the Japs. They spend all their time fighting the guerrillas, and they furnish American equipment to the goddam Japs to use against the Chinese Reds.

"Who the hell are we supposed to be fighting for? Why, the Japs are using Douglas bombers. I've been shot at by them! My ship almost got knocked down once by a Douglas bomber made in Japan! They're using them all the time; that ship is one of their most important planes.

"And then I listen to some dumb bastard who says the world is suffering because it's become too sexy! Why don't they try to learn the truth about things, instead of preachin and prayin and savin souls? It's enough to make anybody blow his top. If I have to fight a war for my country,

I don't want to get killed by my own countrymen I'm supposed to be fightin for."

Freedie tossed off his drink. He signaled for the waitress belligerently. "Ahhh, to hell with it," he said.

Four coastguardsmen from Owensboro came in and set down at a table beside that of the young woman in the red dress.

Freedie eyes the coastsguardsmen silently. "Christ!" he burst out. "Who the hell knows I'm not going to get knocked down by American flak, shot out of American AA guns, made in an American defense plant—to help win the war? What are you going to believe in, if it's run like that. Guys like me are just suckers. I . . . Ahhh, to hell with the bastards."

Freedie got up from his chair and limped across the room to the table at which sat the dark-haired girl in the skin-cling skirt. Al and Johnny watched him talk to her for a moment, and then he sat down. They grinned briefly, and then they began to talk about the things that Freedie had just told them. Five minutes later, Freedie brought the girl over to the table and introduced her to Al and Johnny. Behind her back, he winked and grinned. He held up three fingers, pointed to himself and each of them and nodded elaborately.

Half an hour later, the party in Room 507 on the fifth floor was going strong, and the word got around. The bottles overflowed off the dressers and the people overflowed at the door. The bathroom was pressed into service, but Al and Johnny and Freedie would have none of it. Freedie sat on a pile of coats on one of the beds, getting drunk, hating all the foolish people, and enjoying the noise and presence of the crowd. No wonder, Freedie thought as he held a glass to the lips of the girl in the red skirt. No wonder God's got a bitch against Evansville.

Freedie took away the glass and kissed her tentatively.

Jones wrote in his diary that his Uncle Charlie was trying to "break" him "thru fear and humiliation." Jones was even more outraged when he learned his uncle had opposed his transfer to George Field in Vincennes, making him closer to Lowney. Jones wrote his uncle: "Just forget that I am a part of the Jones clan; just teach yourself that I you have no nephew named Jim."

"You Are AWOL" reflects Johnny's pent-up resentments against his hypocritical relative. The break with the lawyer/businessman relative decisively moves Johnny into Sandy's orbit, for she, unlike Erskine, had come to believe Johnny could become a major writer.

YOU ARE AWOL

AT THE ERSKINE CARTER HOME, AUTUMN 1943

"WHEN DO YOU EXPECT TO leave?" Erskine asked.

"I hadn't thought about it," said Johnny. "Maybe another week. Why?"

"Well," said Erskine in a tone usually reserved for haranguing juries, "you are AWOL, and although you may not know it, I am breaking the law when I allow you to stay here, knowing you are AWOL. That makes me an accessory after the fact. Besides that, I've just had a visit from the chief of police."

Johnny looked surprised.

"You didn't expect that, did you?" said Erskine, "when you went all over town bragging openly that you were AWOL? The chief was very decent about it. But even you can hardly expect him to just overlook such a breech of the law.

"If you had come here to see me and Fanny it might be different. If you had not been so loud about being over the hill, the chief would not have had to recognize the fact. It seems quite evident to me that you have brought whatever happens to you upon yourself. And quite frankly, I don't feel I have any responsibility to intercede for you. You have used our house as a resting up place between drunks and fornications, and for nothing else. I do not like that. You seem to have utterly no sense of gratitude or of responsibility. I do not like that."

Johnny cut in on him: "We've been all over this."

"Yes," said Erskine, "and we'll probably be all over it several times more. Since you seem to prefer the company of Sandy Marion to that of your own family, why don't you just move into her house."

"That's an idea," acknowledged Johnny.

"That is, provided Eddie will let you." The implication caused by leaving Eddie's name out of the previous statement was strengthened a great deal by this postscript. The postscript was unnecessary, however, because Johnny had already got it. When he still ignored the strengthened implication, Erskine went ahead.

"The point I am coming to is this: I don't want you to stay here any longer as long as you are AWOL. And as long as you feel you must act as you have been acting, I don't want you to stay at all. I want you to plan to leave sometime tomorrow."

"Then I take it you'd rather I did move down to Sandy's?" Johnny asked mischievously.

"You are of age," said Erskine. "You are free to do as you see fit. Of course, what the chief of police does after you leave here is also your concern."

"All right," said Johnny. "I'll leave tomorrow night. I wouldn't want to get you into any trouble with the law; I wouldn't want to ruin your business or your reputation."

"Fanny and I," said Erskine, "have taken a number of years to build up the reputation of the Carter name in this town from where it was when your father died. I loved Joe as much as any brother ever loved another—even if he was only my uncle; nevertheless I cannot condone some of the things he did."

"Yes," said Johnny. "You have told me this also."

"I'll drive you to Evansville, and put you on the train for camp."

Johnny laughed harshly, his eyes squinting up a little in sudden anger, "Don't you think I'm capable of taking care of myself?"

"I don't know whether you are or not, frankly." Erskine took his hands from behind his back and folded them over his chest. Johnny remembered suddenly the legend of Endymion that the only man who could ever make Erskine Carter holler uncle was his Uncle Joe, Johnny's farther. Erskine must have seen what was in Johnny's eyes, because he unfolded his arms and hung his thumbs in his belt.

Johnny tossed off the remainder of his drink and stood up. He was directly in front of Erskine and facing him.

"All right," he said. "Now I'll say something. As you said, I'm of age. I'll do as I darned please. You won't take me to Evansville to put me on no train, no time. I'm leaving tonight. Your jurisdiction goes just as far as your front door. No farther. When I leave this house, I don't expect to come back in it. That's not because I dislike you. Neither is it because I feel I've been treated badly. I don't. I agree with you when you say whatever happens to me is my own fault. I wouldn't have it any other way." Johnny stopped for breath and found that he was leaning forward toward Erskine. His fists were clenched and he could feel a tension in him that seemed to be begging for a wrong word, or for a wrong movement. He forced himself to relax a little and lean back.

"When I leave here, just mark me off the roll, forget that you've got a Carter relative by the name of Johnny. You and I have nothing in common except the name of Carter. I've tried to explain some of my ideas about things several times to you. Your picture of me as a punk kid coupled with your own natural lack of foresight makes you too goddamned narrow to listen. That's your tough luck, not mine. I don't feel hurt and I'm not mad at you. I'm mad at what you represent. You and I haven't even any common speaking ground.

"I've told you about how I liked the kind of life you folks live: good food, good liquor, good fun. I still like it. But any poor ignorant son of a bitch can live like that without any effort. That kind of life is fine, but it is no end in itself, and it's no justification for itself. That kind of life is false, as long as everybody in the whole damned world doesn't live it also. There's a great change coming on this earth when this war is over. People like you will be left out of it, because people like you are enemies of change. As long as you try to keep your 'fine life' for yourselves, you will remain enemies, not only of change but of *real* progress. I don't expect you to understand what I'm saying. But someday you'll remember it, when the world moves away from you and your kind.

"Just remember what I said: Mark me off the roll, forget you know a Johnny Carter." Johnny stopped talking, realizing that he was unable to say what he wanted to say.

"Fine," said Erskine. He stared back at Johnny, eye for eye. His jaw muscles were set tight and his mouth was very thin. "Don't expect to come running back to me when somebody kicks you in the tail."

"Every Time I Drop an Egg . . ." is a powerful story, but it is not subtle. Jim Watkins is an American Nazi who loves war, death, and destruction. Every time he dropped an egg, he told Johnny, "I'm going to kiss it goodby and pray it kills a thousand of those bastards. That's the life. That's where the excitement and the fun is."

"George and I are lost," Johnny says. "But old Jim is double-lost."

Jim Watkins is a good soldier.

EVERY TIME I DROP AN EGG . . .

LAST DAY IN ENDYMION, AT THE MARION HOME, AUTUMN 1943

"HE SAID HIS NAME WAS Lieutenant Watkins," said Eddie, who had taken the call. "He sounded as if he wanted to make sure I heard the 'Lieutenant.' He called Erskine's for you and Erskine told him you were down here."

Johnny laughed. "And I didn't tell Erskine I was coming here. That's Jim Watkins," he added after a moment. "Though I didn't know he was home. He enlisted in the Regular Army the same time I did."

"Who is he?" asked Sandy.

"His father's a farmer down south of town. He and I both enlisted for Hawaii. After the war started, he went through flight training and got a commission. We were pretty good friends in Hawaii."

"I told him you weren't here," Eddie said, "but he said you'd be here soon. He's going to stop by to see you."

"Yeh? I'd like to see him, too," Johnny said. When Jim Watkins came, Johnny answered the front door. The man who stood in the doorway was tall and heavy. He was dressed immaculately in an officer's woolen uniform, and the second lieutenant's gold bars glittered on the shoulders of his blouse. The uniform fitted him perfectly; he looked very trim and neat and military in it. There was a heavy stolid look about his face that seemed out of place in a man so young.

"You're out of uniform," said Jim jokingly. Johnny had taken off his tie and shirt in the kitchen and wore only a cotton T-shirt above the waist.

"Hello, Jim," he said, sticking out his hand. "Come in and have a drink."

Jim Watkins took Johnny's hand, and shook it firmly, as if he were doing so with a deliberate thought. Yet when he smiled, there was genuine friendship and liking in his face.

"No thanks," Jim said, a little awkwardly. "I can only stay a minute. I just wanted to see you and say hello. The heater's running; come on out to the car."

Johnny inspected Jim's face for a moment, then he said: "Okay. You go on out while I get a shirt or something."

Jim went out to the car, and Johnny shut the door. He took his topcoat from the chair on which he had tossed it and went out into the kitchen. Sandy and George and Eddie were sitting at the table.

"Jim doesn't want to come in," he grinned. "I think he's heard all about our reputation."

He overlapped the topcoat without buttoning it and tied the belt in a loose knot and went out the back door. Jim was standing beside his oar in the dull gray-black winter dusk.

"How've you been, old boy?" Jim asked him. "How's the leg? Mother wrote me you'd been sent back Stateside in the hospital. You're a lucky bastard, you know it?"

"Yeh," said Johnny. "I used to think I'd never get back."

"That wasn't what I meant. I meant you're lucky you got to see all that action."

"Oh."

Jim Watkins laughed. "The same old Johnny, aren't you? What the hell are you doing wearing an officer's topcoat?" He grabbed Johnny's upper arm with a large strong hand. "You know the old ARs."

Johnny shrugged, playing the part Jim's attitude forced him into. "Well, you know me," he laughed.

Jim slapped his arm a couple of times. "The same old Johnny. Wild and woolly. I heard about you being over the hump. When are you going to settle down a little? You'd probably be an officer now if you weren't so damned bullheaded. Then you could wear one of those topcoats without trouble."

"I'm wearing it now."

"Sure, but you couldn't wear it in camp without some chickenshit shavetail jumping on you."

"I guess you're right, Jim. I shouldn't have turned down that chance I had to go to OCS."

"You turned down OCS?" Jim was incredulous. "How come?"

"Oh, I don't know," Johnny shrugged. "Just don't appeal to me. And I wanted to go into action with my outfit."

"Oh," said Jim. "Then I don't blame you. You ought to get married, Johnny. Did you know I'm married?"

"No. Congratulations. I hadn't heard about it."

"Thanks. That's what you need, old Johnny. Makes you grow up. This war is serious business, you know. You ought to quit playing around, and start taking this war serious."

"So I've heard. Say, Jim, come on in the house and have a drink. Sandy's frying you a steak by my orders. She's got some fine tenderloin."

Jim's eyes flickered away from Johnny's gaze almost automatically.

Johnny could almost see a film form over them. "I can't make it, Johnny." Jim said, not looking him in the eyes. "I left mother and the wife downtown, and I've got to pick them up. Besides," he added, "I don't drink anymore."

"Don't drink!" Johnny was genuinely surprised; he and Jim had been on some glorious bats in Honolulu. "How come?"

"Drinking and flying don't mix." Johnny nodded. Al had told him the same thing. The sudden thought of Al sent a sharp jolt through his stomach.

"I don't want anything to throw me off stride," Jim went on. "Not even an inch. I've quit smoking, too, and I always go to bed early. I want to be in perfect shape when I get to start laying those eggs in."

"Oh," said Johnny. "What are you flying, Jim? Twenty-fours?"

"Nope. The big boys. B-17s. Fly from here to hell and back and drop a load of Nazis on the return trip."

"Oh," said Johnny.

"So you can see what I mean," said Jim, warming up to his subject. "I'm taking this war serious." There was a set hard look on his face. Johnny had seen it before. In his outfit, they called it the killer's look.

"I've got a ten-day delay in route," Jim said. "I'm going east to pick up a plane and then we're going over. I've been waiting for this a mighty long time. I want to get even for what those bastards did to us on The Seventh. They blew Hickam to hell. You were lucky you were gone. It's alright to be able to fight back, but when you can't do anything, it's not so much fun."

"Yes," said Johnny. "I was at Schofield. We just got a little strafing."

"That's why I envy you, Johnny. You've been where you had a chance to do some killing on your own side. It isn't on as big a scale as flying a bomber, but it's killing just the same."

"That's right," Johnny said.

"Every time I drop an egg, I'm going to kiss it goodby and pray it kills a thousand of those bastards. That's the life. That's where the excitement and the fun is." He jerked his thumb toward the east. "I've been sweating and training for this a long time. You don't know how lucky you are. There's thousands of guys who won't ever get overseas, and here you are back already and maybe getting a chance to go over again."

"Yes," said Johnny. "That's right, Jim. Are you sure you won't come in and have a steak and a drink? Oh, that's right, you don't drink."

"Nope. Nor anything else that might make me soften up."

"There's a fellow in the house from Vincennes who lost a leg on Attu," said Johnny. "Maybe you'd like to talk to him."

"No. Those cripples give me the creeps. They're nice guys and all that, but they're all through and they know it."

"That's right. Well, Jim, take it easy and keep your head down."

"Not me. I'm going to see all I can see and get all I can get. To hell with the ducking." The hard cold look stared at Johnny out of Jim's face.

This was not the boast of a callow youth, bragging about something he didn't know anything about. Jim was not bragging.

They shook hands and Jim climbed into the car.

"What're you going to do after the war, Jim?" Johnny asked suddenly.

Jim's grin drew his lips back from his teeth. His eyes threw out bright splinters of the dial light, "Well," he said. His laugh was a bark. "I might stay in the army and get to be a goddamned general; that's not a bad idea. But I ain't worried about that. I've got too much egg-dropping to do."

He started the car. "Well, old Johnny, so long. Maybe I'll see you in London, hey?" He leaned over and shook hands with Johnny.

"Maybe," said Johnny. "Goodby, Jim."

Johnny watched the car drive away, and then he turned and went back into the house shivering slightly with the cold.

"I need a drink," he said to George. "I need a real drink."

"What's the matter, old son?" George asked.

"I just said goodby to a guy I used to like." He took the drink George handed him, and stood staring down at the glass in his hand.

"I wish I knew what it was that did that to Jim. Jim and I were buddies in Wahoo. Something sure's happened to him. It might have been The Seventh; he was at Hickham, and Hickham got hit hard. But I've seen worse than that since then. It must just be what's in the individual. Some people are affected one way and some another." He took a long deep drink from his glass.

"Jim," he said, "is an American Nazi." He looked at George meaningly. "He doesn't drink anymore nor smoke, and he goes to bed early every night. He's cut himself off from everything that might weaken him. He does everything he's told and believes everything he's told—which is worse. He lives for one thing and one thing only. He lives to kill. An American Nazi: America should rule the world: Everything for The State. A fanatic, and like all fanatics, unbalanced. Where's he going to be when this war is over?

"George and I are lost. But old Jim is double-lost." Johnny's shoulders were hunched and he stared at the tablecloth. "I wonder where it's all going to end. Or if it's ever going to end. Jim's the kind of man the army wants. The army tries to teach a man to be the way Jim is. Jim's a good soldier. He's a perfect soldier. But where's it going to end? After Germany, what then? Russia? England? Bankruptcy? Russia's got more men like Jim than America. So had England. America has less than any other country, but America has too many, and getting more. America has gradually set up an ideal for men to emulate, and that ideal is Jim. Everything you read preaches it, everything teaches it. Even the magazine advertisements subtly teach people that a man like Jim is a perfect ideal to build toward.

"Look at all the big corporation advertisements. Millions of dollars a year. Do you think they're doing that to sell things? Paintings of GIs, made-up letters to Dear Mom, telling everybody to trust in God, telling Dear Mom not to worry her head, that's not to sell products, that's indoctrination. That's the subtlest and most deadly propaganda there is." Johnny looked around the kitchen, nobody answered him, or had anything at all to say.

"There is no ending. It just goes on and on, deliberately creating killers like Jim and holding them up as examples. Don't think, don't reason, don't even feel except what you're told to feel. Advertising has become the greatest danger this country ever faced. Our big boys learned a lot from Hitler and he from them.

"I guess the best thing to do is just die and get it over with. The only trouble with me is I can't enjoy it the way Jim does." He looked up and grinned a shy sad smile that was out of place in the gaunt fighter's face he had recently acquired. There was infinite pain in his eyes that went deeper and deeper and never seemed to end.

"Come on, George," he said. "Let's have a drink. You're the lucky one, George. You're all through. Unless Russia lands troopers in the Middle West in the next war. I'd trade places with you in a minute. I'd cut my own leg off to trade places with you, George.

"Come on, drink up. A toast!" he said, raising his glass and standing from his chair.

"To the end of the war!"

Johnny, broken to the rank of private for being AWOL, was reduced for a time to latrine duty. This extended account of Johnny the expendable "crumb" now back in a different company, is filled with specific details that increased the realism of his later war novels. "Stranger in a New Company," however, is primarily expository, and Jones's masterful dialogue is largely missing. Still, this story helps us understand Johnny and his fellow renegades and castaways in the authoritarian army.

"This war is going to last a long time," the captain said to Johnny, "and you might as well reconcile yourself to it."

STRANGER IN A NEW COMPANY

FORT CAMPBELL, KENTUCKY, LATE AUTUMN, 1943

HE WOULD RIDE THROUGH THE gate in the cab of the truck that met all the trains and he would look at the two MPs on duty at the gate, and once again the old familiar feeling of being trapped by a great indifferent power, the insignificance of being no more than a rifle or a grenade, another expendable crumb beneath the grinding thumb of Authority and the leering grin of Fate. Somewhere the wrong gears had meshed to throw the old balance of life out of kilter and every man's life had been affected. Your life was your own and the only one you had, but now it was no longer yours; it belonged to Authority. Each man owed his life to Society. And this might go on for years, for scores of years, before a new balance might take form. Authority accepted for the moment might not be thrown off as easily as it had been accepted. A mystery, Authority, that came from whence nobody knew where, that could not he pinned down to any one man or group of men, a strange formidable power that grew and grew without seeming to take nourishment. You owed a debt to Society, and Authority was the cop with the tin badge and billy club to see that you paid. But Society owed you nothing.

And you were the goat. You were the crumb that was expendable.

He would ride back through the gates where the two MPs stood, and the gates would close up with a clang and swallow him forever.

It was a feeling all soldiers, all the nameless millions who were only the pawns of Society, often have.

It was not a good feeling to have when he was reporting back.

The first thing that happened to Johnny, after he had been assigned to a regiment and to a company, was that he was broken to a private. This action was not unexpected, neither was it particularly resented. Because he was a non-commissioned officer with a rating to lose, and because he was a veteran of overseas combat, he got off without being court-martialed.

The 26th Division was being flooded with combat veterans released from hospitals all over the country and being sent back to duty. Johnny was one of the first, and after these first few came the flood. The sight of men wearing combat ribbons became a commonplace one, and after a while ceased to excite awed comments among the green men. The bright ribbons infiltrated into all the PXs and movies and Service Clubs, particularly into the sections of the various Post Exchanges (there were around twenty on the post) which dispensed the regulation 3.2 beer. At almost any time after Retreat up until closing time, a group of these men could be seen sitting together around several pitchers of beer, discussing the war, the new outfit, the army.

Johnny was the first combat veteran to be assigned to his company, and so he enjoyed the pleasure of being somewhat of a celebrity. He was looked upon as some sort of strange alien creature who had been through combat. The men in his new company were typical of the whole division. The majority of them were young men with close-clipped GI haircuts, strong rugged bodies, and unlined faces. They constituted almost all of the privates and PFCs; very few of them were non-coms. They had all been drafted recently and had just completed their Basic Training; few of them were over twenty, none over twenty-two. There was an eager bright look, in their eyes, and they got a great kick out of Military Discipline and saluting officers and standing at attention. The whole thing was a great lark to them, a great adventure that allowed them to get away from homes, schools, or jobs that bored them. They were having a world of fun out of field problems with live ammunition.

Standing out amidst this group were the non-coms, most of them old men in the division, having been with it all over the United States during the three years since it was activated. The 26th Division—or YD Division—was a National Guard outfit and the non-coms and officers had been in the company before the division was activated. The majority of the non-coms spoke with a soft slurred New England drawl. The cooks, clerks, supply men were all old timers who had had their specialist jobs since activation, jobs that were gravytrain, and for which a man needed a good bit of pull with somebody in order to get the job—a job that stood no formations, made no marches, did not have stand Reveille or Retreat.

The company commander was a small, bowlegged, pinch-faced captain who wore gold spectacles and was a strict disciplinarian—so the non-coms said, having known him before the war when he was an assistant manager of a hardware store. The non-coms did not like him and enjoyed dwelling upon the fact that he had been a lieutenant in the CCCs after quitting his job in the hardware store in Boston, whence most of them came. He was in good with the colonel and was slated for a majority soon, they said, and prayed that he would make his majority very soon.

Johnny was in the company a week before the final orders on his bust came through. The first thing he had done in the company was to take a medical examination which marked him unfit for field duty. Since the company spent most of its time in the field, Johnny stayed alone in the barracks with the clerks and a few of the cooks, those who were not out with the company running the field kitchen. He was a corporal, and he was treated as one. There being no jobs befitting the prestige of a non-com available, he laid around and did nothing. He had to be out of the barracks and simulating some kind of work during each morning until after the battalion adjutant made his inspection of the barracks while the companies were out in the field. Although he had a medical chit excusing him, it was considered bad policy for the battalion adjutant to find any man doing nothing. The company went out at daylight and stayed out till dark, taking their noon meal in the field, thus giving him twelve hours to do nothing.

When the company was in, Johnny's corner bunk became a gathering place for the boisterous eager-eyed kids. None of them suspected that Johnny was no more than three years older than the youngest of them. They misinterpreted Johnny's hard set face and short clipped sentences, and they saw him as sinister and ominous, when in actuality he was only disgusted and dissatisfied. They congregated around his bunk and plied him with questions about the Japs; when he was drinking beer in the PX, they offered to pay for it, and plied him with questions about combat. He was a romantic picture to them, and they could see themselves being tempered by the fire of war into tight-lipped, cold-eyed, nerveless men who could kill or be killed without batting an eyelash.

They listened eagerly to his stories when they could get him to talk. He refused to talk much, and they jubilantly construed this to be because his experiences had been so terrible that he could not stand to talk about them. Actually, it was because Johnny's personal experience and understanding of combat was so opposed to what they wanted to see and hear in his words that it irritated him to try to explain it. They listened almost breathlessly to what stories he did tell—such as the one about the time the Jap jumped into his slit trench from behind in the middle of the night. They thought this very exciting.

And also stories about him got around in the company. One night during the week he remained a corporal, there was a non-com's meeting in the company dayroom, a long low building, the other half of which held the orderly room and supply room. The dayroom contained a ping-pong table with a broken leg and a badly warped surface, a magazine rack without magazines, a number of straight-backed wooden chairs, and a Coca-Cola machine. The captain gave a lecture on gas and the use of gas masks from behind his gold spectacles. After the lecture was over and the non-coms had stopped fidgeting, the captain said; "Corporal Carter, perhaps you'd like to tell us what provisions were made concerning gas masks and gas in your company while it was in combat."

"We didn't use them, Sir," Johnny said. "When my outfit went up to the line the first time, everybody threw their gas masks in the bushes." This was the literal truth.

A couple of the non-coms sniggered, and the captain's eyes narrowed behind his gold spectacles, his pinched face became more so. "Weren't you ever worried about being gassed? Wasn't your company commander somewhat anxious about what might happen if his company were in a gas attack?"

"It's not as simple as that, Sir," Johnny said. "None of us were worried about gas masks. We had too many other things to be worried about. Besides that, the Japs had discarded their own gas masks, too."

"That seems very inefficient to me. But I suppose that is the way the Regular Army works."

Johnny returned the captain's pinch-faced stare without looking away, something not considered a wise action in the association between enlisted men and officers. "Combat is always inefficient, Sir," he said. It was evident the captain did not believe this. "There are too many elements which are not taken into account. In fact, all possibilities can never be taken into account. The same thing never happens twice in the same way. From my own experience, I'd say that a man has to unlearn everything he's been taught from the Soldier's Handbook and begin all over again as soon as he gets under fire. Then he begins to pick up little tricks of the trade that keep him from getting killed, for my part, I don't believe combat will ever reach the point where it can be efficiently mass-controlled."

The captain blinked behind his gold spectacles at this. "Well," he said. "We didn't know as much detail about modern combat when your outfit went in as we do now. But there are men who have devoted their whole lives to the study of combat. We have found that the best way to prevent casualties and defeats is to follow a prearranged set pattern of action in which each man does his particular job obediently, synchronizing the whole into a welded action."

Johnny said nothing to this, realizing that especially in the army is discretion the better part of valor. But he immediately thought of his old

CC, Captain Rosen, who had refused via sound power phone an order from the battalion commander, who was eight hundred yards to the rear and out of danger; the battalion commander ordered Captain Rosen to proceed with a frontal attack as planned. Captain Rosen informed the colonel he had lived with the men in his company for a year and that the colonel could kindly kiss his ass. By this action Captain Rosen saved his company from annihilation, made a flanking attack and captured the objective, and was at once relieved of his command and sent back to the States in the Judge Advocate General's Corps, for which transfer he was duly grateful, even though it was considered a disgrace in the army.

The story of Johnny's tilt with the gold-spectacled captain made a very good joke on the captain, who was not liked by the men in his company. The non-coms spread it around, and while they enjoyed the story, they looked upon Johnny as a damned fool for deliberately antagonizing the CC. No man who argued with his CC could be classed as intelligent.

The barracks were very lonely when everyone was gone. Johnny bought several pocketbooks at the PX, but those books had to be hidden away during the mornings when the battalion adjutant inspected the barracks. They could not be kept under the pillow, and they could not be kept in the wooden footlocker, for the adjutant was also a disciplinarian and inspected the footlockers of all the men who were not out in the field with the company. Johnny found a library in the main Service Club, but this library was ordered to be closed until after Retreat which was at five-thirty.

The barracks were lonely even when the company was in. Johnny was a stranger in a new outfit, an outfit in which there were no old friends, no men who saw things as he saw them, no men with common experiences to be remembered and talked about. Johnny spent a good bit of time writing poetry, most of which he tore up and threw away. His new attitude of mind acquired in Endymion was not conducive to the writing of poetry, which never explained enough, and he found he had no aptitude for writing it anymore. He was concerned with more prosaic things. After the comparative freedom of expression in a combat outfit and in a hospital, the severe regimentation of this outfit was hard to take. If he had had a job, he might not have been so depressed and dissatisfied.

As soon as his bust orders came through, the job part was taken care of. As a private, he was made permanent latrine orderly. The captain called him in and informed him of his reduced status. As is customary, he was offered a chance to appeal this decision to a court-martial if he was dissatisfied with it. While political pull in the army, just as in civilian life, is never acknowledged openly, there is no man but what knows of its existence and governs his actions accordingly. The captain's friend, the colonel, would sit as president of the court-martial if Johnny requested one; it would be asinine to imagine he might get an honest judgment from such a court, even if the reduction in rank was unjust—which it was not. He was not dissatisfied with the judgment, which he considered abnormally light; he was dissatisfied with the outfit, with his place in it, and with the army in general. He made no appeal, and the captain informed him of his new job.

Being a latrine orderly is usually acknowledged as being a particularly odious task. Usually, it is worked on the duty roster so that the job rotates daily among the privates, a portion of whose lot in life it is to do such jobs when their turn comes. One of the inducements offered toward becoming a non-com is that a man no longer has to pull such details. It is a policy that a non-com is used more for his brain than for his back. While it is not physically one of the hardest jobs in the world, being a latrine orderly is not as easy as generally supposed. When a company comes in from the field and mobs a latrine, of which there are two for something like one hundred and fifty men, they leave it in a poor condition. Sergeant George Baker has aptly handled this situation in one of his *Sad Sack* cartoons. It's not an easy job to clean it next morning after they've used it again so that it is fit to pass the daily inspection.

Johnny Carter, being physically disabled, was a fit person to fill this most disliked of jobs. He was not able to go out in the field, and his disability did not keep him from being useful here. Of course, he could have been a cook's helper, or a permanent KP, or an additional clerk, or an aid in the supply room—all of which jobs, like clerking and supply, he had had previous experience in, as his records testified.

Being a malefactor and in no position to gripe, Johnny forced himself to do the job, and which is much harder, forced himself to say nothing about it. The gold-spectacled captain had every ground for being in the right: Johnny had been over the hill, had been busted, had been ostensibly insolent, was not fit for field duty. But to Johnny—especially knowing the army as he did—the captain's attitude was just a shade too personal and too righteous. Johnny was in a position where he could do nothing or say nothing, could not protest or fight back. His only alternative was to get himself into a worse situation. Only a man who has been in such a position can appreciate or understand what a man goes through in that kind of setup. It's a kind of setup very common in the army. Johnny thought that it must be the way many criminals must feel in prison under the personal jurisdiction of a guard, and he did not wonder that now and then a criminal goes berserk and becomes a Public Enemy of a society which fosters such things. Of such a nature was the legend proudly displayed by guards armed with pick handles in the Post Stockade of Schofield Barracks: They pridefully informed prisoners that John Dillinger served six months in the Schofield Barracks Post Stockade, and forever after swore that if it took the rest of his life, he intended to get even with the United States.

To Johnny his job was an indignity. He saw it as a deliberate attempt on the part of the captain to humiliate him or to break him to heel. He could not walk out as he had done with Erskine, he could only force himself to act like he liked it and thus dull the captain's pleasure a small bit. For him, with his experience and his intelligence, it was the worst kind of slap in the face a man could give him. He had to keep forcing himself to turn the other cheek. When the captain made his own personal inspection, as he often did before the battalion adjutant came around, his praise of Johnny's "work" and his impersonality were much too studied and much to obvious to be believed. Johnny would look up unexpectedly and catch his eyes now and then and detect the faintest kind of a twinkle of relish behind the gold spectacles.

In the midst of all this, Johnny received regular letters from Sandy Marion and from Eddie. These were like messages from another world, a world in which he was able to think rationally and clearly, a world in which there was good food and good liquor, a world in which he was able to read and to draw conclusions and to think out things that were too general and too far removed from his present position for him to even attempt. It was as if intelligences and processes of thoughts and ideas had dropped out of his mind as that world had dropped from around his body. There seemed to be nothing compatible between the two worlds, although he saw posters in the latrine every day that stated openly and honestly that this war was being fought for the existence of such a world for all men, not just a few. This seemed to be a vast incongruity, but his brain was not in the proper condition to dwell upon it and find the fallacy—if there was one. The world of thought and conversation faded more and more from his mind between letters, and with it faded his capacity and desire for the kind of thinking that generated such conversation. His face became more bony, his cheekbones more gaunt, his lips thinner, his eyes more burning. When he answered those letters, he did not mention what was going on with him.

After he had been on the latrine orderly job three weeks, the captain called him in. He walked into the office, saluted, and stood at a rigid attention. The captain began to talk without giving him the customary command of "at ease."

"You will be transferred out of this company as unfit for combat infantry duty, Carter," the captain said. "The papers are going through, but they are taking quite a while. We're getting ready to shove off, and there will be an exodus of such transfers, all taking place at the same time. What kind of outfit you'll go to, I don't know. It will probably be some kind of QM outfit."

"Would the captain mind giving me at ease. Sir?" Johnny asked, using the correct third-person address to a superior.

The captain was momentarily confused. "Yes," he said, waving his hand. "At ease." Johnny moved his left foot twelve inches, crossed his palms behind his back and slumped. The captain's eyes narrowed behind his gold spectacles and his pinched face seemed to grow tighter. The first sergeant and the clerk were listening to all this in the outside room, the captain having neglected to have the door shut.

He looked up at Johnny from behind his desk. "I realize that your disability is the result of a wound and that you are not to blame for it. Also that you are not malingering. At the same time, there are a lot of jobs in my company that you could do, even overseas, if you wished to stay in it." He raised his hand when Johnny started to speak.

"Wait just a minute. You've been a corporal and have enjoyed the privileges of a non-com. But you've forfeited all that by going AWOL. You're starting back at the bottom. I've looked at your Service Record and your 201 file, and I know that you've had a lot of various useful experiences—you had a platoon once, didn't you?"

"For two weeks, Sir. Temporarily, in combat."

"Yes," said the captain. "I know all those things." He permitted himself a slight smile, which however was lost on Johnny who stared straight ahead at the wall over the captain's head. "I also know that your AGOT score was extremely high. What I want to point out is that all these things are commendable, but they do not give you the right to set yourself outside the pale. You are just as subject to discipline as anybody else. I play no favorites in my company; you can ask the men." Johnny had already talked to most of them on this subject, but he did not attempt to refute the captain's statement. "And neither do I pick on anybody.

"You're at the bottom again, and you might as well become used to it. As I said, there are lots of jobs that you could do in my company that would not be hindered by your disability. How would you like to be a clerk in my company? It would be better than the job you have now. But you would have to start at the bottom and work up. There are things that could be done in this office on your time off from your other duty, for instance, this stove needs to be cleaned. My clerks aren't as efficient as I'd like them to be. This office hasn't been cleaned properly for some time. If you went to start in that way, and show me you've got the stuff, fine. You'll have to prove it to me, though. But if, in time, I see that you are conscientious and mean to work hard, I'll treat you accordingly." The captain smiled up at Johnny magnanimously, but the look in his eyes did not seem to go with his smile. Johnny thought suddenly of the ancient saying: "What you are speaks so loudly, I cannot hear what you say." He was momentarily shocked at the audacity of this man who could so magnanimously offer him the honor of cleaning his stove—on his time off, in addition to his other duties.

"The captain is mistaken, Sir," he said, not dropping the formal third person, "if he thinks I am dissatisfied with my present job. I'm quite content where I am—until my transfer goes through. I have no desire to remain in the captain's organization."

The captain's face became more pinched, until it was almost prissy. His eyes squinted narrowly. "Very well, Carter," he said. "This war is going to last a long time, and you might as well reconcile yourself to it. You may go." It was apparent that the captain was pleased with his own generous humanitarianism. As he left, Johnny wondered if the captain could actually believe those things he obviously felt about himself. He couldn't really believe them, and yet he apparently did. It was obvious that the captain would not be too displeased if "this war lasted a long time." Being an officer in the army seemed to have the strangest effect on most men! If the people of the country could only understand the way their army worked.

A week later, Johnny was transferred from the 26th Division to the quartermaster, along with about a third of the captain's company. They were assigned to a newly activated Gasoline Supply Company which had only a cadre of seven men from which to build itself.

A month after his transfer, he was made a buck sergeant.

At about the same time, the captain got his majority as a reward for his efficiency, sincerity, and success as an officer in the AUS and immediately began bucking for his lieutenant colonelcy.

Jones, assigned to the 842nd Quartermaster Gas and Supply Company, was promoted to sergeant on March 1, 1944, but he was, as Frank MacShane wrote in Into Eternity, *soon distressed that a Jewish officer he admired was forced out. Earlier, in Hawaii, Jones had been helped by Captain William Blatt, another Jewish officer. Blatt knew about Jones's interest in writing and encouraged him. Blatt was admired by his men on Guadalcanal because he ignored orders he knew would result in many deaths. Instead, he chose an alternate plan that achieved the desired result but with fewer deaths and injuries. Because of his disobeying an order, Blatt was relieved of his command.*

Jones was not afraid to expose anti-Semitism in the army.

ARMY POLITICS AND ANTI-SEMITISM

CAMP CAMPBELL, EARLY WINTER, 1943–1944

THE NEW OUTFIT TO WHICH Johnny Carter had been transferred was suffering its birthpangs. It was in a state of metamorphosis, from idea to reality, and was encountering all those problems which are never provided for. Compared to the much older though inefficient 26th Division it seemed to be fluctuating wildly, grasping at straws.

With the exception of the original seven-man cadre, the new company was composed completely of men who had been officially marked unfit for the rigors of Infantry duty. Over fifty percent of them were men who had seen overseas service—overseas *combat* service—that designation is important, particularly to a man who wears the Combat Infantryman's Badge, because the greatest percentage of men who go overseas never are in combat. These men, like Johnny, had been shipped back because of disabling wounds, or evacuated because of severe cases of malaria or dengue fever or jungle rot or trench foot or yellow jaundice—for any one, or several, of the fifty or sixty diseases combat soldiers are subject to and have to suffer in addition to danger.

The other fifty percent of the company were men who had not been overseas at all. Most of them had been in the 26th Division for three years, going from one maneuver area to another. They were also classed as physically unfit for Infantry duty. A great many of them were, because of illnesses or wounds contracted on maneuvers. Some of them weren't.

The most disabling thing about all of them, including the combat men, was their morale. It had been knocked, cut, cursed, blown, and beaten out of them.

A man in the Infantry, to get himself classified as physically unfit for the Infantry—even if he is—must raise more hell and create a bigger stink than any congressman who tries to get his favorite pet bill passed. To raise that much hell, a soldier must have reached the saturation point of disgust, to where he doesn't give a good goddam about his officers' opinion of him, his comrades' opinion, or anybody else's opinion of him. And most men care more for other men's opinions of them than they care for their own, or would like to admit. The men in this company were a great contrast to the short-haired young kids who comprised the greatest part of the privates in the 26th Division.

Whether this emphasis on other people's opinions is deliberately created to test the sincerity of a man's disability is hard to tell. It may be that it is a natural outgrowth of certain social mores like *patriotism* or *self-sacrifice* or *heroism* or a continuation of the schoolroom authority. And it may not. In his *Decline and Fall of the Roman Empire,* Gibbon says: ". . . and it was an inflexible maxim of Roman discipline that a good soldier should dread his officers far more than the enemy." Whether or no, it exists and every soldier must surmount it first before he can even think of getting himself out of the Infantry. He has to fight shavetail college-boy doctors at dispensaries, has to fight company commanders, battalion commanders, regimental burgeons, clinical psychiatrists, and as likely as not, face a court martial. So the men in Johnny's new company were a wild and wooly bunch.

The first thing this new company did as soon as it had its men assigned to their barracks was to proceed to give them a Basic Training course, which consists of hikes, forced marches, creeping and crawling, extended order drill—in short, all of the things that are taught to a raw recruit the minute he's inducted. And which he must forget as soon as he gets into combat. This to a group of men none of whom had been in the army less than two years, and a great many of whom had seen as much as nine months' continuous combat duty.

The first thing Private Johnny Carter did when he was assigned to his new barracks and heard this news was to offer his services as an experienced clerk in the Orderly Room! They were accepted.

A Quartermaster Gasoline Supply Company is a separate company. It is connected with no battalion or regiment or division, except the one to which it ministers gasoline at the moment. The men in this new organization were there because of physical disabilities. They soon learned that their new job consisted mainly of loading and unloading "bays" of five-gallon cans in and out the back ends of trucks that reached to their chests. A "bay" consists of 125 five-gallon GI cans. Rectangular ones with three parallel handles across the top, the same type can the Infantry carries water in. And the company had something like twenty-five or thirty bays. Hoisting these cans in and out of trucks four or five times a day is a man-sized job, even for a soldier who is physically fit for Infantry duty. One man in the company was unable to wear a helmet because of a wound scar in his head from a shell fragment encountered in the second battle of Kasserine Pass. He was apt to pass out from extreme physical exertion and fainted four times in two weeks. He was refused a transfer by the medical officers. Another man had had half of his calf muscle torn out by a shell fragment. He, too, could not get a transfer. Several men were constantly dosing themselves with atabrine begged from the dispensary. The wild and woolly bunch became wilder and more woolly.

The cadre, consisting of acting first sergeant, mess sergeant, supply sergeant, two section sergeants, one cook, and a clerk, were supposed to be trained for the job they undertook. It developed more and more obviously that none of them but the cook and mess sergeant knew what they were doing. After two weeks, the acting first sergeant quit and went back to the ranks, and a big burly red-headed staff sergeant who had come down from the 26th Division was appointed to take his place. The acting clerk became Johnny's assistant, and Johnny was instructed to teach him how to make out a Morning Report, Sick Report, and most important of all, the Payroll.

The ratings were completely tangled up. All the men who had come from the Infantry had been transferred In Grade, so that there were at least three rating for every job, almost as many non-coms as there were privates. The total number of ratings was fifty percent higher than that allowed by the company's Table of Organization.

The company commander who stepped in to take over this mess was a first lieutenant, a young Jew, tall, stoop-shouldered, sad-eyed, and self-conscious. He brought with him another first lieutenant, a fiery Scotsman. Both men had been commanding Negro companies—what is known as a crummy detail at every white officer's club. Both men worked themselves half to death, spending all day with the company, and half the night in the Orderly Room trying to straighten out the newborn records and reports. Johnny usually stayed with them and more and more assumed responsibility for the clerical work. His previous experience and natural quickness of thought were invaluable. The new acting first sergeant knew nothing about the job except how to handle men, which was no mean job in itself in this company, and frankly admitted his ignorance. Johnny spent a couple of hours a day teaching Red the first sergeant's clerical duties. The company copy of Army Regulations became so dog-eared and thumbed that a new one had to be requisitioned and the old one salvaged.

From the moment he first stepped into the Orderly Room, Johnny worked savagely. He worked with a fanatical drive that carried the others along on his wave of energy. His mind was like a water-starved sailor, soaking up every drop of intense thought it could find. He worked constantly and gloried in it and in the release from himself that it brought. He forgot the existence of Johnny Carter. He cursed and threatened and raved at the old cadre clerk and the new assistant imported to help out. His intensity made them efficient at the things they hardly knew, in spite of themselves. His mind had been atrophied by looking at latrine walls, and it burst out now like a brilliant explosion which startled even him. He spent one whole day, worked clear through the night, and the next day till three p.m. making out the first Payroll and got it through the Finance Inspectors. It was the first Payroll he had ever made out in his life. He didn't even take the rest of the day off.

The new company began to grow and take form as an embryo grows and takes form in its mother. But in this case the mothers hated the offspring. The men hated the company, the administrative staff hated the company, even the Jewish company commander and the Scotsman hated the company. Johnny hated it completely, but he nurtured its files like a midwife, worked like a maniac—as they all worked who actually had any work to do. The two platoons of men, sections as they were called here, hated it the worst, because they did not have the sanctification of unending work. Everybody hated the company, but it imperceptibly became the Company, instead of just the company. It became their pride, their place, their home—as near as soldiers can be said to have a home.

To the surprise of all the men who had known him in the 26th Division as a malcontent, Johnny became a sort of sparkplug, a dynamo of energy that you could attach your own plug-in to. His drive for speed and more work carried over even to his meals, so that he gulped his food down almost without chewing, even when he had no work in particular to do after the meal was finished. It was mostly for this drive that he got his sergeant's rating, when the TO called only for a corporalcy for the company clerk. He immersed himself in the life and work of this company until he had forgotten the existence of any world outside.

This attitude was apparent in his letters. Sandy was puzzled by the change in them. They were more infrequent. They seemed very preoccupied. His typing fingers seemed not able to keep up with his racing mind that flew from one furious thought to another with such speed and cramming that the letters were hard to follow. He told her his new address and that he had a new job, but he didn't have time to explain it in detail. His letters pounded the theme of work; work, work, work; a man's life must be dedicated to work. Sandy was puzzled by the letters, but also less worried. He seemed to have made a contact with something. As the company began to take shape out of chaos, a new property began to show itself. The rating situation had finally been straightened out, not without great upset. Big Red ceased to be "acting" and became actual first sergeant, and acquired that subtle touch of authority that is so lacking in an acting non-com. A number of men had to be busted to get the TO back to normal. This caused a big stink, and the blame was placed by the men upon the company commander. The usual procedure is to absorb ratings—that is, if a man is broken because of inefficiency or insubordination, a new rating is not made, and the old extra one is absorbed. But Harry Weidmann, the Jewish first lieutenant, received explicit orders from higher up to get his ratings down, as soon as possible even if it meant breaking men who had done nothing wrong. This was where the new weight first began to make itself felt.

The effect on the company morale was bad and immediate. Several of the busted non-coms went over the hill for a week's vacation. At night Johnny sitting in the Orderly Room working, with Weidmann across the room working, could hear some of the boys coming back from the PX 3.2 beer garden, drunk, and singing in close four-part harmony: "Oh, I'm just wild about Harry, and Harry's wild about me!" and "My vild Irish R-r-rose, dah sveet-iest flour det grows." Sometimes they even sang it: "My vild Jewish Rose." Weidmann would look up and grin a tight painful grin and murmur something about thank God men have a sense of humor for a safety valve.

The company was under administration of the local Second Army headquarters, whose main headquarters was in Memphis. The Second Army headquarters in the camp controlled all the auxiliary troops, quartermaster and separate companies, under a "Provisional Headquarters." Johnny, being in the office, was able to see and hear all this new force that was being directed at the company. Weidmann was given orders that he could issue no three-day passes. Other companies around them were giving them out. As a result, more men went over the hill and took their three-day passes. Weidmann was called up on the carpet because he couldn't handle his men.

Weidmann was given orders that he could not give furloughs longer than four days. Other companies around them were giving ten-day furloughs. As a result, men from the company deliberately overstayed their furloughs by four or five days. There were several summary court-martials. Weidmann was called up on the carpet because he couldn't handle his men, and warned that his inefficiency, if continued, would cost him command.

Reports began to be sent back because of misspelled words or small typographical errors or misplaced punctuation. Things that occur often in all outfits and are usually disregarded. Johnny was forced to redouble his efforts at perfection; nothing less was acceptable. He worked superhumanly, checking every paper that left the office. He had constantly to check and recheck the two men working with him for insignificant errors. They had to do a lot of work over two or three times, and they naturally resented it. Only Johnny's force of drive kept them in line.

Every day or so, inspectors from Second Army would come around to inspect the company—the barracks, the area, the Orderly Room, Supply Room, company administrative and supply records, the mess hall, the menus—everything there was to inspect. They invariably found a great deal wrong, as an inspector can always find something wrong if he refuses to allow for the human element, which does exist, even in the army.

A new officer had been added to the company, a quiet meek older man named Bird. He was a graduate lawyer and had studied international law. He was a second lieutenant. He was placed in charge of the motor pool. The inspections of his motor pool were invariably masterpieces of derogation, no matter if Lieutenant Bird spent the whole night before checking his motor pool. Bird complained to Weidmann that he didn't know a carburetor from a head gasket, but Weidmann could only shrug. Second Army refused to have him shifted to another job.

It went from bad to worse. The inspections became more frequent and much stiffer. Weidmann and Bird and Thompson, the Scot, held consultations in the Orderly Room at night, they could decide on nothing. There was nothing they could do but sit and take it. You can't talk back in the army. Johnny, working late and being in the Orderly Room all day long, began to divine a form emerging from this heavy weight.

One day a colonel came into the Orderly Room to inspect the company fund record. This was another thing Johnny had shown Weidmann how to handle, using a few old Regular Army tricks; in the Regular Army, the company fund is one of the most used and most important clerical items.

Johnny and one of his assistants were working away hard. Both were wearing field jackets because it was cold. Neither looked up when the colonel entered. The colonel slammed the door and walked loudly into Weidmann's office. Neither Johnny or the other clerk, being engrossed in their work, looked up or paid the slightest attention. The colonel came back into the outer office.

"What's the matter with you, Sergeant?" he asked. Johnny looked up absentmindedly without speaking. "Haven't you learned yet, Sergeant, that you are supposed to call attention when an officer enters?"

Both Johnny and the other snapped up to attention, dropping their work.

The colonel looked at the private and then back at Johnny. "Who's in charge here, Sergeant? You?"

"Yessir," said Johnny.

The colonel was gray-haired and small. "I don't want you boys to think I'm unduly harsh," he said. "I've been in the army a long time. The army runs on discipline—unfailing, automatic discipline. Without it, the army wouldn't be worth its salt. Your outfit is getting ready to go overseas. When you men get overseas, you will find you must be trained to instant discipline. You must act automatically upon an order. An instant's hesitation may mean death to a thousand men. It's different overseas than it is here," he explained in a fatherly tone. "Overseas the war waits on no one. If you don't learn to obey quickly, it may get you killed. You're no good to the war effort dead. That's why we insist upon these things. We want you to be trained right when you get overseas."

"Yessir," said Johnny when the colonel finished.

"All right," said the colonel. "Carry on."

Johnny and the assistant went back to work. The colonel went into Weidmann's office. Johnny could hear him in a low voice giving Weidmann holy hell about Military Discipline. While the colonel was in the office, Johnny took his field jacket off and hung it over the back of his chair and went back to work.

When the colonel came out, Johnny called out "Attention!" and he and the other clerk leaped to their feet. Johnny stood with his chest stuck out, gut sucked in, eyes staring straight ahead, the position of a soldier at attention. As the colonel passed him, the colonel saw the ribbons pinned to Johnny's shirt. Just the two main ones were all he wore in camp; the Purple Heart, and the Asiatic-Pacific with its three stars. The colonel stared and stopped, for a second, but he didn't speak. Weidmann was watching from the doorway, and Johnny saw his eyes develop a twinkle. Johnny winked once, swiftly, with his off eye. The colonel left without saying anything else. The clerk broke out laughing but stopped when Weidmann stared at him. A suggestion of a smile flickered over Weidmann's face; Johnny kept his face perfectly deadpan. Weidmann went back in his office and shut the door. Johnny went back to work, and the other clerk collapsed into his chair shaking with silent laughter. Johnny never referred to the episode, because Weidmann was a man for discipline. And neither did Weidmann mention it. Neither of them needed to.

The form Johnny saw beginning to take shape behind these unduly rigorous inspections and pass restrictions became more and more apparent as time passed. Weidmann, Thompson, and Bird had gotten their orders to take over the company from Washington, direct from the War Department. Such orders naturally superseded any plans or orders of the local camp Second Army headquarters. Weidmann was a Jew. Both he and Thompson were "nigger" officers. Bird was a Casper Milquetoast, and intellectual, a natural affront to any old line officer. Host of the gray-headed officers in Second Army were old Regular Army men, West Pointers, as near to a Junker class as America has allowed itself to come. And they all thought of themselves as being much more similar to that ironbound Junker class—ironbound both socially and physically—than they really were. Like anybody else they had their friends, their favorites. They were well schooled in that old game of putting straws on camels' backs, army politics. They had absolute dominion over every company that fell under their jurisdiction, and like the Junker class they tried to emulate, they had come to believe in the divine superiority of their iron sway, thus absolving themselves from any necessity for conscience, or association with the "Ninety-Day Wonders." Behind their superiority was the means by which they kept it. When they didn't like a man, good or bad, strong or weak, that man hadn't a chance in the world to make good. These men would have been surprised and insulted if they had found out at the same method they used in the officer caste was the identical one used in the higher non-com caste in most companies. To Johnny, who had seen the same situation among non-coms a number of times, the nonpareil attitude of these men should have been a constant source of amusement. But it was a hard thing to laugh, while seeing Weidmann, Thompson, and Bird as victims of this power.

In spite of everything, the work went on in the company, at a furious pace. In the 26th Division, Johnny had been very near going over the hill a number of times. In the new company, the thought would pop into his head now and then after some especially pungent edict. He thought about going over the hill as an antidote to the very bad taste in his mouth. But he never had time to think about it long because his thoughts were too much needed elsewhere.

Most of his spare time, when there was not work of a more pressing nature, was spent on Service Records. The Service Record is the most important part of a man in the army—as a chief clerk had once stated. Practically everything a man did or did not do was recorded in his Service Record. The Service Record of each man had been sent down with the men from the 26th Division, and they were in terrible shape, filled with errors of both form and information. And there was an adjutant general's inspection due in a month. Johnny had to do all this work himself, because Weidmann would not let him trust it to either of the other clerks. He worked himself to sleep several nights and the CC would wake him up so he could go to bed.

Weidmann was fighting his fate with clenched teeth. He had to fight not only local Second Army, but he had to fight the men in his own company. His men couldn't understand why they had no passes, why they had no longer furloughs, why they invariably spent several more hours of duty every day than the other companies around. The men blamed it all on Weidmann who was, they said, a driver. Johnny and Red, the first sergeant, were two of the very few who took Weidmann's part.

Johnny would sit evening after evening working in Weidmann's office, checking Service Records with Form 20s. There was a small white church across the street from the Orderly Room, and at this church during the week were held the Jewish services. There was a frail, sallow, hook-nosed, sensitive-mouthed Jew in the company named Isaac Rabinowitz, who had been a well-known actor on the Jewish stage. He had come over from Russia in Chekhov's special troop. The trip didn't make money, Isaac had stayed in New York when it broke up. Isaac was the cantor for the Jewish services.

Isaac had a magnificent tenor voice, and Johnny would sit in the Orderly Room at night and listen to him from across the street. There was a deep melancholy of the earth in Isaac's voice, a song of infinite pain and degradation—brought to God's Chosen People because they, too, had been arrogant and once tried to conquer the world. The chants were plaintive with a sort of puzzled sorrow, an anguish that could not understand the reason for its own existence. The chants were sung in wrenching minors, one piled upon another, going up and on up until there seemed to be no ending to their wail of unhappiness. The shouting, singing, and laughing in the nearby PX made an incongruous backdrop to the haunting sound of Isaac's voice.

Often, for the first time since he had left Endymion, Johnny would find himself listening to Isaac and thinking of Al, what had happened to him, where he was, how he was making out. It was hard to associate the existence of Endymion and Camp Campbell on the same planet. He and Al had become very close, particularly on their trip to Evansville and their mutual sympathy for Freedie, who hated. There seemed a close similarity between the haunting voice of Isaac Rabinowitz and the haunted eyes of Al Garnnon. It was as if Isaac, who had lived through the last war in Russia, was singing of and for Al Garnnon and those like him who needed succor from their own kind and from the earth. Every man needed a friend—such unspoken implications as were in that simple word—a friend to whom he could turn, in whose company he could find the understanding that he needed, without explanations or questions or answers. And Johnny felt he was Al Garnnon's friend—as Al was his.

Johnny would shake the obsession of Isaac's voice from his brain and go back to work.

In his new job, Johnny's brain had seemed to awaken from its torpor, and in his scattered moments of free time, he did a lot of thinking. The things that had happened to him since he left Endymion seemed inextricably wound together. The people of Endymion, the pinch-faced Infantry captain, latrine orderly, Weidmann and his persecution, the new job as clerk, Al Garnnon and Isaac Rabinowitz. They all went together, each a panel in the same door, and for that door there was a hidden key, a special significance in all these facts that he could not quite grasp, even knowing it was there. If he could find that key and unlock that door, he would learn some general conclusion that fit them all and explain them and was what he was seeking to learn.

The obvious yet subtle persecution of Weidmann was a focus of his thought, because it was always present. The voice of Isaac Rabinowitz coming distinctly from across the street seemed to be an extension, an underscoring of Weidmann with his silent bitter smile, his fighting with clenched teeth. In those evenings in the Orderly Room working alone with Weidmann, the two had come to do a great deal of talking, each about himself. It was pleasant to lean back from your work and relax your mind in idle intelligent conversation for a little while before plunging in again. But in all this talking, never once was the predicament of Weidmann mentioned, or the reason for it.

Surely, Johnny kept questioning himself, surely, it could not be simply because Weidmann was a Jew? The stopping of such persecution was one of the planks in the platform of this war which the Second Army was—in its abortive way—helping to fight. Such persecution with whips, torture, and murder was a universally acknowledged evil. But the same persecution enacted without physical violence was ignored. It was the ancient difference in the Bible between the Old Law and the New Law. Any savage could understand the meaning of *Thou shalt not torture with whips*, but how many civilized men could understand the meaning of *Thou shalt not torture with guile*? Who will admit as a proved fact that you can kill a man just as easily with politics as you can with a rifle? And are not the two evils equally bad? Nay, isn't the subtler evil more dangerous, simply because of the difficulty of understanding it? Wars are never fought against subtle evils. Hitler was being fought because he openly used whips and so was obviously a danger, but what of the subtle forces that fostered Hitler, backed Hitler, gave Hitler power he could never have gained without their aid. No whips, no violence, and because of that more dangerous. Who had the vision to conduct war against these subtle powers? And where could they be found? Their origin could be found in social forces, but who was willing to fight to change these social forces?

In America, there was certainly discrimination and it existed likewise in the army. Everybody knew that and accepted it. But how about when it came to a showdown? when efficiency and work accomplished must be sacrificed in order to propagate the persecution? Was it allowed to exist even then? It seemed it was.

At times, Johnny felt like angrily grabbing Weidmann by the shoulders and asking him if he was blind, if he didn't know, and telling him to do something about it, to write Washington, or to go to Second Army Memphis, to fight back without suffering pointlessly. But the immense reserve Weidmann kept wrapped about him forced Johnny to be silent. Washington and Memphis were pipedreams anyway, and Johnny knew it. Occasionally his sense of injustice boiled over into anger, and he would quit work and spend the rest of the evening in the PX distending his stomach with 3.2 beer in a fruitless effort to get drunk as hell. But he never went on the evenings Isaac sang.

One evening, Weidmann stepped to the open door to listen. Isaac's voice came across the cold air clear as a bell, each note distinct yet the whole slurred slightly together, as a man in great pain will slur his sentences. Weidmann stood tall and stooped, leaning on his hand against the wall, relaxed as if he were accepting without reservation, were escaping into the tortured music of Isaac's voice.

"It's beautiful, isn't it?" Johnny asked, feeling he ought to talk. After he uttered them, the words sounded crude and blunt. The chants of Isaac's voice were too far above description to be labeled with anything so commonplace as "beautiful."

Weidmann turned back with his peculiarly twisted smile. "Yes. Yes, it's beautiful." He sat down at his desk and cocked his feet up on it. It was an unthinking gesture of possession, and Johnny could not help wondering if Weidmann did it because he did not expect to be able to do it long. "Isaac's voice is beautiful because Isaac's religion is a part of him, as much as his testicles or the hair on his arms. Isaac's religion is a formality that goes above formality and becomes informal, an intimate part of each man."

"It gets me. I've never heard anything quite like it before."

"And you never will again—outside of a Jewish synagogue. But it's been going on for centuries, always the same. And I suppose it will continue to go on for centuries, probably till the world ends. That stuff about two thousand years of pain and agony is old and trite: Every poet's had a crack at it, and now the radio commentators are getting their chance. Still it's there: It's true, none the less. Isaac knows it, it's bred in him, he feels it, just like he feels his teeth. He couldn't escape it if he wanted to."

"Why should he want to?"

"Want to? I don't know. Lots of us do. Maybe it's because he wants to feel that he's the same as other men, acceptable to other men as they accept each other. But the moment he *wants* acceptance, he's admitting that he doesn't have it. I guess other people feel that, and they immediately think he's trying to leap over his own sense of inferiority. Did you ever notice that as soon as anyone *wants* something badly, almost everybody else automatically tries to stop him from getting it?"

"Yes. I've noticed it." Johnny was thinking about what Eddie Marion had told him about work and efficiency: People don't want you to love your work. The minute they find out you do, they try to talk you out of loving it and take up playing pool. People instinctively seem to fear a man who loves his work and is efficient in it. That may be because they sense their own inefficiency; or it may be because they feel such a thing is inhuman. I've fought it all my life.

"The most common way is through money," Weidmann said. "A Jew thinks if he makes enough money, he'll be acceptable and so will be able to escape that indescribable loneliness in Isaac's voice. But in the end it's always useless.

"For the next thousand years the Germans may have to undergo what the Jews have suffered for the last thousand. A race without a home. A race turned back upon the memory of its former glory. It's all in Isaac's voice. A punishment for too great an arrogance."

"The Wandering Jew," said Johnny musingly. "Then that's a symbol, isn't it?" Weidmann nodded. "I think that's one of the most sorrowful stories I've ever heard."

Weidmann smiled, "It is. It's a pitiful story. And that's just the trouble. Pity implies condescension."

"I've never thought of it just like that before." Johnny put aside his work and lit a cigaret, leaned back in his chair. "I've thought about it a lot, too. The reason for it, I mean. Fear maybe, hatred, arrogance—all on the part of the Gentiles, too. I never can quite figure it out. I find I have a strong antipathy to most Jews. Miami Beach is the place to experiment with your own reactions. It's hard for me to be civil to most Jews, especially there. They hog the sidewalk, they bull in ahead of you, they run the rents racket there. They're loud-mouthed and crude to boot."

"I know," Weidmann said. "They do do that. It's a very hard thing to be pitied. It's almost worse than being hated. I find I have a hard time trying to keep from wearing a chip on my shoulder—because I'm a Jew, and because I know how most people feel toward a Jew." Weidmann took down his feet and leaned back in his swivel chair.

"I'd like to go over some time and hear Isaac sing," Johnny said.

"Why can't you?"

"Oh, you know how it is. I'd feel like I was intruding where I had no right to be. I feel it's something private—I saw a guide taking a bunch of tourists through a Chinese church in Honolulu once. Besides, I'm afraid seeing Isaac would spoil it. When I hear him now, it's like hearing a disembodied voice. I can't associate Isaac in ODs with that voice."

"You needn't worry on that score. He'll be wearing the formal robes. We're like the Catholics: We'll have our robes and formality, even here."

"Have you seen him?"

"No," said Weidmann shortly. "I haven't. I stopped going a long time ago. I wanted to live my life and make my way as an individual, completely apart from any race or creed." His twisted smile was like a sardonic laughter at himself. "How are you making out with those Service Records?" It was a polite indication that he wanted to go no further with that line of conversation.

"Pretty good," said Johnny. He stuffed out his cigaret and drew his chair back up to the desk.

"I've got a new job for you tomorrow," said Weidmann with a grin. "A good one. A new Second Army idea. A chart with fifty-six items on it, a line for each man in the company. It's to see at a glance if each man's prepared for overseas. You have to check each item with each man's Service Record and enter the data on the chart."

"Jesus Christ!"

"Shouldn't take you over two weeks' hard work."The work went on. The thumbscrews tightened around Weidmann, but still the work went on, just as if there were no impending disaster. Weidmann refused to give up his belief that he, as an individual, could make his own way, his own success. Johnny watched him going down with admiration. For some reason, it is always the man who goes down fighting overwhelming odds that is the most greatly admired. Perhaps it is because other men always wish they had the nerve to forego their security and fight for what they really want against the million to one odds that say they cannot attain it. They ache to take up arms in their own fruitless lost cause, but they so seldom do.

The first blow fell on Big Red, the first sergeant. An old Regular Army first sergeant was imported to take Red's place. He was one of those unofficial inspectors who go around from outfit to outfit straightening them out. This time his job was more to seal it up and affix the stamp of doom. Big Red was offered a sop: He could have his old staff sergeant's rating back and take a transfer to another company. Red thought it over and turned it down. He would rather stay in the company as a private. After he was busted, he was transferred anyway, on the grounds that a former first sergeant serving in the same company as a private was bad for discipline. Red stayed in camp, but in another company. He spent all his time off over in the old company barracks, talking to the guys. He was glad to be a private again, he said, no responsibility, no work, just do as you're told. He would grin, but his boisterous grin seemed to have taken on some of the characteristics of Weidmann's twisted one.

Several of the men protested to Weidmann, but Weidmann was powerless. Red's bust had come down from Second Army. The new first sergeant was working direct from there. He ran the company his own way, through Weidmann, and if Weidmann tried to argue with his suggestions he went over Weidmann's head.

The new first sergeant worked with Johnny in the office. He was surprised to find another Regular Army man here who seemed to know the clerical ropes. He spent a good bit of time telling Johnny what was wrong with Weidmann as an officer, as if he were trying to justify himself. He knew the whole story on the setup and told it to Johnny.

There were several officers up at Second Army who had nothing to do. They had been promised commands in one of the new companies being activated, but orders from War Department had superseded that promise. They were being used temporarily as inspectors but that couldn't go on forever. If they were found no place, they'd have to go into "nigger" companies. These boys had worked together before, and they were all well connected at Second Army, Weidmann's company was being opened up for them.

With Big Red gone, the Company muled and balked. Several men went over the hill. Nobody could get any work out of them, least of all Weidmann.

A week after Red had gone, Johnny walked into the office and found a stranger sitting behind Weidmann's desk, a big husky ham-handed flat-nosed captain named Dupree. Johnny recognized him as the recent supply inspector. He had been in position to do himself good, and he hadn't let it go by: The supply reports were some of the worst marks against Weidmann. Captain Dupree handed Johnny a copy of the new Special Orders, just cut. They stated that Captain Frank M Dupree was to proceed immediately to take over Lieutenant Weidmann's command.

Dupree was a disciplinarian. As he told Johnny, he had come up the hard way, from the ranks, and discipline was the thing; Dupree knew. Weidmann stayed in the company as second in command. This was a deliberate slap in the face.

The furlough and pass restrictions were immediately lifted, as soon as Dupree took over. He gave out three-day passes and fifteen-day furloughs galore. Weidmann had to sit by and watch. The men in the company became happy again. AWOLs dropped down to nothing.

Thompson was the first to go. He was given command of a Negro Gasoline Supply Company, for some reason considered a comedown for an officer who had been with white troops.

Johnny's name came up on the furlough list, but Dupree couldn't spare him. He kept on doing the work he had done before. He made the papers out and laid them on the desk and Dupree signed them. Dupree was a disciplinarian. Johnny would be working in Dupree's office and Dupree would be sitting behind the desk. The phone, which sat on Dupree's desk, would ring and Dupree would say: "Get the phone, Sergeant." Johnny would have to get up, walk across the room, answer the phone, and hand it to Dupree when the party asked for the company commander—as they always did. Then he could go back and continue his work.

Needless to say, Johnny did not like Dupree any better than he liked the pinch-faced captain in the 26th Division, but at least here he had the solace of losing himself completely in the details of work. He still worked savagely, because there was never time enough to do all that needed to be done, there were always two or three unfinished jobs that needed attention. But he did not enjoy working as he had enjoyed it before Dupree took over. Intangibly, the sense of unity in the office had been destroyed when Dupree came. When Dupree worked, he worked for approbation; the work in itself or the satisfaction of a job well done held nothing for him. Dupree was less concerned with the work and getting the work done than he was with the impression he and his company made on higher Second Army officers. Dupree, with an utter lack of self-consciousness, used Weidmann whenever he needed his advice or help, Johnny detested seeing Weidmann sitting around doing nothing in his former office at the beck and call of Dupree, waiting for Dupree to ask questions and advice about how such and such a thing was done.

Weidmann didn't seem to mind the indignity. He let Dupree order him around like a lackey without any sort of protest, spoken or unspoken. The only change in him was that he didn't work hard; he didn't seem to give a damn if all the work got done or not. The only hint of the humiliation he was suffering came from his smile; where before it had been sardonic, now it was caustic; where it had been bitter, it was now vitriolic. Johnny was surprised when Isaac Rabinowitz told him in the course of a conversation that Weidmann had started coming to services. Isaac was surprised, too; it was the first time he had seen Weidmann in church.

Dupree was especially hard on Lieutenant Bird, the motor officer. Bird was what Dupree considered a diapered intellectual, and Captain Dupree made no effort to soft-pedal his sarcasm, even in the presence of enlisted men. He made it quite plain that he wanted to get Bird out of his company as soon as possible. Bird was unhappy and he picked Johnny to talk to, probably because he and Johnny had had some longwinded conversations about books and literature. Johnny made a mental note of this. It seemed invariably that the main tiling which broke down the class distinction between officers and himself was intelligent conversation; literature seemed to be the love that laughed at the locksmith of military discipline. Of course, that didn't fit with a man like Dupree, but to Johnny it was for some reason a consoling thought. He wondered what provision army policy made for literature. Bird had ideas; he had written Washington applying for the Allied Military Government School. He figured his training in international law would get him in. It was the only way he could see to beat the rap that was being pinned on all of them, he was sitting on pins and needles hoping the order came from Washington before he was kicked out and assigned to another outfit.

After Thompson, the Scot, Weidmann was next to go. He was also sent back to commanding a "nigger" company. When his orders came in, Johnny was sitting up in the room he shared with the two other non-coms, and Weidmann came up to say goodby to him, an unprecedented thing for an officer to do. Johnny was the only person in the company Weidmann said goodby to. He thanked Johnny for the help he had been, even if it hadn't turned out so well, he added with his grin of gall. He left then, and Johnny never saw him again. He was the only officer whose home address, civilian address, Johnny had ever asked for. Johnny found out from Isaac that Weidmann kept on coming to church. Isaac couldn't understand it; Isaac didn't like religion, he only went to church so he could sing.

As each officer left, he was replaced by a new man from Second Army, it was evident at once that Dupree had worked with these officers before. They all knew him and slapped him on the back and asked about such and such an old company. The new officers under Dupree were all youngsters, and Johnny found them pretty dumb. Of course, it was possible that he was prejudiced.

Bird beat them under the tape. His orders came in from Washington before he was reassigned. When he got them, he was happy as a child. When he had his last talk with Dupree, he allowed himself the luxury of raising his eyebrow, but, strangely, he was very decent about not rubbing it in. He could have, because Dupree no longer had any jurisdiction over him. Dupree's face was congested red, but he said little to Bird. There was nothing he could do to supersede or revoke Washington's orders; Bird was out of his hands then. Bird's good fortune made Dupree very angry for some reason, it was evident he thought Bird a milksop and a nincompoop, unfit to be an enlisted man in the army, let alone an officer. Second Army thought so, too, apparently.

The Regular Army traveling first sergeant was replaced as soon as Bird left. His job was taken by another old timer who had been in local Second Army headquarters as a personnel sergeant major for a long time. A tall, silent, very competent man; Dupree let him run the company pretty much as he saw fit.

After all the old officers were gone, the company settled down a little into a routine. Johnny continued working at the same furious pace and day by day began to get caught up. The greatest part of the clerical work of activation had been completed before Dupree took over, and after

Dupree took over, strangely enough, Second Army relaxed their vigilance. Work that had had to be done over two and three and four times, checked and rechecked, now could he dashed off and sent right in. It saved Johnny a great deal of work, but he was not pleased.

Dupree would congratulate Johnny profusely whenever he did an especially involved job and did it well, and Dupree would give him holy hell whenever he wasn't just up to what Dupree considered par. Dupree was greatly puzzled by what he regarded as Johnny's stolidity. He did not become elated when Dupree praised him; he did not become chastened when Dupree gave him hell. Johnny was unaffected by either opinion. This was something Dupree could not grasp. The only time he could ever invoke interest in Johnny was in the explanation of the technical details of some job or other, and usually it was the cryptic first sergeant who did such explaining. Dupree was at a loss to what to do about Johnny's indifference to approbation. He considered it abnormal and practically insubordinate, but since Johnny was doing fine work, and since Dupree could not actually put his finger on anything, he decided to let it go.

By the end of January, Johnny had the Form 20s, the Service Records, and the Second Army chart in good enough shape to pass an AGO inspection with a marking of satisfactory, which was superior, under the circumstances. He had repeatedly asked for his overdue furlough, and Dupree repeatedly refused it. The company was scheduled for maneuvers at the end of February, and from maneuvers it was scheduled to proceed directly to a POE, provided it passed the maneuvers tests.

Finally, Johnny accosted Dupree and insisted that he be given his furlough. If he didn't get it, he said, he would quit the office, and Dupree could see how well his office would run. This was an unprecedented thing for any enlisted man to say to Dupree, and Dupree raised hell. If Carter refused to work in the office, he would be court-martialed for malingering. Johnny said he doubted that, because as long as he was willing to work in the ranks, he couldn't be tried for malingering. Dupree said he could be tried for refusing a direct order, and threatened to have such action taken. Johnny agreed with this, but pointed out, laughing, that Dupree would he cutting off his own nose to spite his face by putting his most, or only, valuable clerk in the stockade. Dupree had had no experience with this type of mental blackmail, and be finally agreed to give Johnny his furlough. From that time on, the association between Dupree and Johnny was that of an armed truce.

Dupree stalled for two weeks, until Johnny threatened to quit, right here and now, unless the furlough papers were made out and signed. He pointed out that his work was all caught up and that the company would not lose any ground if he had his furlough. Dupree made out the papers and signed them, but he withheld them until Johnny had made out the Payroll for the month of February, Johnny worked one whole night and all the next day to get it done, turning the daily work over to his two assistant clerks. He finished it the second night and left camp immediately afterwards. He was tired and had had no sleep the night before, but he felt if he spent ten more minutes around Dupree he would desert and go over the hill for good.

By the time he argued Dupree into the furlough and made out the Payroll, he had only six days left before the company would leave to go on maneuvers. Consequently, he only got a four-day furlough with one-day travel, instead of the usual fifteen that Dupree had been handing out so munificently. He suspected that Dupree had deliberately arranged this, but he couldn't prove it, and if he could have, there was nothing he could do. He did not know why—unless it was just Dupree's nature to be like that. But it was also probable that Dupree had seen that Johnny's sympathies were with Weidmann and was exacting payment for it.

Johnny had been writing to Sandy Marion. When he mentioned to Sandy that he was getting a furlough, she had written back and invited him to spend it as hers and Eddie's guest. He had not declined her offer, but he decided to go to Miami Beach to his brother's—the only relative he had left now, discounting Erskine. Five days was hardly enough time for the round-trip bus ride to Miami. So he made up his mind to brave Endymion again, a place he had meant never to return to.

He took a camp taxi up to Service Club No 1, which was also the bus station. The bus for Evansville was just loading. After it finished loading, there were at least fifty men left milling around the outside of the bus for whom there was no room until the next bus, in the morning.

The greatest percentage of the camp was shipping out to maneuvers with orders to proceed direct to a POE after the maneuvers were over. It was February of 1944, and there was a heightened activity about the whole camp that left a pall of suspense over everybody. The camp was emptying fast, outfits were shoving off every day. There was the rush and noise of moving out, followed by a sense of emptiness that was like a vacuum; silent empty buildings, unused lightless streets, whole sections of the camp had that sense of desolation that comes to manmade places when the men have gone, almost sinister, like a medieval city from which there had been a great exodus to escape the plague. Trucks rolled every night, leaving behind them a hollow sound like the inside of an empty tank. There were big things in the wind. All the rumours said England—which could mean only one thing; the invasion of France.

Johnny had been through it all once before, and he knew the impending frenzy. It disheartened him and left him a little cold inside. He had seen men throw away valued possessions before, because they had no place for them in their crammed "A" and "B" bags: "What the hell? I won't need this stuff where I'm goin." It disheartened him more when he looked at the dejected shoulders and lowered heads of the men who had missed the bus. The next one wasn't till morning. Twelve hours lost! Many of them turned silently away and started back to their barracks. Many of them walked away cursing loudly in futile voices. Many of them went silently into the PX nearby to expand their stomachs with 3.2 slop; it made him think suddenly of the rumoured Japanese torture where they shoved a garden hose down a man's throat and turned on the water full force until they ruptured his stomach with water.

A wild unreasoning rage rose up in Johnny. He picked up his little canvas furlough bag and commenced walking on toward the Main Gate. The four-lane highway was dark and far ahead up a gradual rise were the lights of the sentry box at the gate. He trudged along and the rage ate into him like acid. It was too late to catch a ride with anyone driving out, and he walked all the way to the gate, limping along in his low quarter issue oxfords.

When he went out the gate, he walked across the highway and stood waiting in the dark, hoping to catch a ride. To hell with this hanging around for twelve hours, dejectedly waiting for the next bus and maybe then not being able to get on! It was Highway 41, a truck route, and it ran all the way to Florida. There might be some tourists on their way home from Florida who would pick him up. It was strange, but there still seemed to be tourists in this savage insanity of a world. A way of life may crumble, but the individual bricks like tourists always remain undamaged and are fitted and cemented into the new wall.

It was cold and he turned his officer's topcoat up around his ears. Dupree had warned him that he must get rid of it, send it home or sell it or throw it away. The topcoat collar, tall as it was, was not much protection from this February wind, and Johnny set down his canvas furlough bag and put his gloved hands up over his ears. He stood that way, his hands over his ears, his breath a mist that wafted away on the steady wind, and he looked back into the camp where lights were beginning to wink out.

From across the highway, Johnny looked past the brightly lighted sentry box with its two shivering MPs, looked down the long hill that met the camp and then rose again, undisturbed, on the other side. The camp with its bleak buildings and abortive amusements lay sprawled along the narrow little valley that ran along the road. It covered an immense amount of ground and the lights ran along, becoming smaller and smaller until they faded into sightlessness on either end. Behind each light lived men, each group in its own little vicinity, its own PX and its own movie, almost unconscious of the other groups beside it. In each group lived men whose lives were being decided every minute. Men like Big Red who had been a staff sergeant then a first sergeant and now was a private in another company, men like Weidmann who were making changes of terrific import every day, men whose lives—infinitesimal but none the less important to *them*—were being affected tremendously; things of great importance were happening to their personal lives. Things that could not be seen from the highway looking down the hill. From where he stood, he could see it whole. He was like a man who has been transported into space to look down upon his planet objectively. He could not see from the moon the wars and murders and things that were important to the people of his planet.

If he did not know what was going on inside this camp, he would not suspect the existence of so many important things. He might be a tourist or a truck driver passing by the camp in several seconds and saying to himself: "Here is a camp with many soldiers inside of it. Many soldiers live inside this camp, sprawled out over the countryside, its lights winking on and off." But the words would have no meaning, no significance. "This camp has no relation to me. I drive by this camp and I see a camp with many soldiers who are part of my country's army. Then I drive on, I pass, I do not see this camp, I go about my life which is foreign and unrelated to this camp. Then this camp is gone. I have driven by. But it is still there. I am not gone, because I'm always here. They are only soldiers in a camp, and my here must go on by this camp; it must go about its travel and its living."

The third truck that passed glimpsed the soldier standing with his hands over his ears in the flickered glare of the passing headlights. The driver applied the air and stopped and picked the soldier up.

"Where you going, Bud?"

"Endymion, Indiana."

"Going to Evansville, then East."

"I'll ride along. To Evansville."

"You just come from the camp here? You stationed here?" A jerk of the thumb.

"Yeah. Just come. I live here."

Pause. "Pretty big camp, this one. Ain't it."

Pause. "Yeah. Pretty big."

From Jones's poem "The Hill They Call the Horse," the dead pass by:

> *Set Lechessi—*
> *Belly ripped wide open, still gasping:*
> *Help me. Help me.*
> *Can'tcha see? I'm gonna die!*

Memory will not allow Jones to forget the scene of the steady march of the dead.

The poverty-stricken Lechessi family remains in Massachusetts. Johnny cries for them. He cries for Set, for himself, and for humanity.

Sandy tries to console Johnny, but she is rejected. She didn't see the line of the dead. As Johnny says to her, "You don't know anything about it. What do you know about it?"

HE WAS A WOP

THE MARION HOME, ENDYMION, EARLY FEBRUARY 1944

STANDING IN THE CENTER OF the room, he told her the whole story about Weidmann. Sandy listened sympathetically, nodding every now and then. He stood motionless in the center of the floor and talked and talked.

"There was a guy in my old outfit named Set Lechessi," he said. "He was a wop. He was a wop and he was from Boston. Cambridge, Mass. He was a curly-headed wop and he had the most magnificent physique I ever saw. He had to have a wonderful body. He needed it. He worked with it all his life. He didn't go to high school because he had to work. All he ever did was work with his muscles. Railroad gangs. Cement gangs. Stuff like that. That was all the work he ever got a chance to do."

Johnny's voice was choked and there were tears threatening to overflow from his eyes. His mouth was open and he worked it spasmodically to keep himself from breaking down and crying.

"I don't know anything about economics," he said. "I don't know the first thing about economics, or philosophy, or psychology, or history. But I know Set Lechessi worked all his goddam life with his hands because he didn't get a chance to do anything else; he couldn't get any other kind of work, and he didn't have an education, he was dumb. He wasn't one of these examples of the Great American Success Story. He didn't rise out of the slums to become president or a great financier. He was too honest for that; he was too innocent; he was naive. When people told him things, it never occurred to him to doubt that they were telling him the truth. He was just plain dumb; he believed everybody was as honest as he was. He was dumb, but if he'd had a chance to go to school, even to high school, he might have developed the brains he had so he could have gotten a clerking job. That was his greatest ambition in life: to have a white-collar job as a clerk or an accountant.

"Set wasn't bitter or hard, although Christ knows he should have been. He had plenty of reason to be. His was the kind of life to make a 'Public Enemy of Society.' Society makes its own enemies, and then calls them 'criminals.'

"Set had to quit school in the eighth grade and go to work because his father got crippled on a construction job. He was fifty years old and working as a laborer. And then he got smashed up, and Set had to quit school to support his two kid sisters. All the older kids were already married with their own families beginning to grow, and they couldn't help much.

"So Set had to work to try to support all four of them on what he could make as a kid laboring on construction jobs and railroad gangs. That was during the depression and they were laying off men everywhere. Everybody's forgotten all about the depression now. Everybody's working in defense plants now. And they all say a man can always get a good job if he's got the stuff. 'No man ever needs to go hungry, if he really wants to work.' People forget things awful easy.

"Set kept getting laid off one job after another. And finally he got a job digging and cleaning cesspools. He cleaned cesspools under the ivy-covered walls of Harvard; that's as near as he came to an education. He didn't like it much. I don't guess anybody would like working with his hands in shit all day, with the smell of it in his nostrils all day long. He didn't like it; but he did it, he did it because at least he got some money to feed himself and his father and sisters. He could have gone on the bum and done better than that, but he didn't want to. He could have got in the CCCs, but he wouldn't get enough money to feed them all. And besides, he was a wop, a dago. His family meant everything in the world to him. And finally, he got laid off the cesspool job even. And he couldn't get any work at all, no matter how hard he tried. His crippled father and two sisters were hungry all the time. They never had enough to eat.

"So finally, he joined the goddam army. Joined the army at twenty-one bucks a month. So he could get some money for them to eat.

"This makes a mighty dull story, doesn't it? There wouldn't be much to write a novel about there, would there? People want to read adventurous exciting things like Ernest Hemingway writes, and they don't want to hear about this. It's depressing to read about drunks and failures and bums—unless they're romantic and adventurous. 'Why do writers want to write about the poor in life and those of low estate?' they say. 'There are too many happy things to write about.' They don't think working in shit all day is exciting enough, and they don't want to hear about it; it offends their good taste.

"I don't know a damn thing about economics or tariffs or world trade or any the rest of that crap. But they sure don't seem much good to me, when guys like Set Lechessi have to live like they are forced to live—and die like they are forced to die."

Johnny was crying now. His sentences were punctuated with long racking sobs and great sighing intakes of breath as he tried desperately to keep himself from crying. Four drinks on an empty stomach; but this was no crying jag. Any spring released from heavy pressure will bound out, expand, recoil upon itself. The liquor was just enough to loosen the bonds he had clamped down tight over Al, and Weidmann, and Isaac Rabinowitz, and over Set Lechessi. That much liquor is usually necessary, even when the pressure is released; it is taught to men that it is a woman's prerogative, and therefore unmanly, to break down, even when your soul is begging you to cry. This was the first time he had allowed himself to tell about Set, about all that had been festering in his soul for a long time.

"The third man in the company to die. He got hit in the belly with a burst of machinegun fire. It tore his belly wide open. A bunch of guys were going downhill and they got ambushed. Everybody got back over the top of the hill except Set and one other guy. Johnson. He was killed outright—but Set wasn't.

"We laid on the back of the hill and listened to him yell for three hours, before he finally died. Our company had only been on the line for three days; we hadn't had time to get numb yet. We could still feel. And we lay there scared to death with our faces pushed down into the grass and the heat and dust and seeds choking us and listened to Set yell. Guys who'd lived together for three years. Guys that used to get drunk together and go to whorehouses together. In a company like that, everybody gets to know all about everybody else's life and family and plans, everything about a man. And we had to lay there and listen to Set yell and call on the Virgin Mary and think all the time we were glad it wasn't us—and then feel ashamed. We even begged the company commander to let one of us go down over the hill after Set. He wouldn't do it because he said we wouldn't have a chance. There were tears in his eyes when he said it.

"A couple of guys even squirmed out into the fire and tried to get in position so they could shoot him. But nobody could do it.

"Finally, he bled to death."

Johnny stopped talking and dropped into a chair.

"That's a fitting epilogue to a life like he had, ain't it? There's an epilogue for him, and for Weidmann who got kicked out of his command because he was a Jew and some son of a bitch had a brother-in-law. They're all in the same boat. It ain't so much that they died or that they lost out. It's the injustice and the waste and the uselessness and the indignity. It makes you sick to your stomach. It makes you hate. But you don't know what to hate. It's rottenness, just plain goddamned rottenness, and nobody you can put a finger on. It's not that we owe them a monument or a revered memory. That don't do them any good. That don't mean a goddam thing. We owed them a life. Society owed them a life.

"He laid out there for three hours, three whole hours, I tell you. And all the time he was screaming and yelling for someone to help him, please somebody help him. He kept yelling he couldn't die because he had to take care of his father. He sounded like he expected God and the Virgin Mary to miraculously heal him as soon as they understood they'd made a mistake; God hadn't meant to kill him because he had to take care of his father. I guess he forgot about his ten thousand insurance."

He buried his face in his hands, and great choking sobs shook his body. Sandy got up from the divan and went to his chair.

"There, there," she said helplessly, trying to quiet him somehow. "Go ahead and cry; it'll do you good. You've had it coming a long time."

"You don't know anything about it. What do you know about it? It's easy enough for you to say there, there."

"Go ahead and cry; it'll do you good. You've had it coming a long, long time."

To the end of the war. There was no end to the war. Worse than that, there was no beginning to the war. The war was not yet begun.

The AWOL story
before it was edited.

Source:
Archives / Special Collections
University of Illinois at
Springfield
Springfield, Ill.

for the next war to bolster up the nation falling into debt and depression!

Johnny grinned to himself. Well, here was one vet who couldn't be frightened into keeping his mouth shut. He had fought for "Freedom of Speech". And he intended to have it. Even if it meant being looked upon as neurotic and a danger to the "Minority Groups" of society. Johnny took Sylvia's arm and squeezed it a little.

Johnny had made no bones about telling everybody he met that he was AWOL. To a few people he had deliberately flaunted it, but to most of them he did not care one way or the other, whether they knew it or not. Having been in the Regular Army, he had acquired a Regular Army outlook toward Absence Without Leave: it was nothing disgraceful even if you didn't get away with it, and it was a sort of game played against Authority. Civilians had never entered into the question one way or the other; they neither approved nor disapproved; they weren't even aware of it, and it made no difference to them. What Johnny failed to realize was that now that there was a war on, everything was changed. The civilians took an active interest in AWOL, because it meant that each soldier who was AWOL was dishonorable and a traitor to them personally, because he was refusing to fight for them and their country. Civilians had become very conscious of AWOL and they were indignant about it when a man went over the hill; one could almost say they were intolerant. But that reaction was natural to them, because they realized that if the whole army went over the hill, they would lose everything they had, including their freedom of speech.

When the Chief of Police came around for an informal chat with Erskine, Erskine blew his top. He had known something like this would happen. The Chief was almost apologetic; he hated to have to be the instrument of punishment for a boy who had been through as much as Johnny. But there it was: it must be faced: Johnny was AWOL. People had been complaining to the Chief about it. If Erskine could not do something, the Chief would have to write a letter to Camp Campbell and inform them of the situation and ask for instructions. Erskine assured the Chief that he would do something. The Chief departed with a final apology to the effect that if Johnny would have made it a little easier on himself and not gone around telling everybody that he was over the hill, it might have carried on for some time. The Chief had his own position to think about.

The possibility that Johnny might be thrown in jail--really thrown in--was the crowning black smirch on Erskine's character. Erskine was lawfully indignant at the thought of his business, reputation, and social position--all going down the drain on account of his cousin being thrown in the clink. The possibility was even worse than the fact, which had not occurred yet--and would not occur if Erskine could prevent it. The fact was a fact, and it could be faced when it had to be. The possibility was much worse, because it could only be faced with the imagination, which conjured up all kinds of terrible results.

Erskine called for a showdown. He caught Johnny at home the next evening.

Johnny had come home to pick up a stack of Japanese photographs, souvenirs of Guadalcanal, to show to Sylvia. It was a weekday, but it seemed like Sunday to him. Something about the old Carter house had seemed to capture the lazy, comfortable, coldly religious air of Sunday of an era ago. The house was a product of the 1900's, a modernized copy of a southern colonial, and as such it stubbornly remained, inside and out--with its lightning rods, its angularly bulging gables, its ornately pressed tin gutters, it high ceilinged rooms with their ornamented scrollwork cornices, it Ionic columns supporting the second story front porch.

Johnny was met at the door by Fanny who informed him that Erskine wanted to see him. He nodded and went on upstairs to his room. When he came down, he walked through this overly ornate labyrinth that was the house, back to where the "sunroom" was. It had been, he remembered, the back parlor in his grandfather's day, but since Erskine and Fanny had taken over the house they had renamed the "back parlor" the "sunroom." The room didn't mind. It remained as it had been, too obviously a back parlor to be changed by Fanny's redecoration. It seemed not to realize it had weathered one era of American life and was now embarked upon another.

Erskine was sitting in the long lounge chair reading the paper when Johnny entered the sunroom. When he saw it was Johnny, Erskine put down his paper. He displayed quite obviously that he was being fair and trying to control his patience. Johnny went into the kitchen that opened off the diningroom and the sunroom and mixed himself a drink. He came out of the kitchen into the sunroom with his drink in his hand and sat down on the couch. Erskine still had not picked up his paper. He sat, his body immobile, staring at Johnny with a sarcastic look frozen on his face.

Erskine remained that way until Johnny was finally settled on the couch, drink in hand. Then Erskine got up out of the lounge chair and stood with his back to the glowing fire in the open fireplace, his hands behind his back. He teetered back and forth from his heels to his toes with studied reflection. Johnny looked at him with detachment from the couch and decided that Erskine's paternal air would look authentic if one failed to note the deep lines of sarcasm that ran from his nose to the corners of his mouth and dilated his nostrils.

"Well," said Erskine in his deep courtroom voice. "It's certainly nice of you to come home. I had begun to think you might no longer be in town."

"Okay, Bootleg," Johnny said. "Take it easy."

Bootleg was the nickname given Erskine by some of the town wits for his part in the Prohibition scandal exposed by Goodman Spurgeon's uncle. It was a nickname Erskine did not particularly like, and it was the first time Johnny had used it since coming home.

"When do you intend to leave?" Erskine asked, coming directly to the point and dropping the irony while retaining the note of sarcasm. As a good a lawyer should, he controlled his voice very well.

"I hadn't thought about it," said Johnny. "Maybe another week. Why?"

"Well," said Erskine in a tone usually reserved for harranging juries, "you are AWOL, and although you may not know it, I am breaking the law when I allow you to stay here, knowing you are AWOL. That makes me an accessory after the fact. Besides that, I've just had a visit from the Chief of Police."

Johnny looked surprised.

"You didn't expect that, did you?" said Erskine, "when you went all over town bragging openly that you were AWOL? The Chief was very decent about it. But even you can hardly expect him to just overlook such a breach of the law.

"If you had come here to see me and Fanny it might be different. If you had not been so loud about being over the hill, the Chief would not have had to recognize the fact. It seems quite evident to me that you have brought whatever happens to you upon yourself. And quite frankly, I don't feel I have any responsibility to intercede for you. You have used our house as a restingup place between drunks and fornications, and for nothing else. I do not like that. You seem to have utterly no sense of gratitude or of responsibility. I do not like that."

Johnny cut in on him: "WE've been all over this."

"Yes," said Erskine, "and we'll probably be all over it several times more. Since you seem to prefer the company of Corny Marion to that of your own family, why don't you just move into her house."

"That's an idea," acknowledged Johnny.

"That is, provided Eddie will let you." The implication caused by leaving Eddie's name out of the previous statement was strengthened a great deal by this postscript. The postscript was unnecessary, however, because Johnny had already got it. When he still ignored the strengthened implication, Erskine went ahead.

"The point I am coming to is this: I don't want you to stay here any longer as long as you are AWOL. And as long as you feel you must act as you have been acting, I don't want you to stay at all. I want you to plan to leave sometime tomorrow."

"Then I take it you'd rather I did move down to Corny's?" Johnny asked mischievously.

"You are of age," said Erskine. "You are free to do as you see fit. Of course, what the Chief of Police does after you leave here is also your concern."

"All right," said Johnny. "I'll leave tomorrow night. I wouldn't want to get you into any trouble with the law; I wouldn't want to ruin your business or your reputation."

"Fanny and I," said Erskine, "have taken a number of years to build up the reputation of the Carter name in this town from where it was when your father died. I loved Joe as much as any brother ever loved another--even if he was only my uncle; nevertheless I cannot condone some of the things he did."

"Yes," said Johnny. "You have told me this also."

"I'll drive you to Evansville, and put you on the train for camp."

Johnny laughed harshly, his eyes squinting up a little in sudden anger. "Don't you think I'm capable of taking care of myself?"

"I don't know whether you are or not, frankly." Erskine took his hands from behind his back and folded them over his chest. Johnny remembered suddenly the legend of Endymion that the only man who could ever make Erskine Carter holler uncle was his Uncle Joe, Johnny's father. Erskine must have seen what was in Johnny's eyes, because he unfolded his arms and hung his thumbs in his belt.

Johnny tossed off the remainder of his drink and stood up. He was directly in front of Erskine and facing him.

"All right," he said. "Now I'll say something. As you said, I'm of age. I'll do as I damned please. You won't take me to Evansville to put me on no train, no time. I'm leaving tonight. Your jurisdiction goes just as far as your front door. No farther. When I leave this house, I don't expect to come back in it. That's not because I dislike you. Neither is it because I feel I've been treated badly. I don't. I agree with you when you say whatever happens to me is my own fault. I wouldn't have it any other way." Johnny stopped for breath and found that he was leaning forward toward Erskine. His fists were clenched and he could feel a tension in him that seemed to be begging for a wrong word, or for a wrong movement. He forced himself to relax a little and lean back.

"When I leave here, just mark me off the roll. Forget that you've got a Carter relative by the name of Johnny. You and I have nothing in common except the name of Carter.

I've tried to explain some of my ideas about things several times to you. Your picture of me as a punk kid coupled with your own natural lack of foresight makes you too goddamned narrow to listen. That's your tough luck, not mine. I don't feel hurt and I'm not mad at you. I'm mad at what you represent. You and I haven't even any common speaking ground.

"I've told you about how I liked the kind of life you folks live: good food, good liquor, good fun. I still like it. But any poor ignorant son of a bitch can live like that without any effort. That kind of life is fine, but it is no end in itself, and it's no justification for itself. That kind of life is false, as long as everybody in the whole damned world doesn't live it also. There's a great change coming on this earth when this war is over. People like you will be left out of it, because people like you are enemies of change. As long as you try to keep your 'fine life' for yourselves, you will remain enemies, not only of change but of <u>real</u> progress. I don't expect you to understand what I'm saying. But someday you'll remember it, when the world moves away from you and your kind.

"Just remember what I said: Mark me off the roll. Forget you know a Johnny Carter." Johnny stopped talking, realizing that he was unable to say what he wanted to say.

"Fine," said Erskine. He stare back at Johnny, eye for eye. His jaw muscles were set tight and his mouth was very thin. "Don't expect to come running back to me when somebody kicks you in the tail."

Johnny did not answer, and they stood that way, both

tense, Erskine with his thumbs in his belt, Johnny with his hands straight down at his sides, staring at each other for a long moment of silence. Their gaze filled the air with a tension so unbearably strong that any movement or sound from either would have broken the tension and pitched them at each other's throats. Fanny stood out in the kitchen, wringing her hands miserably.

With an abrupt movement Johnny turned on his heel and went upstairs to pack his bag. They could hear his heels beating angrily on the mellow worn stairs. Erskine sat down in the lounge chair and picked up his paper. It shook imperceptibly, and he had to exert his will and force himself to read it. He thought suddenly that he was getting a little old, and he wondered if he really could have taken the boy. He was young and strong and had a fine build, a real Carter physique, and he had had a lot of fight training in the army, plus that Golden Gloves tournament when he was in high school. Erskine really wondered. It had been that close.

Maybe the boy was right, in a way. Maybe he *was* getting old, maybe his ideas were old fashioned and an impediment. But youth was always wild, always radical for change. They grew out of it.

There were no farewells. They only heard the front door slam. Both of them wished simultaneously that the Chief of Police would not have to turn him in. When the door slammed Fanny turned to the pantry. She fixed herself a hasty toddy and then walked in and sat down by Erskine and looked at him. Erskine studiously read the paper. The headlines blared about the Munda airstrip.

NOTES FOR THE INTRODUCTION

Jones to Maxwell Perkins, March 16, 1947, is quoted in George Garrett, *James Jones*. San Diego: Harcourt Brace Jovanovich, 1984, p. 89.

General biographical information about Jones is from Garrett, *James Jones*; Frank MacShane, *Into Eternity: The Life of James Jones American Writer*. Boston: Houghton Mifflin, 1985; George Hendrick, ed., *To Reach Eternity: The Letters of James Jones*. New York: Random House, 1989.

Helen Howe and Don Sackrider provided information about Robinson.

Jones on Thomas Wolfe is from MacShane, *Into Eternity*, p. 32.

Jones on the possibility of being dead within a month is from MacShane, *Into Eternity*, p. 149.

Jones on soldiers' acceptance that their names are on the roll of the dead is from James Jones, *WWII*. New York: Grosset & Dunlap, 1975, p. 54.

Jones on loss of confidence is from Hendrick, *To Reach Eternity*, p. 27.

Attu information is from Simon Rigge, *War in the Outposts*. Alexandria, Virginia: Time-Life Books, 1980, pp. 122, 135, 141; C. L. Sulzberger and others, *The American Heritage Picture History of World War II*. New York: American Heritage, n.d. pp. 16, 54–55, 330. The cry of "Japanese drink blood like wine" is from Sulzberger, *The American Heritage Picture History of World War II*, p. 330.

Jones's "The Hill They Call the Horse" is published in Hendrick, *To Reach Eternity*, pp. 32–35.

Jones's comments about his lovemaking in Memphis is from MacShane, *Into Eternity*, p. 63.

For information about the interest of Lowney Handy and James Jones in Eastern religions, see Steven R. Carter, *James Jones: An American Literary Orientalist Master*. Urbana: University of Illinois Press, 1998.

For Lowney Handy's account of meeting Jones, see A.B.C. Whipple, "James Jones and His Angel," *Life*, May 7, 1951, p. 144. See also, George Hendrick, Helen Howe, and Don Sackrider, *James Jones and the Handy Writers' Colony*. Carbondale: Southern Illinois University Press, 2001, for an account of their relationship.

Jones on Lowney's subjecting herself to him is from MacShane, *Into Eternity*, p. 77.

The summary of Jones's talk with a psychiatrist is from MacShane, *Into Eternity*, p. 68.

For general information about Maxwell Perkins and James Jones, see A. Scott Berg, *Max Perkins: Editor of Genius*. New York: Dutton, 1978; John Hall Wheelock, ed. *Editor to Author: The Letters of Maxwell E. Perkins*. New York: Charles Scribner's Sons, 1950; Burroughs Mitchell, *The Education of an Editor*. New York: Doubleday, 1980.

For a thought-provoking M.A. thesis, see Greg Randle, *James Jones's First Romance: An Examination of "They Shall Inherit the Laughter."* Sangamon State University (now the University of Illinois at Springfield), 1989. For Wheelock to Aley and Perkins to Jones, see p. 6.

Aley's letter to Jones, March 25, 1945, is from the Handy Collection, Archives/Special Collections, University of Illinois at Springfield.

Jones to Perkins about *Laughter* lacking "resolution" from Hendrick, *To Reach Eternity*, p. 49.

Burroughs Mitchell on the faults of *Laughter* is from Mitchell, *The Education of an Editor*, p. 57.

ACKNOWLEDGMENTS

My thanks for the assistance of Helen Howe; Ray Elliott; Kaylie Jones; Librarians at the University of Illinois at Urbana-Champaign, the University of Illinois at Springfield, and the Urbana Free Library; Jean Thompson; and Don Sackrider.

—George Hendrick

Portions of the manuscript of *They Shall Inherit the Laughter* are published with the permission of the James Jones Estate. The new title is *To the End of the War.*

The manuscript of *They Shall Inherit the Laughter* and various documents concerning that unpublished novel are in the Handy Colony Collection, Archives/Special Collections, Norris L. Brookens Library, University of Illinois at Springfield and are published with permission.

cover design by Karen Horton
interior design by Danielle Young

ISBN 978-1-4532-5823-1

Published in 2011 by Open Road Integrated Media
180 Varick Street
New York, NY 10014
www.openroadmedia.com

OPEN ROAD
INTEGRATED MEDIA

CPSIA information can be obtained at www.ICGtesting.com
Printed in the USA
BVOW03s1314090814

362258BV00001B/6/P